Her Deadly Inheritance

by

Beth Ann Ziarnik

To DEB —
Love you, dear friend!
All God's Best to you.
Beth Ann Ziarnik

Lighthouse Publishing
of the Carolinas

HER DEADLY INHERITANCE BY BETH ANN ZIARNIK
Published by Lighthouse Publishing of the Carolinas
2333 Barton Oaks Dr., Raleigh, NC, 27614

ISBN: 978-1-941103-60-9
Copyright © 2016 by Beth Ann Ziarnik
Cover design by Elaina Lee, www.forthemusedesign.com
Interior design by Atritex, www.atritex.com

Available in print from your local bookstore, online, or from the publisher at
www.lighthousepublishingofthecarolinas.com

For more information on this book and the author visit: www.bethziarnik.com

Brought to you by the creative team at Lighthouse Publishing of the Carolinas:
J. Christine Richards, Rowena Kuo, Eddie Jones, Meaghan Burnett, Shonda Savage, and
Deb Haggerty

Library of Congress Cataloging-in-Publication Data
Ziarnik, Beth Ann.
Her Deadly Inheritance / Beth Ann Ziarnik 1st ed.

Printed in the United States of America

Praise for *Her Deadly Inheritance*

Beth Ann Ziarnik's debut novel, *Her Deadly Inheritance,* doesn't disappoint. Set in a small town in Michigan's Upper Peninsula, I could imagine the characters walking its streets and along the shores of Lake Superior. The story's suspense kept me turning the pages. If you enjoy reading inspirational romantic suspense novels, you'll want to pick up this one except you won't want to put it down! A great story.

~ **Andrea Boeshaar**
Bestselling Author of *A Thousand Shall Fall*
Co-founder, American Christian Fiction Writers

I loved Beth Ann Ziarnik's novel, *Her Deadly Inheritance,* and couldn't put it down! She drew her characters out so clearly. A top job.

~ **Sally Bair**
Author of *Willliwaw Winds* and *The Trouble at Fish Camp*

I really enjoyed Beth Ann Ziarnik's debut novel, *Her Deadly Inheritance.* It had a great balance between the suspense and the romance, and kept me turning the pages!

~ **Kathryn Springer**
USA Best Selling author of *The Dandelion Field*

Beth Ann Ziarnik did a great job with *Her Deadly Inheritance.* Her heroine's motivation and Christianity come through beautifully."

~ **Gloria Clover**
Author of Children of the King series

I really enjoyed *Her Deadly Inheritance.* Beth's characters were well developed and had great interaction. I could see their body language, and it was easy to picture each setting in my mind's eye as I read. There was something to keep my interest throughout the entire story.

I love, love, love *Her Deadly Inheritance*. The story had enough twists and turns to keep me turning pages, made me feel like the characters were real and believable including Button (nice touch) and appreciated the way Beth wove the gospel into the story so that it was clear without becoming preachy. She has written a wonderful book that doesn't just entertain people, but speaks to their hearts!

I had a hard time putting *Her Deadly Inheritance* down. I had to know how it ended.

I finished *Her Deadly Inheritance* at 2:00 am this morning. Beth's fault that I'll be blurry eyed today. Her debut novel definitely captured and held my interest. I'm proud of you, Beth.

To my beloved husband

Acknowledgments

Through the years, so many have helped or encouraged me that I could never name them all. Please know that I will always be grateful.

Special thanks go to:

My husband, Jim, who painted a two-story house to pay for my first writers' conference, saw me through years of learning and minor successes, and insisted, "You worked hard, and you're a good writer. If no one publishes your novel, I will!" Thank you, sweetheart, for believing in me.

David Worel, a forest ranger with the U.S. Department of Agriculture in Northern Michigan. He enthusiastically showed me around Grand Island, taking me to the places that made up my novel's setting. He also risked his life to save mine by grasping my bike handle and dragging me firmly away from a cliff where the path had washed out just enough to be dangerous.

Oshkosh firemen Brett and Eric, and especially Chris, who patiently answered my many questions about the nature of house fires. Thank you for sharing your expertise.

Lin Johnson and the Write-to-Publish Conference. Returning year after year, I learned how to answer God's call to write, the skills of writing and marketing, and met many wonderful writers, editors, and publishers who encouraged me and helped me to grow. God bless you, Lin, for all your hard work.

Jim Hart, my agent at Hartline Literary Agency. Ten days after receiving my novel's proposal, he requested the full manuscript. Two weeks later, he declared he loved my novel and offered to represent me. From that point, he never wavered in believing a good publisher would offer a contract.

Rowena Kuo, acquisitions editor at Lighthouse Publishing of the Carolinas, who championed my novel. I met her at Write-to-Publish, pitched my novel, and six months later, she made a contract offer.

Editor Chris Richards whom I met at the same Write-to-Publish Conference. She gave my novel one of four big awards at the conference banquet. Now an editor at Lighthouse, she has worked with me to polish this novel and get it ready for publication. Thank you for your enthusiasm and expertise, Chris.

My American Christian Fiction Writers critique group: Karen Witemeyer and Gloria Clover. Both of these dear friends have combed through every version of my novel, helping and encouraging me all the way.

My Word & Pen Christian Writers critique group: Kathi Bloy, Kris Orkin, Ruth Schmeckpeper, and Chris Stratton, who fearlessly red-penciled my novel to help me to make it better, and cheered me on.

My faithful prayer team: Carol Belongea, Lois Wiederhoeft, and Michele Zraik. Each week they take my requests before the Lord and share in praising him for his answers. I am blessed to have them in my life.

Most of all, I thank my beloved Lord God. He not only called me to write but has guided me along the way and brought me into the land of published books. I am so grateful for his tender love and care.

"The Lord is my strength and my shield;
My heart trusts in him, and I am helped."

~ Psalm 28:7, NIV

Chapter One

5:00 a.m. Twelve hours before a judge would declare her legally dead.

Clutching her cell phone to her ear, Jill Shepherd turned away from the red numbers glowing on her bedside clock and paced in the room's pre-dawn shadows.

"Say you'll come, Jill."

"Don't ask me, Uncle Drew. You know I can't." She squeezed her eyelids shut and struggled against the tightness in her throat. "The minute Lenore finds out I'm alive and you knew, she'll think we planned this."

His wife would turn on them both for snatching the house on Michigan's Grand Island from her at the last minute. "She'll leave you."

"I'll take my chances. More important things are at stake here."

His quiet resignation clawed at her conscience. She clenched her teeth. She would remain strong. He deserved that much.

"I can't."

"Yes, you can."

She swallowed hard at his pleading.

"I have to go," he said, "but please come. The company plane is waiting at O'Hare. You have the pilot's number. Call him."

Jill pulled in a shaky breath. "She'll never forgive you."

"I'll meet the plane when you get here. On the way to Windtop, we'll decide how to break the news. Everything will be fine."

He disconnected the call.

Everything would not be fine. Even he knew too well that someone would pay. The same woman who had driven Jill's fragile mother into seclusion would see to it.

1

Jill laid her phone on the bedside table near her Bible and ran her hand over the book's leather cover. She often drew comfort from touching it. Nothing this time.

Jill chewed her lip as she paced. She wouldn't go back. Let Lenore have Windtop. She deserved that rotting old place.

After light rapping at her bedroom door, it opened with a slight squeak, hall light knifing through the shadows. "Are you awake, Jill? I heard talking."

Retreating to her bed, Jill turned on her lamp and crawled onto the rumpled sheets where she scooted back until she had trapped the pillows against the headboard. "Come in, Nona."

In yellow bunny slippers and pink flannel pajamas, her older housemate padded across the carpeted floor to sit at the foot of the bed. "For what it's worth, I think you should go."

Jill shook her head. Nona had no idea of all the trouble that would follow if Jill took her well-meaning advice.

Tenderness born of their friendship shone in the older woman's gaze. "Isn't it time you faced the truth about your mother's death? Isn't it time you found peace?"

"Peace at Windtop? Impossible!"

"God specializes in the impossible, Jill."

"You don't know Lenore."

"God does."

"I can't just leave the Rogers' project." Nona had entrusted it to her. In these hard times, failing to meet the deadline could cripple her friend's genealogy business.

"Take it with you. When it's ready, send it by attachment, and I'll take care of the rest."

The woman could sure be stubborn. "But—"

"Give God a chance, Jill. He won't fail you." Nona stood up and walked to the open door where she paused. "The decision is yours. Make sure it's the right one, okay? I'll be praying for you."

The door closed, and Nona's parting remarks left Jill numb, but she had to do something. Easing herself to the edge of the bed, she swung her legs over and let them dangle. What was she supposed to do? Go to Windtop and expose the lies, take whatever her aunt dished out, and maybe shatter a marriage? Or hide out in Chicago, go on as before, and leave her aunt blissfully unaware? One choice frightened her. The other sickened her.

Argh! She buried her fingers in her hair and clutched her head. Flopping backward onto the bed, she stared at the ceiling. "God, I don't need Windtop. I don't even want that rotten house and its ugly memories." Tears trickled down the sides of her face, wetting the hairline around her ears and dropping to her rumpled sheets. "So what if I'm declared dead? Staying out of Lenore's reach would be worth it."

Of what use was an aging pile of wood and bricks that had driven the family apart? Nothing but a haunting reminder that her mother and Maggie were gone from this earth.

And she had failed them.

Returning now didn't make sense. She couldn't undo the past. If only her pastor hadn't spoken last Sunday about the God who loved her but also hated a lying tongue. The words had reached deep into her heart, and as much as she tried, she couldn't forget them. If she really wanted nothing to stand between God and herself, how could she go on living a lie? How could she go on hiding the truth from Lenore and trapping Uncle Drew into doing the same?

Her uncle never wanted to deceive his wife. He only gave in to Jill's pleading. She was ashamed, now, to admit she had taken advantage of his regrets about his sister's death. How she had manipulated him.

At the time, she hadn't been a Christian, but what did that matter now? That sinking feeling in the pit of her stomach refused to go away and made her choice clear. She had no excuse. A lie, even for the right reasons, was still a lie. Yet wasn't destroying a marriage wrong too?

As the pink of dawn spread its pale light through her bedroom's lace curtains, a fat tear slipped down her cheek. In her twenty-two years, she had made enough miserable mistakes. She couldn't bear to make another one. Not of this magnitude.

Nona thought she knew the right answer.

"But, Lord, I don't know," Jill whispered. "Which way should I go? Please tell me what to do."

A tender silence hung in the room, yet no word came to her heart.

Jill picked up her Bible, left the bed, and crossed the room to turn on a floor lamp near a bank of windows overlooking an empty Chicago street. She snuggled in an overstuffed armchair and opened the book. As she did, a photograph slipped from its pages. Snatching it midair, she turned it over. Uncle Drew had given it to her.

She found it hard to believe that Windtop no longer resembled the decaying heap she'd left behind three years ago. The brick was now clean. The Victorian balconies, turrets, and porches were repaired and painted a rich chocolate brown. Even the stained-glass panes circling the cupola on the roof gleamed in the sunlight—no doubt thanks to the restoration contractor Lenore had hired.

Her gaze moved to the young man with dark hair, broad shoulders, work jeans, and a long-sleeved cotton shirt who stood in the foreground. He stared into the camera with guarded surprise. Funny, as many times as she had studied this picture, something in his eyes tugged at her heart.

She snorted "No way," and slid the photo inside her Bible's back cover. She'd never get close enough to meet this Clay Merrick. Restored or not, what Uncle Drew called her rightful inheritance was more of a deadly inheritance she had no desire to claim. The old house had brought nothing but sorrow and strife to her mother. Jill could expect nothing better.

Returning made no sense.

Flipping her Bible's pages open to where she had left off the day before, Jill lost herself in the story of Jesus and a demon-possessed man in Mark's Gospel. Crazed and living naked among tombs, the man had no one to rescue him.

Until Jesus came.

She drew back. The sudden sense that she had something in common with this man startled her.

Okay, she'd never been crazed or lived among tombstones, but a year ago, she'd felt as trapped. Learning of her mother's suicide had nearly driven her to do the same. Jill would never have known the good life she had now if Nona hadn't reached her in time.

Then why did it feel as if God were nudging her back to Windtop, to all the chaos, all the pain? A loving God wouldn't do that, would he?

Of course not.

She released a shuddering breath and returned to her reading, blinking as the next words jumped off the page.

"Go home to your family …"

Clay Merrick frowned as his gaze swept the summer sky over Hanley Field. He had no business getting involved with Drew Bradwell's personal life. Why hadn't he just said no?

He knew why. Because he couldn't come up with a decent excuse fast enough. So here he stood in the deserted airfield's one-lane parking area, waiting for his client's niece. And she wasn't his only problem.

Gravel crunched beneath his leather boots as he crouched to peer beneath his old Ford F150. Not a kitten in sight. Slick little creature. He stood and popped the truck's hood once more. At least it hadn't climbed up onto the air filter. He slammed the hood.

The niece and the kitten—two unaware and helpless creatures. His mother would have said, "You can't save the world, son." Maybe not, but he would try. He gritted his teeth and tapped the hood. He'd check again before he left—hopefully without Jill Shepherd.

Shading his eyes from the noonday sun, he scanned the clear blue sky again—still no plane. He dropped his gaze to the thick wall of evergreens surrounding the secluded field. Bradwell sure knew how to spirit the girl into the community unseen. Not another soul or plane was in sight. Not that it would matter once the man's wife found out.

He ground his jaw. What kind of world was this where innocent people were hurt for no good reason? Bradwell's niece had no idea what she was walking into. He should warn her. Bad idea. He'd have to blow his cover and throw away two years of hard work just when he was so close to success. And for all he knew, she might not stay long enough to get into trouble. In the meantime, he'd do whatever he could to ensure her safety.

He blew a frustrated breath. Too bad she chose today to show up. Two more weeks, and he'd have solved the problem. She could've come home in safety. As it was, he needed one last piece of evidence to convince himself he had trailed a killer to Windtop.

Sure, telling Jill Shepherd was the right thing to do, and he wanted to do the right thing. But why should she trust a stranger?

A Cessna buzzed overhead. He jerked around to watch the single-engine plane circle and float to the grassy runway as if this were any ordinary day. It taxied within a few yards of where he stood and swung broadside.

His gut clenched as a passenger peered from a side window. He hooked his thumbs in the back pockets of his jeans and emitted a grunt. Bradwell's niece had arrived.

With a fading whine, the plane's engine shut down. Moments later, the pilot emerged and opened a side door to help a petite beauty with golden hair step down.

Clay pressed his lips together as he sized her up. She couldn't weigh more than a hundred and ten pounds. If it came to defending herself, she didn't stand a chance.

Her green blouse rippled in the summer breeze, and several spiraling wisps of hair swept across her face. She brushed them aside with a slender hand and looked around as if expecting someone.

He strode forward. "Jill Shepherd? I'm Clay Merrick."

A whisper of wariness flashed in her violet eyes. She looked away and then fully engaged his gaze. "The contractor my aunt hired."

She had a gentle way about her yet remained cautious, her stance poised for flight. Maybe he had underestimated her.

"My aunt knows I'm here?"

"I don't think so. Your uncle sent me." He pulled a paper from his shirt pocket and handed it to her.

A slight lifting of her shapely eyebrows indicated she recognized the handwriting. She opened the note.

Earlier at the paper mill, Bradwell had briefed him on its contents. Visiting executives had him tied up in an unannounced meeting. He urged her to go with Clay to present herself to the judge as proof she was alive, then on to Windtop to wait. He would join her around 4:30 p.m.

She lifted her gaze to study him as if weighing her options. "I would like to talk to my uncle."

Do the smart thing, he wanted to say. Get back on that plane and go home. Instead, he stood there as she pulled out her cell phone, turned her back to him, and walked away a few paces. However, she hadn't gone far enough to prevent him from catching the drift of the conversation.

"Uncle Drew? What's going on? Yes, he's here. No, I'm not comfortable doing that. She won't? You're sure?" A long pause. "All right, I'll do as you say, but I still don't like this."

Clay didn't like it either, but it wasn't his decision.

Tucking both the note and her cell in her purse, she returned. "Let's go then. I hear the judge is waiting."

"Uh, right." He checked his watch. "The ferry is too."

She tensed. Her eyes widened. "The public ferry?"

"Your uncle arranged for private passage."

She didn't move.

"Is something wrong?"

She raised her delicate chin and squared her shoulders, stirring his reluctant admiration. "Nothing. Nothing that matters."

He swallowed a grunt and tipped his head toward the two large leather bags beside her. "Yours, right?" When she nodded, he reached for them.

"Mr. Merrick."

At the quiver in her voice, he wiped his hands against his jeans and gave her his full attention.

"On the way, could we?"—her words choked off and she tried again—"stop at the island cemetery?"

The pain etched in her eyes strafed his heart. He knew all too well the source of that pain. He grabbed her bags. "We'll make the time."

He turned away, scowling. Without even trying, she had cracked his defenses.

The aging truck shuddered as Jill settled on its stiff bench seat and clicked her seat belt into place. She looked over her shoulder and through the rear window. The man whose eyes had mysteriously drawn her in the photo adjusted her luggage among trees with balled roots and flats of red, white, and blue petunias. He slammed the tailgate.

Strange. He wore quality denim yet drove a truck almost as old as he was. Then again, maybe her aunt had purchased the Ford 150 for Windtop. Grand Island residents preferred using sturdy, old vehicles on its unpaved roads.

Merrick approached the driver's side, but instead of joining her, he reached inside and pulled a lever to pop the hood. He opened and then slammed it, returning to slide behind the steering wheel.

"Trouble?" she asked.

"Just checking." He turned the key in the ignition, and the motor sprang to life.

She shrugged. Everything must be all right then. Or maybe not. Merrick seemed awfully tense. Almost as if … as if he were worried about something. Did that something have anything to do with her? Surely not. Yet she couldn't help but wonder why her uncle sent this man in his place and insisted her arrival be such a secret.

I'm glad you came, Uncle Drew had written in his note.

Glad, for what reason? Even her uncle was hiding something from her.

She shivered. Suddenly, it seemed the smart thing might be to turn back while she still could. *Go back to your family.* Yes, there was that. The moment she read those words this morning, she knew she must face Lenore and the truth about her mother's death. Unfortunately, she could only do that at Windtop where all the trouble began.

Clay revved the motor, and her stomach lurched as the truck moved, carrying her away from Hanley Field into an unknown future with a stranger at her side.

Uncle Drew should be here. At the very least, he should go with her to meet the judge. "To cancel proceedings declaring you legally dead, he has to have proof that you're alive," her uncle had said. "Don't worry. Lenore won't be there. I'll take care of letting her know once you're on your way to the island."

Don't worry? She shook her head. How was that possible? Right now, all she was running on was pure trust in God.

And she wasn't very good at that yet.

If only she'd had more practice, this whole situation might not loom quite as frightening.

Yellow dust billowed behind the old truck as it sped over the sandy road along Grand Island's southern shore. Jill swiveled back to stare ahead through the windshield. The island had changed. The forest crowded the edges of the road and blocked out the sunlight more than she recalled.

Cold prickles danced over her shoulders. This wasn't the Grand Island she once knew. She'd leave this dark place as soon as possible.

On the plus side, her meeting with the judge had gone well. She and Clay found him waiting at Powell's Point before they were to board the ferry. She had glanced around and found no one else who might know her, but being a family friend, the judge had recognized her instantly. Before they parted, he mentioned, as a favor to Uncle Drew, he would delay processing the order and keep their secret until her uncle got back to him. Drew had asked to inform Lenore himself. As the judge drove away, she and Clay Merrick had boarded the ferry.

Now, with a rumble, his truck pulled off at the side of the road below the island cemetery. Clay shifted into park and Jill peered through the windshield at a lone path rising through the forest. At its end, she would find her mother's grave, a prospect that left her numb.

The door on the passenger side opened, and Clay stepped back as he held it. She bit her lip and slid from the bench seat. Putting off this visit to her mother's grave would only make it harder to face what lay ahead at Windtop.

Jill followed Clay around the hood of the vehicle where he leaned with his back against the driver's side fender. He crossed his arms.

"I'll wait here," he said, his voice a gravelly growl. He broke their mutual gaze and stared at the ground to hide … what? Anger?

She turned to the forested pathway, forcing one foot in front of the other. Her mother had died too young. Was her death Jill's fault? Jill found the question hard to shake and needed an answer before she left this island.

The path gave way to a quiet clearing where sunlight filtered through a high, leafy canopy. In the glow of green and gold, she passed thirty weather-worn stones marking the resting places of the island's early settlers, some her ancestors, but her proud heritage would not help her now.

Her stomach churning, she found her grandparents' graves, and beside them, a newer red granite slab embedded in the forest floor. She crouched down to touch it and cold seeped into her fingertips as she read the inscription. *Susannah Bradwell Shepherd. Beloved mother of Jill Ashley Shepherd.*

She closed her tired eyes. *Beloved mother.* Yes, certainly, but was she her mother's beloved daughter? Or had her flight on that long ago stormy night driven her mother to suicide?

Hot tears spilled over and splashed on the marker. She palmed their tracks from her face. Too late for tears now.

She never meant to cause her mother's suicide. How was it even possible? The Susannah Bradwell Shepherd she knew would never have done such a thing. Yet the police had come to that conclusion and people did change. She had. Had her mother changed enough to take her own life?

Frantic cries echoed unbidden through her grieving heart. *Come back, Jill! Please! Come back!*

Tipping her face heavenward, Jill whispered into the agonizing silence, "Too late, God! I've come back too late." With her mother gone, all her arrival could accomplish was to end the lie. Something her mother would want her to do, yes, but small comfort at a time like this.

A bird trilled in the quiet of that place as if to encourage her. Nona said God would help her find peace. How?

"Is it my fault, Lord?"

Her shoulders shook as she gave way to tears. Nona said tears would help cleanse her of this terrible grief. Yet no relief came, only a searing, choking pain.

How long she wept, she couldn't say, but when at last her sobs stilled, she opened tear-blurred eyes to find Clay Merrick standing near. A quiet sympathy shone in his clear gray eyes. Without a word, he extended his hand. Placing her own within its warmth, she found the strength to rise.

Clay gripped the steering wheel and pointed his truck north on the forest road along the island's east side. Jill's too-quiet form beside him worked knots in his gut. Tears glistened on her lashes. Her chin trembled, and the memory of her weeping at her mother's grave disturbed him to the core.

He stared grimly ahead. She shouldn't have come. He wanted to tell her that before they crossed the channel at Powell's Point but couldn't force the words past his lips. Instead, he watched for the slightest hint that she had changed her mind. In a heartbeat, he would have whisked her back to the airport. Instead, she'd lifted that small, determined chin of hers and boarded the ferry while he muttered a few choice words under his breath and out of her hearing.

Now, his jaw twitched. More than ever, he ached to tell her all that he suspected but couldn't yet prove. For her sake, as well as that of other innocent people who might die if he failed, he couldn't risk it.

He clenched his teeth. He might not be free to stop her, but—he flicked a glance heavenward—Someone Else ought to! At one time, he would have asked that Someone to change Jill Shepherd's mind. However, a long time had lapsed since his last prayer, and he didn't plan to resume the habit anytime soon.

He turned the truck toward Windtop's entrance gate. As it swung wide, he drove through, and Jill tensed beside him. When the gate clanged shut behind them, she jumped like a startled bird. Any moment, he expected her to cry out, but she clamped her mouth shut.

Did returning to Windtop stress her that much? Then why did she keep going?

He glanced at her pale face. *For pity's sake, turn back!* The words burned in his gut. Yet he, too, clamped his mouth shut.

Chapter Two

Jill trembled as the truck sped past Windtop's brick gatehouse, racing toward nothing but trouble. Uncle Drew might be optimistic, but she had no such illusions. She couldn't have arrived at a worse time—the very day Lenore expected to own Windtop. No plan she or her uncle could devise would soften that blow.

Fear not, child.

The gentle words warmed her heart as the truck emerged from the forest shadows into sunlight streaming over a velvet green lawn. As the great house swept into view, Jill drew a sharp breath. Windtop shone like a jewel in the forest. The photo her uncle had given her offered a poor representation of all this man had accomplished.

Clay Merrick glanced her way and smiled as if she had paid him the greatest of compliments. "Restoration can work miracles," he said.

Restoration. Is this what you have in mind, Lord?

A lump of uncertainty rose in her throat while the man beside her parked the truck before Windtop's main entrance.

He placed a key in her hand. "Go ahead," he urged. "I'll bring your things."

She stared at the brass object warming in her palm. For better or worse, the moment she used this key, her life and that of the Bradwells would change. She snatched up her purse.

Standing before Windtop's massive door, she inserted the key, turned it, and pushed the door open. The entrance hall yawned before her. As she stepped across the threshold, a sad silence seeped into her bones. No familiar voices greeted her—not Mother's, not Maggie's.

Never again.

While suffocating pain wrapped itself around her, she remained in place. Why hadn't she come back while Mother and Maggie were still alive? Before nothing remained but this shell of the past? Breathing in shallow gasps, she forced herself forward.

Her footsteps echoed on the parquet floor as she crossed the hall. Standing at the bottom of Windtop's grand staircase, she let her gaze follow its square ascendency to the third floor. As she peered up through the heart of the house, a burst of sunlight brightened the cupola's stained glass windows, showering down bits of luminous color like rainbow promises. God's rainbow promises.

Would he really make all things work together for good in this dark, dark place?

Clay finished stocking the kitchen with the groceries he'd bought in town and returned to the back of the truck. He hefted Jill's luggage from its bed and set the bags on the gravel drive while he closed the tailgate. As he bent to retrieve them, a tiny tail swung down from the front wheel well.

So that's where the kitten went.

Abandoning the bags, he snuck up to grasp the waving tail but missed. "Clever kitty," he whispered before hunching down to reach into the wheel well.

Mewing in protest, the little creature jumped down and sprinted across the lawn, heading for the wraparound porch. He scrambled after it, first to one bush, then another, until the kitten disappeared through the porch's latticework and spun around to look out at him with big eyes.

Great! He'd never fit his hands through those narrow openings. He'd have to coax it out. "Here, kitty-kitty."

The kitten cringed and scrambled backward, keeping him in view.

As little as it was, it seemed to know how to care for itself. First, it clung to the wheel well all those miles since Hanley Field, and now quickly found this hiding place. "You're one clever little character."

A little character he needed to get his hands on. But he'd already frightened the kitten enough with his rejected rescue attempts. If he left it alone for a while, it might calm down and be ready to let him take it home. "All right, but I'll be back."

The kitten maintained eye contact as Clay backed away.

"Stay put now." Scant chance of that, but Jill Shepherd had already waited too long.

Clay eased the luggage to the entrance hall floor to keep from disturbing Jill. What a picture she made, so vulnerable as she stood before the fireplace, gazing up at her mother's full-length portrait. Making as little noise as possible, he closed the distance between them. She glanced his way with a sad smile, the small gesture stirring something in his heart he shouldn't welcome.

His gaze moved from Jill's quiet presence to the portrait he had often studied this past year. Susannah Bradwell Shepherd. Serenity itself in an ivory satin gown, her bright golden ringlets had been swept up and cascaded to her bare shoulders. A single strand of pearls graced her slender neck and a wisp of a smile lit her fine-boned face while something profoundly sad shadowed her soft, brown eyes. He'd often wondered about that.

Now, here was her daughter. "You look like your mother," he whispered into the silence.

She smiled. Just a trace, and though he had no right, would never have a right, it helped to know he had comforted her.

Mother and daughter looked enough alike to be mistaken for one another, except for one thing. "Except for your eyes."

She sucked a sudden breath and her smile vanished. Lowering her lashes, she hid deep violet eyes with their fascinating flecks of gold and brown.

Somehow, he had offended her.

Jill shifted away. It wasn't Clay's fault. Not really. He had simply stumbled on her longtime family wound. Her mysterious eye color marked her as different among the Bradwells, an outcast in her aunt's estimation.

15

Bradwell eyes were brown, something Lenore often pointed out as if the color of Jill's eyes somehow cast a slur on the family name. Had she inherited her eye color from her father? The man whose name her mother had taken to her grave?

She rubbed her upper arms to chase away the sudden chill. Dwelling on the mystery of her father had only brought arguments and tears until finally, she had run away to find him. She had come back to end her lie, not to solve her parentage. She might never know her father, but now that she had returned to Windtop, she would do all in her power to make things right with her mother's family. She wasn't sure how, but she would try. Maybe that's all God expected of her, and it was time she started.

Combing her fingers through her hair as if to free herself of dark thoughts, she leveled her gaze at the man beside her. "Thank you for your help, Mr. Merrick—"

His gray eyes engaged hers. "Clay."

"Clay." His simple invitation warmed her heart but didn't unravel her resolve. She wouldn't keep leaning on him. "I can handle it from here."

His jaw took a firm line.

"Really," she assured him. "I'll be fine until my uncle arrives."

He didn't appear convinced. "Humor me, Miss Shepherd—"

"Jill."

He nodded once. "Jill. I promised your uncle I'd see you safely settled in. I'd like to keep that promise."

The conscientious type. She shrugged. "It's a long trek to the third floor."

His eyebrows raised in surprise, but he didn't ask questions. Gathering up her luggage, he said, "Lead the way."

On the third floor, she entered the one room in Windtop where happy memories and bright sunlight lived. The room once inhabited by Maggie Pierce.

Jill surveyed the place where the housekeeper had poured all of her "mother love" on Jill as she grew up. Other than fresh wallpaper in a tiny blue rose print, Jill was relieved to find it as she remembered. The brass bed, the rosewood wardrobe, and Maggie's bentwood rocker before the fireplace all remained as if the dear woman would return at any moment.

Clay lowered her luggage to the floor inside the bedroom door. A slight frown creased his brow. "This house has better rooms."

Jill laid her purse on the glass-topped table. "This one is right for me."

He shrugged. "If you're hungry, I've stocked the kitchen. If you need anything else, just let me know."

When his retreating footsteps became inaudible on the thickly carpeted stairs, a crush of loneliness rushed upon her. Her heart thudded in her ears as she steeled herself to keep from sprinting to the rail and calling him back. For what? To hold her hand until her uncle arrived? Ridiculous! With God's help, she could handle this. After all, He had made it clear He wanted her here, hadn't He?

Go home to your family and . . .

And what?

Kneeling on the varnished floor, she dug her Bible from her suitcase and sat back on her heels. She flipped the pages to Mark 5:19. *Go home to your family and tell them how much the Lord has done for you.*

She blinked. Really? He wanted her to talk to Lenore about the Lord? That would take a miracle. Yet Nona insisted the Lord was still in the business of miracles.

A hollow rumbling from her stomach reminded her it was well past lunchtime and she hadn't taken time for breakfast this morning.

Rummaging through the refrigerator and food pantry, Jill found the makings of deli ham on bakery rye bread. She poured a glass of cold milk and carried both to the back porch to savor their flavors while sitting on the top step and basking in the sun's warmth.

"Me-ew."

The soft sound rose from the bottom step just as Jill finished the last bite of her sandwich. Struggling to climb to the next step, a tiny gray kitten regarded her with large golden eyes.

What a cutie! "Who are you?"

"Me-ew."

She glanced around the yard. "Where's your mama?"

The golden eyes blinked.

"All alone?"

"Me-ew."

A familiar stab pierced Jill. She released a long, low sigh. "Me too."

She dipped two fingers in her milk glass and held them out. The kitten sniffed, and then licked them with its raspy tongue.

"Hungry?"

The big eyes watched her pour milk onto her empty sandwich plate. Again, she dipped her fingers in and held them out to the kitten before lifting its thin body to the edge of the plate.

She smiled as it sniffed and plunged in, cleaning the plate more than once. With its little tummy full, it climbed onto her lap and curled up. Giving her a last searching look, the kitten closed its eyes.

Jill stroked the soft fur, feeling a contented rumble beneath her fingers. She gazed wistfully at the tiny creature. She'd once received a kitten as a Christmas gift. With all her five-year-old heart, she had loved that kitten the moment her mother put it in her arms. So cute with a big red bow around its neck, but she didn't have it long. The kitten died when four-year-old Carver played with it a little too roughly. An accident really, but she cried inconsolably. Aunt Lenore had scolded her for making such a fuss and hurting Carver's feelings.

Jill continued stroking the sleeping kitten. Half-opening its eyes, it peered at her. Closing them again, it nestled deeper into her lap. Could this kitten be a gift, a promise of more good to come? Was God giving back what had long ago been taken from her? Warmth crept into her grateful heart. She closed her eyes and raised her face to heaven.

Clay stopped short the moment he caught sight of Jill on the back porch, her eyes closed, and her beautiful face aglow with contentment. In her lap, a little ball of gray fur lay sleeping. "You found the little dickens."

Jill blinked. "The kitten? Oh. It's yours." A delicate disappointment overtook her gaze.

"Not really. The little rascal hitched a ride from Hanley Field in one of my truck's wheel wells. I spent the last half hour looking for it. At least some island predator hasn't made a snack of it. I should get him back to his mother." Closing the distance between them, he reached for the kitten.

Jill pulled away. "Do you have to?"

"Does your landlord allow pets?" Maybe she hadn't thought about that.

"Nona won't mind." She seemed certain.

"Are you sure you want it? Pets require a lot of work."

The kitten climbed to her shoulder and nudged her under her jaw. "Please."

He stepped back. "If you're sure. When I go back into town to pick up your uncle, I'll see what the kitten's owner has to say. If it's all right, I could pick up some pet supplies."

"You'd do that?"

"Not a problem. You'll need 'em."

He walked away, trying not to rap himself on the head. What was he doing? Instead of discouraging her stay, he'd just volunteered to aid and abet it. Not smart. For her own safety, she had to leave as soon as possible.

Smiling dreamily, Jill observed the kitten asleep on Maggie's bed. It only took this tiny creature and a certain contractor's kindness to push back Windtop's shadows. Maybe Uncle Drew was right. Maybe everything would turn out all right.

The kitten yawned and stretched from the tip of its tail to its tiny pink nose. It relaxed, examined her with quizzical eyes, and then sprang to the edge of the bed.

"Wait!" She lifted him to the floor, amused as he explored the room. He settled at a bottom corner of the rosewood wardrobe and sniffed delicately. Then he dug in, intent on snagging something with his paws.

Jill chuckled. He was as curious as the child she'd been in this very room. Whenever she became restless, Maggie would say, "Let's play the game, Button."

Button! What a perfect name for her kitten. She bent to stroke its fur, but Button refused to be distracted.

What did he find so interesting? It couldn't be … could it? She nudged the kitten aside to check the hidden compartment Maggie'd devised years ago. Her heart thumped as she pulled it out. A piece of paper was wedged in it.

Excitement surged through her as she stared at the housekeeper's handwriting. Her eyes rimmed with moisture as she gazed at Maggie's last message. Knowing just how to comfort her hurting heart, God had brought her here to find it.

"Button, you little dear. You've led me to Part One of Maggie's game: Start with the paper message. Now for Part Two: Decipher the key."

Jill sat on the floor. Button climbed into her lap, nosing her hand as she turned her blurred gaze to the words on the paper. They would direct her to Maggie's real message. She brushed the moisture away in order to read. "If you bear to puzzle it out, you will see clearly under glass."

The words didn't make much sense but wasn't that the point? So first, pick out the main words. "Bear ... puzzle ... see ... clearly ... under ... glass."

Put some of them together. "*Bear ... Puzzle.*" She said it faster. "Bear puzzle!"

A favorite childhood toy. But where would she find it now? Whoever cleaned Maggie's room might know. More likely, Maggie had put it somewhere herself. Not in here where it might be thrown out once she was gone but maybe in the attic where they used to store old toys.

Setting the kitten down, Jill hurried to the end of the hall and opened the attic door. As she stepped inside, Button scampered between her feet.

Sunshine penetrated the bank of gabled windows ahead, making the dust motes visible as she picked her way through aisles of stored trunks and furniture. Deep inside the attic, she found what she was looking for. Shelves jammed with old jigsaw puzzles stood against a far wall. In the attic's stifling heat, she sorted through the many boxes. What if she didn't find it? About to give up, she spotted it in a dark corner.

She removed the lid of the box and turned a piece over. Maggie had printed one word on the back. She stroked the word tenderly, a precious link to a dear friend. Checking a few more pieces confirmed each bore one word.

Closing the box, she glanced at her watch. Just enough time to finish the puzzle before Uncle Drew arrived. She'd have to hurry.

"Button?" A movement caught her eye as the little gray fellow tried to disappear behind a large trunk. She seized his tiny tail. "It's way too hot to play in here."

The kitten protested but came along, contented enough once she cradled it in one arm and shut the attic door.

Back in her room, Jill set the puzzle on the bed and returned to the paper message. "See. Clearly." She needed clarity. *Lord, please help me to see clearly when I face Lenore.*

She returned to the game. "See. Under. Under the puzzle pieces? No. Under. Glass. The glass table?"

Strange how Maggie had made the game so easy. Had she been in a hurry?

Spilling the pieces on the table, Jill turned each one design-side-up as Maggie had taught her. She checked her watch again and stretched enough to see out the French doors to the room's wood balcony. As long as those doors were open, she could hear Uncle Drew arrive and have plenty of time to run downstairs to greet him.

She collected the straight-edged pieces and formed the puzzle's frame before filling in the other pieces. Three more to go.

The hum of a motor approaching floated through the open doors. She jumped up in time to catch the flash of black.

Uncle Drew! Finally, she'd learn how he planned to tell his wife the news. Her throat went dry. It wouldn't be long before she'd have to face her aunt.

Jill scooped up Button and shut him in the bathroom, then hurried down the stairs. She reached the second floor and rushed toward the final flight of stairs as the entrance door below opened.

"At last." A rich, throaty voice caressed the words.

Jill froze.

Chapter Three

Lenore!

Strength drained from Jill's body. Her legs wobbled as she backed into the second floor's deep shadows. Pressing against the dark paneled wall, she struggled for every shallow breath. So this was Uncle Drew's idea of how to break the news. He could have warned her.

"Carver, dear," her aunt gushed to her son. "Leave those things by the door and bring in the rest of our luggage, would you please?"

Jill's heart thrummed in her ears. This was no simple meeting. Lenore was moving in! What was Uncle Drew thinking?

"Dad will be furious," a girl whined.

The childlike voice belonged to Tia. The younger of her two cousins would be sixteen by now.

Jill closed her eyes momentarily. Thank goodness her Uncle Drew had no part in this invasion. He hadn't betrayed her after all. Still, she couldn't quite envision him angry with Lenore. He'd be miffed maybe or frustrated, but not angry.

"He will get over it," Lenore said. "Mrs. Fenton will give your father my note when he arrives at home—which should be any minute—and I will handle him when he gets here."

Feeling sick to her core, Jill sagged. Her aunt had maneuvered this whole thing. Nothing much had changed.

"Dad said to wait until tomorrow," Tia insisted.

At the sound of the grandfather clock's door opening, Jill stretched to see who might be near it. Too much balustrade blocked her view from this angle.

"Your father required we wait one year. It will be over"—the clock began its soft ticking—"at precisely five o'clock when the judge declares your cousin legally dead. Then Windtop will finally be ours." The door to the clock closed. "I've waited long enough and will not be deprived of one more moment."

"But—"

"Tia Bradwell, do not give me any more trouble. When your brother returns, we will take our luggage upstairs and settle in."

A trembling overtook Jill, gaining momentum. At any moment, Lenore would march up those stairs. What was she supposed to do? Greet her aunt as if no bad blood had ever flowed between them? Run for the hills and hide out until Uncle Drew arrived?

She pressed her lips together and straightened her shoulders. No. She would not run or hide. Uncle or no uncle, her aunt would not find her cowering.

Stepping away from the wall, Jill paused and bit her lip. She'd let them know she was here. The trick was seizing the right moment without scaring the life out of them.

Skirting through the shadows, she positioned herself behind the second-floor railing where she could safely observe. Her aunt stood near the clock at the right side of the fireplace. Amazing how the woman never aged. How did she maintain the same flawless skin, the same dark hair, perfectly styled, the same tall and slender figure?

"That will be the first thing to go," her aunt said, flicking a disdainful glance at the portrait above the fireplace. "As for you, Tia, you worry for nothing. No one is left to stop us. Susannah is dead, and—"

"—Jill's body was never found." The girl tossed her silky blonde hair.

Carver dropped the last of the luggage onto the parquet floor. "Tia, you know Lake Superior never gives up its dead."

Her cousin was right. The lake's deep waters remained so cold a body could freeze and remain on the bottom, never to be discovered. A fact well known to locals, which—to her shame now—she had counted on to cover her tracks when she fled during that storm.

"What if she didn't drown?" Tia ventured.

Carver rolled his eyes. "Jill's boat shattered in the storm. Face it. She didn't survive."

Jill shuddered. Yes, according to Uncle Drew, after the storm, pieces of her boat were found floating on the bay. Officials were certain she had not survived. A reasonable conclusion since a storm that great could break huge iron ore ships in half. Another fact which made possible Lenore's request that the courts declare her niece legally dead three years later.

Lips quivering, Tia turned to her mother. "I want to go home."

Lenore arched to her full height. "We *are* home. For the summer at least. Now calm yourself. You know what the doctor said."

"I hate this dingy old place!" With a pout, Tia folded her arms and dropped into a fireside chair.

"What is the matter with you?" Lenore had obviously grown tired of the confrontation.

Carver shook his head. "She thinks this house is haunted."

"Ghosts haunt places where people die tragically," Tia countered.

Lenore's gaze pinned the girl. "Who said that?"

Tia jumped to her feet. "The girls at school and Mrs. Fenton."

"Weak-minded fools," her brother said. "Every intelligent person knows we live, we die. It's over."

A frown flickered across her aunt's face. "I don't know about that, but I do know this—haunted or not, Windtop is ours and, this time, no one will drive us out."

The clock's first deep chime sounded. Lenore whirled toward it as if captivated, a woman full of joy and expecting to possess her dream.

Fascinated, Jill stared as realization rocked her heart. She and the woman who hated her had something in common. Her aunt, whose actions she deplored, also knew what it was like to strain toward an impossible dream. They both suffered from fierce desires driving them to make choices that hurt others, intended or not.

Here was Lenore, on the cusp of owning Windtop, unaware Jill lurked in the shadows, blocking her way. Jill wished she had never come. She had hurt enough people in her lifetime, including her mother and Maggie. She had no desire to hurt one more, not even her aunt.

Yet to stop the lie, she had to reveal her presence, and revealing her presence would force her to claim her inheritance, ending Lenore's dream. Not even Jill had the power to change that. The provisions of her grandparents' will forbid her to sell or give away the old lake house. What her grandparents had meant to protect her from her strong-willed aunt, unwittingly forged a wedge that had divided the family and caused years of conflict.

Nona insisted God had a plan to set things right again. If only Jill knew what that plan was, but time was running out. The moment the clock stopped chiming, her aunt would climb those stairs to possess the house.

If Jill was going to do something, she had to do it now.

Clay gunned the Jeep along the road toward Windtop. He'd been gone too long. Bradwell's meeting at the mill ended later than expected. Then the boat had given them trouble. Nothing he couldn't handle, but it ate more time while something inside him grew edgy.

Drew Bradwell made notes on some business papers and packed them into his briefcase. He set it on the back seat. "Thanks for stepping in to help, Merrick. I knew I could trust you."

Trust. Clay rolled the word around in his mind. Not a word he'd choose, but then his client didn't know his true purpose at Windtop.

Bradwell loosened his tie. "I wish I didn't have to put Jill through all this. Or drag you into it. But I don't have much choice. Did she really seem all right when you left her?"

Clay stared straight ahead. He wouldn't exactly say all right. Jill had too much grit for her own good. But the kitten had helped. "She seemed to relax some."

Bradwell cleared his throat. "Good. Yes, good."

Guiding the Jeep through Windtop's gate, Clay wondered if now was as good a time as any to find out if he should adjust his plans. "I hope you don't mind my asking, but I need to know. Do I still have a job?"

The man leaned back in his seat and stretched. "You didn't bring it up with Jill?"

"No." Somehow he couldn't bring himself to press her. She was so deep in her grief.

"You're nearly done, right?"

"I'll need another two weeks at most." He'd have to stretch the work at Windtop to make it last that long, but he'd adjust his bill to be fair.

"Let me talk to her."

Clay preferred discussing business with a client himself, but technically, Jill wasn't his client. Under the changing circumstances, his situation might be better handled by her uncle. "I'd appreciate it."

"You will still have to fill her in on what you've accomplished, what remains to be done, and get her approval for any further expenses." Bradwell closed his eyes and heaved a great sigh. "Right now, I have a bigger problem. I'm still not sure how to break the news to my wife about Jill."

As they left the forest drive, bringing the house into view, Clay focused on the car parked beside it. "It looks like that's no longer a problem."

"What?" Bradwell jerked upright. His eyes widened. "Hurry!"

Flooring the accelerator, Clay brought the Jeep to the house in seconds. While Bradwell bounded toward the porch, Clay gripped the steering wheel, his shoulder muscles taut.

If only he had the right to barge into that house. He needed to know what was going on.

★★★

The clock's fifth gong hung in the air. Jill stepped out of the shadows and into the light at the second-floor railing. Before she could say a word, Tia glanced up, and her young cousin's face paled.

"Tia …" Lenore followed her daughter's unblinking stare and her own jaw slackened.

Carver looked up with a flicker of surprise. He grinned. "So, cousin, you've returned."

"It's Jill?" Tia whispered.

"How …?" The word died on her aunt's tongue as the front door burst open.

Uncle Drew. Jill closed her eyes briefly. *Thank you, Lord.* She wouldn't have to face Lenore alone after all.

He stopped short, his dark pin-striped suit snug around his stocky girth. He glanced from his wife to his children. A deep pink flush crept up his neck to his round face. "What's going on here?"

Lenore glanced up at her and then back to her husband. "You! You knew!" She spat the words. "You knew she was alive. You knew she was here!"

Jill cringed, but her uncle stretched himself to the full extent of his five-and-a-half-foot frame. "I tried to save you this embarrassment."

Her aunt's face grew red. "How was I supposed to know?"

"I didn't know myself until this morning," her uncle asserted.

"You didn't know what until this morning? That she was alive?"

He looked his wife in the eye, and Jill took hope at his firm but quiet restraint. She never suspected him capable of being so firm. Maybe he was in the office, but never with Lenore. This must be something new since his sister's death.

"I didn't know until this morning," he said, "that she would return."

Lenore crossed her arms and looked down at him. Her words cut like ice. "You knew all along."

"About a year," he said.

Lenore whirled to spear Jill with a glare. "You both let me believe a lie."

Jill tensed and gripped the railing to steady herself. If only she hadn't talked Uncle Drew into their awful agreement. "Blame me, Lenore. It's my fault."

"I do blame you. Both of you!"

"Uncle Drew never wanted to keep the news from you. He only tried to help me through my grief. I talked him into it because I believed we would all be better off if things went on as they were. I never intended to return. This morning, I had no choice but to change my mind."

Lenore's flawless features worked as if the woman were struggling to grasp the nuances of her predicament.

How odd. Jill could hardly believe that her aunt's anguish could touch a tender place in her own heart.

Lenore spun back toward Uncle Drew. "And when did you intend to tell me?"

"By the time I knew, I expected you to be on your way to the auction you told me you were going to today." Her uncle leveled his gaze. "And you refuse to carry a cell phone, Lenore. How was I supposed to tell you?"

"Carver," her aunt barked, "return those bags to the car. We are leaving."

"No!" Jill nearly choked as the word slipped from her lips. She skimmed down the stairs. "Please. Wait." As she stopped on the Persian rug at the foot of the stairs, icy prickles raced along her spine. "We'll have to talk. Why not now?"

Lenore's brown eyes narrowed. Her lips pressed into a thin red line as she folded her arms and glared. "So you can gloat? No. We will not chat as if your inopportune reappearance were of no consequence."

Warmth climbed Jill's face, knowing her aunt had a right to be angry. She swallowed hard. "I have no desire to gloat, Lenore, but you may want to hear what I have to say."

Her aunt quirked a brow, her dark eyes still smoldering.

"At least I hope so," Jill added. *Please, God, convince her. Because if you don't, I'm done here.*

"Five minutes," her aunt said, "and it had better be worth my time."

Uncle Drew forced a tense breath and took his wife's elbow to accompany her, but she jerked away and shot him a venomous glance. "Carver. Tia. Come."

Their two children fell in behind her as she disappeared into the library. Tia paused at the doorway and glanced back, confusion in her gaze.

Once they were alone, her uncle's shoulders drooped. "I am so sorry, Jill. I should have known Lenore might try this."

"It's not your fault." No one controlled her aunt, including her uncle. If anyone were to blame for the mess they were in right now, Jill knew who it was. Her uncle may have gone along with hiding the truth from his wife, but she had made it almost impossible for him to refuse. She used his self-blame about his sister's death to talk him into it at a time when he would have done anything Jill asked to make up for his past failures. "Talking you into lying to your wife wasn't fair to either of you. If I could go back, I'd do it differently."

"But we can't." He paused, wrinkling his brow. "You don't really think talking to her now will help, do you?"

Jill chewed her lower lip. "We can try."

An idea struck her. She grinned and dashed toward the library. "Come on. I think I know a way out of this sticky situation."

Chapter Four

Clay stole into the house through the back door and deposited the newly purchased kitten supplies on the kitchen counter, providing a good excuse should he be caught snooping. He had to know what was going on during Jill's first family encounter.

Moving through the kitchen shadows, he entered the butler's pantry and inched toward the swinging door separating the pantry from the dining room.

Cracking the door enough to peer beyond, he quickly eased it back into place. With one glance through the dining room's arched doorway into the library, he caught Mrs. Bradwell scowling from the red leather couch, her son fidgeting at the writing desk on the far side of the room, and her daughter frowning as she plunked into one of the wing-backed chairs.

This was as far as he could go. Thank goodness for acute hearing and eyesight. Both had served him well in the Army Special Forces.

He cracked the door again as Jill entered the library followed by her uncle. Bradwell's wife crossed her slim legs, then her arms. Her dark eyes narrowed. "Well? You insisted we hear what you have to say. Get on with it."

The woman's brittle words could've pierced metal.

"Yes, cousin," her son said, "tell us why you returned."

Jill gave Carver her full attention. "Simply to let you all know I'm alive."

"And to take possession of Windtop." Her aunt glowered as she ground out the words.

"No. I never intended—"

"Nevertheless, it has happened. You returned. The house is yours." Her aunt glared at her, not a drop of family kindness evident. Clay would have liked to assess Jill's reaction, but she had her back to him.

"You know I have no control over the provisions of—"

"Of course. Your grandparents' will. How convenient," her aunt said.

Clay marveled as Jill continued speaking with a soft appeal in the face of her aunt's spite. Where did she get such inner steel?

"Admit it," her aunt said. "You came back to snatch Windtop out of our hands. It was your plan all along. So just where have you been hiding while waiting to spring the trap?"

"I was looking for my father." The yearning in her voice clutched Clay's heart. A yearning he well understood.

"Your mother didn't want that." Her aunt smirked. "Did you even know his name or what he looked like?"

"Not his name, but I had my father's picture in the locket Mother gave me."

Lenore huffed. "I'm sure that fuzzy little thing was a great help."

"And my birth certificate. I felt sure I'd find him in a few weeks. The problem was it wasn't as easy as I thought, and once I started looking, I couldn't stop. Not until I ran down every last clue. That's when I called home and found out Mom had died."

"So you didn't find him," Lenore snapped. "Serves you right when a simple phone call might have saved Susannah's life."

"Mother!" Her daughter seemed shocked at the cruel accusation.

"Lenore!" Her husband chided.

"What?" the woman said. "Everyone knows your sister killed herself because she believed her daughter was dead."

Jill tensed as if struck, and Bradwell motioned to his family. "I think it's time we all went home."

"No!" Jill said.

No? What in the world was she up to? Bradwell and his family should go home. They'd done enough harm. How much more could the girl take?

With a satisfied smile, her aunt leaned back into the couch. "Well, then, I take it you have more to say. Go ahead. Not that it will make a difference."

"Lenore, I'm sorry I dragged Uncle Drew into keeping my secret from you. I'm sorry I made him promise not to tell you I was alive. I really believed it was best for all of us."

"You actually want me to believe you thought lying to me was best?"

Clay grimaced. Jill was getting nowhere with the woman. Why even try?

"It made sense to me then because I never intended to return and felt sure you'd be happy owning Windtop. Something only possible if I were *dead*."

"And you expect me to believe you would abandon a valuable property like Windtop?"

"What did I have to come back to, Lenore? An empty house? My mother's grave? It just seemed to me that remaining *dead* was best."

Lenore glared at her husband. "And you agreed to this insane plan?"

Bradwell shifted his weight to his right foot. "She needed time to get over the shock, time to adjust to Susannah's death. I owed it to her. For a while."

"At the cost of deceiving me?"

When he made no attempt to defend himself, his wife turned on Jill. "And you. All of a sudden, today, here you are. Why?"

"I realized this morning I was living a lie and couldn't do it anymore."

Tia peered around the wing of her chair. "Why not? Everyone lies." At her mother's disapproving stare, she lowered her voice. "Sometimes."

"True, but I ... I'm a Christian now, and I knew it was time to stop the lie. So I came back to make things right with all of you."

Clay frowned. So that's how she walked right into this trap.

"And how do you propose to make things right?" Her aunt goaded her.

"Just this. I don't know—I don't even care—when or how the fight over this house began, but I want it to stop." When her aunt opened her mouth, no doubt to protest, Jill put up her hand. Good for her! She had gumption. "So here's what I propose."

Clay held his breath.

"We can't change the past, but we can change the future." Jill went on. "What if you and I no longer had a reason to fight?"

Her aunt eyed her suspiciously. "What are you talking about?"

"I admit my solution isn't perfect, but if we try hard enough, it might work."

Clay tensed. Whatever it was, Jill had their full attention.

She stepped closer to her aunt. "I propose we share Windtop. I may not be able to sell or give it to you, but I can let you use it anytime you like. Move in right now. How about it?"

Her aunt's mouth gaped. Tia drew back as if Jill had slapped her, and Carver eyed her as if searching for some hidden flaw.

Her uncle broke the silence. "You don't mean it."

Clay almost cheered. *All Right! Talk her out of it, Bradwell.* Bad enough she was here, but share the house? She couldn't have come up with a worse proposal.

A lopsided smile pulled at one corner of Carver's mouth.

"Look," Jill pleaded. "Windtop is legally mine, but it's also a Bradwell family heritage. It belongs to all of us."

"Lovely sentiment," Carver said, not a speck of warmth in his eyes or voice.

"Think about it, Lenore," Jill said. "You could go ahead with your plans as if I'd never returned. I won't stay long anyway, and when I leave here, I may never come back."

Clay relaxed. That part sounded good. But the sooner she left, the better.

"What do you say?" Jill still urged them.

"No strings attached?" her aunt asked.

"No strings attached."

Uncle Drew coughed. "Jill, I don't think—"

"We accept." Her aunt's voice rapped like a gavel.

"Wait!" Bradwell's daughter jumped up from the wing-backed chair. "I say no!"

"Not now, Tia." Mrs. Bradwell waved her daughter away.

The girl turned pleading eyes on her father, and he slowly shook his head. While she plopped back into her chair and flicked a pouting glance at Jill, the man cleared his throat and coughed.

"So let me get this right," Carver said. "You came all this way to hand the house over to us. Incredible!"

"To let you know I'm alive."

"I hate to clue you in, cousin, but we were perfectly content without that information." His gaze challenged her. "So before I accept your kind"—he laced the last word with sarcasm—"invitation, is there anything else you care to confess?"

"Nothing."

Her cousin didn't appear convinced, and Clay clenched his teeth.

"I have a question," her aunt said. "You say you are now a Christian. How long ago did you make your decision?"

"About six months." A simple, straightforward answer.

The woman's upper lip curled. "And it took you this long to decide you were lying."

"I'm so sorry. I should have come back long ago. Would you please forgive me for waiting so long?" Jill pleaded.

Her aunt stood and peered down at her, her jaw twitching. "I will never forgive you."

"Lenore, dear," her uncle said, "you don't mean that."

"You betrayed me, Drew, and you both lied. What do you expect? A quick apology and it's over?" Her mouth closed in a hard line.

"Please don't blame Uncle Drew," Jill said. "I convinced him we were sparing you needless pain."

Her aunt bristled. "This is sparing me needless pain?"

"If I hadn't come back—"

"But you did," Lenore said, "and now it's over. You've won. Windtop is yours, and I will never forgive you." She glanced from Jill to her husband. "Either of you."

Clay breathed easy again. Jill's plan had failed.

"Now I'm tired of all this talk," Lenore said. "It's been a long day, and if you don't mind, we'll go and settle in as planned. May I ask which rooms are available to us?"

What?

"Um, I suppose any rooms on the second floor will do. I'm already settled in Maggie's room."

Tia blinked. "But that's—"

"My favorite room," Jill said.

"It's settled then," Bradwell's wife said. "Carver, you take the east room and Tia, the tower room. Drew, join me in the master bedroom when you are ready. We will talk." Lenore bustled off, giving orders to Carver and contending with Tia's objections. With a scrunched brow, Bradwell watched his family retreat from the library.

Jill sank to the couch, releasing a sigh. To Clay, she appeared drained but pleased. Her uncle unbuttoned his suit coat and eased down on the couch beside her. "I don't know, Jill. I'm not sure this plan of yours is wise."

Clay jerked. Maybe the man would talk her out of it yet.

"You're not pleased? Lenore is, isn't she?"

He shook his head. "You meant well, Jill, but I don't think she will ever give up her fight for this house."

"But, Uncle Drew, she no longer has a reason to hate me. And maybe this arrangement will make it easier for her to forgive us."

He squirmed. "I'd like to believe you're right."

He didn't? Clay had to agree.

With a hefty sigh, Bradwell slapped his knees. "Well, my wife finally has what she wants. Most of it anyway."

"Why is this house so important to her, Uncle Drew? Did she know about it before you were married?"

He shook his head "We were married four months before I brought her here to meet my parents."

Jill's forehead crinkled. "Then why?"

"I don't know really."

"But if you had to guess?"

Bradwell propped his elbows on his thighs, laced his fingers together, and rubbed his chin with his forefingers. "If I had to guess, maybe the family roots that Windtop represents. Generations of Bradwells have lived here. Lenore didn't have our stability as she grew up. Her parents died when she was a baby. Her grandmother took her in but died when she was ten, and Lenore grew up in a county group home until she turned eighteen."

"What a sad childhood."

Clay agreed. But lots of children grew up in less than ideal circumstances—himself included although he'd never been sent to a county group home.

"It made her strong, Jill. Still, for Susannah's sake and yours, I wish I had been firmer with my wife. Your mother might not have despaired. She might still be with us." He stood, silent for a few moments. "I wish you had told me. If I'd known what you had in mind, I would've stopped you."

"Then I'm glad you didn't. Our family has fought over this house long enough, Uncle Drew. Now, it's finally over."

"It's not over," her uncle said as Clay eased the door to the butler's pantry back into place.

He'd heard enough. Jill had made either a brilliant or deadly move with her sudden invitation. Either she had thwarted or made it easier for a killer who might just go after her.

Chapter Five

At the kitchen counter, Clay was jotting a quick note to Jill when the door to the butler's pantry suddenly *thwapped* back and forth. He jerked his head up, crushed the small paper in his hand, and stuffed it in his pocket.

Fists on her slim hips, Jill grinned. "You remembered. And I can keep Button, right?" She hurried forward and swerved to peer around him. "Wow! A battery-powered litter box and a bag of deodorized litter, kitten-sized food and water dishes, and a five-pound bag of food. And more. You, uh, brought so much."

Had he gone overboard? But then, what did he know? "A woman at the supermarket who has five cats recommended all this."

Jill's eyes crinkled with merriment. "A real authority, I take it?"

Was she laughing at him? No, just having fun in a harmless manner. He liked it. "You might say that."

She ran a delicate hand over the fleece-lined pet bed and picked up a toy mouse. "Thank you so much. Oh! Wait right here. I'll get my checkbook. How much do I owe you?"

"No rush. I take it you plan to stay for a while."

"Not long."

Perfect!

She washed the pet dishes and filled one before stashing the bag of kitten food in a lower cupboard. After stacking them with the rest of the supplies, she hugged them in her arms.

"I could help you carry those things to your room."

"I'm good. See you tomorrow." She shot him a twinkle-eyed smile before she disappeared up the back stairs.

Was he smiling? He wiped the grin off his face and strode to the back door. He had no business developing feelings for her.

He shut the door. For Pete's sake, he'd better get a grip.

Urgent mews greeted Jill as she reached for the knob and opened the bathroom door. Button sprang forward and curled around her ankles.

"Look what I have, fella." She placed the litter box in one corner of the bathroom and the kitty bed in another. After spreading a clean finger towel near the kitten's bed, she set out the food and water dishes.

Button dove in, crunching the dry food while Jill changed into jade-colored jeans and a long-sleeved tee. Her exhausting day had left her craving a bit of fresh air. She sat in Maggie's rocker and bent to tie her running shoes.

Dashing over, Button pounced on the laces.

"You little gray fuzz ball." She picked him up, relishing the nuzzling of his soft, furry head under her chin and the rumble of his purr.

He was so warm-hearted and easy to please. If only people were the same, instead of so often complicated and hard to predict.

She leaned back in the rocker. Setting it gently into motion, she closed her eyes, trying to lose herself in its comforting rhythm. *Lord, is Uncle Drew right? Did I make a mistake?*

Inviting the family to stay at Windtop seemed the right thing to do. If they lived together, maybe they could work out their differences. Not that she held any grand illusions. Her aunt and cousins weren't all that eager to welcome her into the family, and her uncle's first allegiance would be with them. But they had all made a beginning, hadn't they?

If not, it was too late to change anything now.

Button leapt from her lap and scampered under the glass-topped table. Sniffing, he batted an object around with his paws.

The puzzle! She'd forgotten all about it. Joining him, she first picked up the two loose pieces on the table and pressed them into place, then looked for the last. So that's what Button was batting around.

When she reached for it, he sat regarding her with solemn yellow eyes. She flipped it over, and the strength melted from her limbs like gelatin in the sun. She closed her eyes and opened them, hoping against hope. The word jumped at her again, and she groaned.

Murder!

Heart thundering in her ears and fingers trembling, she pushed the last piece into place. Then, dropping to the varnished floor, she gathered the kitten into her arms and looked up to read Maggie's words.

Her breath caught.

They say you are dead. In my heart I know it's not true. I pray you never return, but if you do, that you find my words quickly. You are in danger. Leave if you can. Your mother's death was no suicide. I say murder! If you stay, trust no one. Especially the one who tried to end her baby's life by falling down the stairs. I pray for you. With much love, M.

Her body numbing, Jill struggled to catch each breath. She skimmed the words again, hoping she had read them wrong. But, no, Maggie's message was plain.

Leave … mother's death … no suicide … murder!

Her skin prickled. Choking back a cry, she dropped the kitten and backpedaled from the revolting words until she hit the brass bedpost behind her. Pain shot through her shoulder.

Murder! Leave! Murder! Leave!

The awful words tumbled through her brain, gaining momentum. She grabbed the bedpost, pulled herself to her feet, and bolted from the room.

Keeping to the edge of the forest, Clay peered through its twilight shadows and caught a flash of movement. Jill fleeing the house like a frightened bird.

Something ugly crawled in the pit of his stomach. He clenched his jaw. *The deadly game had begun.* Just when he dared to believe she would be fine until morning. What had he been thinking? He never should have brought her here. But if he hadn't, someone else would have. Either way, she was in trouble.

Jill sprinted across the open lawn and entered the forest a few yards ahead of him. Doubling over, she sucked raspy gasps and looked back at the house. Light shone through lace-curtained windows, but he saw no one. Her ragged breathing slowed, and she hung her head and moaned.

He retreated to melt into the woods before she could turn and discover him, but a twig snapped beneath his boot. She spun, her eyes wide. She searched until her gaze found him.

Arrgh! He stepped forward. "Sorry. I didn't mean to frighten you."

She covered her heart with her hands and expelled a tense breath. "What are you doing here?"

"Checking the grounds. I do it every evening." He offered a reassuring smile though he doubted it made any difference. She seemed pretty shaken. "Are you all right?"

She let her hands drop to her sides. "I'm fine. Just have to catch my breath."

Her guarded expression let him know whatever had frightened her, she found no reason to trust him with it. He was still a stranger. A few hours acquaintance hadn't changed that. "Is there anything I can do for you?"

A long moment of silence passed between them. "No."

The naked vulnerability in her gaze washed through him, and the tenderness stirring in his chest startled him. "Then good night, Jill Shepherd." He moved past her onto the open lawn, certain her frightened gaze drilled his back and followed his every step.

Sadness settled in his heart. If she knew why he had sought out this job at Windtop, she'd be appalled. If she knew, she would never trust him.

He kept moving.

Jill tracked Clay's retreat across Windtop's lawn, certain he had witnessed her wild dash. What he must think! But then why should she care unless he reported it to Lenore. The possibility chilled her. She had seen kindness—or was it pity?—in his eyes moments ago. Had she misread him? No, whatever else he might be, he didn't seem the type to expose her like that.

Trust no one at Windtop!

Maggie's words burst through her heart, scattering every crumb of comfort. She turned away to find the familiar forest path. Though overgrown, it still led to the edge of the island's east cliff where the rock of her childhood days waited like an old friend. She climbed onto its cool, flat surface and hugged her knees to her chin. Tears slipped down her cheeks.

If true, Maggie's warning changed everything. Everything she thought she had accomplished in the past few hours. Worse, it might mean she was truly in danger.

Her mother murdered?

Shoulders shaking, she fought the sobs that came too easily since arriving on this island. "Dear God," she whispered, "please say it isn't true." Tears soaked the knees of her jeans. "It's all some terrible mistake, isn't it?"

Far below, the lapping of Trout Bay's waters worked its comforting rhythm, slowly calming her like a child rocked in her mother's arms. When her tears stopped, she stared into the deepening velvet of the evening sky. A smattering of stars winked at her like promises too far away to grasp.

If her mother was murdered, Maggie was right. Only the Bradwells had anything to gain, and by returning to Windtop, she may have unwittingly walked into a trap. "God, would You really let me make such dreadful a mistake?" Would he lead her into mortal danger?

Crickets broke the silence of the summer night while moonlight danced on the bay's dark waters. Lacking the will to move, Jill revisited the events responsible for bringing her here. Yes, it was God's doing, which meant she was in the right place. No matter how frightening it appeared at the moment, Nona would say to trust him. *Walk by faith, not by sight, right?*

Her gaze found the flames from campfires on the beach below. They grew brighter as the evening deepened. With blankets and baskets, people too small to recognize at this distance emerged from cottages. Soon, the aroma of roasting hot dogs and the soft sounds of guitars and singing floated on the night air.

If only she and the Bradwells could enjoy such happy times. Instead, warnings and suspicions flitted among them. Hopefully, Uncle Drew was wrong.

As for Maggie's warning, she was often right about people. Yet, over the years, she had begun to nurse a deep distaste for Lenore. Had it colored her perception? Maybe the housekeeper was wrong this time. Nothing else made sense.

Jill stretched her legs and slid down from the rock. As she made her way back to the house, forest trees pressed in close around her. She shivered, searching the darkness and hurrying, uncomfortably aware she had stayed out longer than wise on a wilderness island.

When she broke free of the trees, she paused. Windtop's silhouette stood against a moonlit sky while the damp night air stole around her in billows of ground fog. She hurried up the wooden steps of the back porch and twisted the door handle.

Locked!

Chapter Six

Clay's hands stirred a discordant clinking of dirty dishes and silverware in the sink full of hot, soapy water. Scrubbing a plate with more vigor than necessary, he rinsed it in hot running water and dropped it into the dish rack.

Visions of Jill's golden hair, alive with noonday sunlight, filled his senses as he stared into the darkness beyond the window above the sink. Her anxious gaze haunted him.

Her frantic flight earlier coiled in his gut. Something or someone had frightened her enough to drive her from the shadowed house. The deadly clock was already ticking.

He should've said something at the airport or Powell's Point, or the cemetery. He'd had plenty of opportunities to spill the suspicions he couldn't quite prove yet. Would she listen now if he gave her the chance? Or toss him out with yesterday's garbage?

A sudden spurt of adrenaline shot like fire through his veins. He seized the glass casserole dish and scraped at the crusty edge of baked lasagna as if it were the offending party. A determined scrubbing finished the job but did nothing to help him remove the threat to Jill.

Was she still out there, a prey to her enemy? Or had she returned to the house? Either way, Windtop was no sanctuary, and the Bradwells' presence stripped him of easy access to ensure her well-being.

He pulled the sink plug, and dishwater spiraled into the drain, gurgling on its final exit. He rinsed the dishrag, ringing the excess water from it. Snapping it flat, he folded it once before hanging it on the sink's edge to dry.

Focus. Be methodical. Maintain control. If he did that, he might get the job done before harm ambushed her.

Most of all, he had to be careful. Something in him softened a bit more each time he neared Windtop's golden-haired beauty. He couldn't let her sidetrack him.

He flicked the faucet handle and sprayed the sink with clean water, then rubbed it dry.

A little more time. If he stepped up the hunt, that's all he'd need. Then he'd be gone.

Jill released the front door knob. It, too, refused to budge. What kind of game was this? What kind of trick?

Raising a fist, she prepared to pound on the door but pulled back. Why give her aunt the satisfaction? She'd find another way.

Skirting the house, she tested each window of the first floor. All secure. Never in all the summers she'd lived in this house did she have this much trouble getting into it. She dropped down on the bottom step of the front porch. She'd get in without Lenore knowing, but how?

Clay knew the house and might help her. But knock on his door at this hour? Too embarrassing. She'd think of another way.

Rubbing her arms against the evening's damp chill, she moved away from the house and let her gaze roam its shadowed recesses. Honeysuckle vines festooned the veranda to the roof line. Well beyond the eaves, the tower room windows looked out into the night. While a teen, she had used those windows and the roof to sneak in and out of the house after dark. Not tonight. Her old room now belonged to Tia. If she climbed in through one of those windows, she would startle the girl. What a ruckus that would cause.

Letting her gaze drift to the right, she stopped where the porch roof intersected with another section extending over the driveway. Her pulse quickened. That was it! From there she could reach Maggie's balcony and get into her room. She hadn't locked the French doors. All she'd have to do was move quietly and she'd outsmart Lenore yet.

Hurrying up the porch steps, she grasped the roof's first supporting column and pulled herself onto the railing. The rich scent of roses from her mother's bush wafted upward, and her heart lurched. Tending the rose bush had been her mother's joy, and the only reason she would venture outdoors during those last years they had summered at Windtop.

Quick tears blurred Jill's vision. She blinked them away and reached with one hand for the ledge above.

"Need a boost?"

Jill gasped, hugged the column, and peered over her shoulder.

Clay stood below in the moonlight, a quizzical expression on his upturned face.

Warmth crept over hers. "I, uh …" Wait a minute. She didn't have to explain herself. The house belonged to her. She could do whatever she pleased. "You almost scared me to death!"

He chuckled. "Sorry about that. What's going on?"

Obviously, he wasn't about to allow her a graceful way out. "If you must know, I'm locked out." *Good grief!* Was amusement crinkling the corners of his eyes?

He hooked his thumbs in his jean pockets. "Someone must have activated the security system."

"Security system?" Windtop didn't have a security system.

He strode up the porch steps. "Here, let me help you down."

She did feel a bit silly hugging the column as if it was a life preserver, but she certainly didn't need his help. "No thanks. I can manage."

Relaxing her grip too fast, she started to slip. *Oops!*

His broad hands caught her by the waist, but momentum prevailed. She pitched forward, grabbing his well-muscled shoulders. The ploy broke her fall, but she found herself eye-to-eye with her rescuer.

He lifted her down amid the sweet fragrances of red roses and creamy-yellow honeysuckle swirling around them. Her skin tingled beneath his touch, and for a breathless moment, she gazed into eyes of fathomless depth.

This was crazy. She didn't even know him. All right, a little, but really, how much could she know anyone in a mere matter of hours? Besides, he wasn't making a pass.

Clay released her and she shivered. He hadn't answered her question yet. "So, whose idea was this security system?"

"Your mother's."

"Well, you could have told me before!" And even though a bit miffed, she could've spoken to him with a less edgy tone.

His gaze remained steady. "I didn't know it was in use again. After your mother's … death, your uncle ordered it disarmed."

On the other hand, when Lenore wanted anything, she wouldn't let a mere matter of her husband's displeasure stand in her way. To outsmart her aunt the next time, Jill would need more information. "So how does it work?"

"The keypads are inside the front and back doors and in the master bedroom. You can lock every door and window from any one of them. Once the system's engaged, you need a key to enter the house."

So one of the keypads was in Lenore's room? How convenient. Jill hugged herself against the evening chill.

Clay removed his thick cardigan and wrapped it around her shoulders. "I take it you don't have your key with you."

She pulled his sweater close. Its soft volume wrapped her in his lingering warmth and masculine woodsy fragrance. "I didn't know I'd need it." That, and she had left in a hurry.

He shrugged. "You could've knocked."

"And wake the whole house? I'd rather stay outside all night."

His eyes regained that annoying amusement. "I wouldn't advise it."

He was right. Not a good choice on a wilderness island.

"If you want, you could use the phone line between the main house and gatehouse to let your uncle know you're locked out. It's operating now."

At her astonished reluctance, Clay squelched a smile—spunky enough to try and scale the house but balking at using a phone?

"Or I could call for you."

She bit her lower lip, taking her time before nodding.

The moon shone bright overhead and ground fog swirled around their feet. He paced himself beside her as they walked the graveled drive toward the gatehouse. "How is your kitten doing?"

Jill looked up at him with those large, expressive eyes. "Button loves everything you brought."

"Button?"

"Don't ask," she shot back as if he didn't need to know everything. A few steps later, she bent her head. "Okay, he's so curious, he reminds me of myself when I was growing up. Button was my nickname."

"Button, huh? Well, one thing's sure. You're both fast on your feet." He grinned.

Her cheeks pinked as she slid him a sideway glance then shrugged. "I was merely taking a walk."

Right! "Pretty fast walk."

"Walk. Run. It's all exercise." She lifted her chin and picked up the pace as if to prove her point.

Since she had closed the subject, he'd drop it for now. He picked up his own pace to catch up with her. She was a feisty little thing when she wanted to be. It would either serve her well or get her into even more trouble if she stayed. Good thing she planned to leave soon.

Clay opened the gatehouse door and stood aside, allowing her to enter first. A nightlight near the kitchen sink cast a soft glow and outlined her shapely silhouette. He flipped on the overhead light and grabbed a poker to coax life into the dying embers in the cottage's fieldstone fireplace.

As he added a log to the fire, pages rustled and he tensed. Jill had wandered to his drawing board and its blueprints.

"Windtop?" she asked.

He nodded. "Do you read blueprints?" *Please say you don't.*

"I learned the skill to help with my research on house histories."

His gut clenched as she peeled back another page. He steeled himself against stopping her. He'd have to distract her before she went too far. "An interesting hobby."

"It's my job. I write up house histories for interested clients. It's a type of genealogy."

"I know." He also knew her skill could spell danger for both of them. "Let's take care of your phone call."

★★★

Moonlight glowed across the landscape and the house loomed ahead as Jill strolled beside Clay. The unmistakable current flowing between them made no sense. Neither was staying around long enough to develop a meaningful relationship. She would leave in a day or two and he'd finish his work here and go back to his life, wherever it was. As attractive as he was, she wouldn't get involved with this Clay Merrick.

To be honest though, she was curious. Where did he live? What kind of life did he know away from Windtop?

He broke the companionable silence. "You're leaving soon."

She glanced up and caught his scrunched brow. Was he hoping she might stay? She shrugged. "That's the plan."

His shoulders relaxed. Was he relieved? So much for his possible interest in her, and maybe it was best. The last thing she needed was another relationship so soon after Brian.

"And then?"

Clay's intense gaze caught her off guard. She pulled his sweater close. "Back to Chicago. How about you? Where's home when you're not working on a restoration project?"

He thrust his hands into his windbreaker's pockets. "Willowbrook."

Jill peered up at him. "Illinois?"

He nodded.

Not far from Nona's. "Quite a distance from here. How did you hear about this job?"

He continued to walk, focusing ahead. "Word of mouth."

"And there's no one back home to keep you there?"

Stopping, he stared at her with such dark intensity she regretted the flippant question. "If you're asking about family, they're all dead."

Jill's breath caught in her throat. Everyone? How awful for him. "I'm— I'm so sorry."

He barely nodded, but she'd already glimpsed his pain. So that explained his quiet sympathy at the cemetery and the kindnesses he had shown her since. He understood grief.

She stared into the night, hurting for him as well as herself as they approached the house.

Long fingers of light pierced the windows of Windtop's entrance hall and flooded the porch. She paused at the bottom step, reluctant to end her time with him. "Thank you for helping me."

His gaze lingered, his eyes solemn. "Good night, Jill Shepherd. Be careful."

She stared at him. Careful of what?

Before she could open her mouth, he strode away. The night shadows swallowed him even as the front door opened. Uncle Drew stepped out.

"Jill, is it you?"

Lenore hovered behind him in a red satin nightgown and wrapper, her eyes bright with too much interest. Clay's troubling words followed Jill as she hurried up the porch steps.

Uncle Drew moved aside to let her enter before closing the door. "I'm sorry for all this trouble, Jill. If only you had told us you were going out."

A smug smile clung to her aunt's lips. The woman's dark brown eyes sparkled with a cold mischief.

Jill shook her head. Trying to befriend her aunt was a wasted effort, just as Uncle Drew suggested.

She turned to him. At least she could talk to him. "Why didn't you tell me about the security system?"

"Why, I … it slipped my mind, Jill. We haven't used it since—" He closed his mouth, and a trace of gray followed his jawline.

Lenore lifted her chin and smiled. "Since Susannah died."

Jill clenched her fists. Why did the woman continue to goad her? She'd never done anything to earn her aunt's animosity. At least nothing she knew of.

Uncle Drew leveled a stern gaze at his wife. "From now on, Lenore, we will refrain from using the security system."

"If you say so." Her aunt's cool gaze flicked to Jill. "Anyway, little good it did your mother, locking out help while she bled to death in plain sight."

Jill's knees buckled. She grabbed the back of a nearby chair to steady herself. Her mother hadn't died of an overdose? Hadn't died in her room as Jill supposed?

In a swirl of red satin, Lenore turned away. "I'm going back to bed, Drew. Please don't be long."

As his wife withdrew, Uncle Drew put an arm around Jill's shoulders. "I'm sorry you heard it this way, Jill. Come on. Isn't it time you let me tell you how your mother died?"

Jill let him guide her into the parlor where he switched on the Tiffany table lamp beside the couch. He helped her to sit and took the space beside her.

She peered at him, trying to fathom what her aunt had said, trying to wrap her mind around it, but couldn't. Her uncle was right. It was time she knew how her mother had died. It was time to stop running from her pain.

Leaning forward, he placed his forearms on his knees and examined his short, square hands. "My sister—your mother—wasn't well her last year. The doctor said she had become deeply paranoid, afraid of everyone but Mrs. Pierce."

"Paranoid?" Before Jill left, her mother had only cut herself off from her brother and his family out of necessity. How else would she find peace from Lenore's verbal attacks?

As for her mother trusting Maggie Pierce, that made sense. Their long-time housekeeper had been their staunch and loyal protector, no matter what trick Lenore attempted. A protection her mother failed to experience from her brother.

He cleared his throat, drawing Jill's attention back. "The day your mother died, Mrs. Pierce had gone to town on errands."

Jill pictured her mother waiting alone in this house, easy pickings for anyone.

"Only for a few hours, and before she left, she made sure Susannah activated the security system." He shook his head. "If only she hadn't. Everyone tried to talk Susannah out of installing it, including Merrick."

Clay? "What did he have to do with it?"

"He hired the subcontractor and oversaw its installation to make sure it didn't alter Windtop's historic value. He also made sure it was everything Susannah wanted."

Jill imagined the metallic racket of locks and bolts slamming into place though she was certain home security systems made no such noise.

"He explained how dangerous it might be if Susannah were alone and the house caught fire. Or she had an accident. But she insisted and signed legal papers absolving Merrick and the subcontractor of any liability."

Jill bit her lip, not wanting to hear more, yet knowing she must. How else could she put Maggie's suspicions to rest? How else would she find peace about her mother's death?

Her uncle's face pinched as if he were in pain. "Mrs. Pierce insisted Susannah was happy that morning. She even accompanied her to the front door and said she would be all right."

A strange change because before Jill left, her mother would beg Maggie not to leave the house. She would pace and agonize until the housekeeper returned.

"When Mrs. Pierce returned, she found the house locked and Susannah lying at the foot of the stairs. She searched her purse but couldn't find her key. She rapped on the window and shouted, but Susannah didn't move." His voice choked off.

Strength drained from Jill's body, yet as difficult as it was listening, she had to know the rest. "Please go on."

"Are you sure?" His gaze held great concern.

Bracing herself, she nodded. No more running. No more hiding. No more pretending.

"Mrs. Pierce found Merrick at the gatehouse where he was packing. He'd already turned in his key, so he drove her back to the house and ran to the garage to find Windtop's handyman."

"Sam?"

"Yes. He had a key, but by the time they got to Susannah, she was barely alive. She died before the sheriff and the emergency medical team could get to the island. The sheriff and the coroner determined Susannah had jumped from the second-floor railing."

Jill moaned. So her mother had committed suicide. *And, Lord, I'm to blame. If only I hadn't run away. If only I had come back sooner.*

She sat beside her uncle in muted silence until chimes from the grandfather clock invaded their grief. He wiped his eyes with a monogrammed handkerchief and blew his nose. "I should go. Lenore is waiting. Will you be all right?"

All right? She'd never again be all right. Yet she nodded. Uncle Drew carried enough of his own pain. He didn't need to carry hers too.

Looking somehow older, he stood and rested a hand on her shoulder. For a long moment, he looked into her eyes, then turned and walked away.

Seeking the comfort of darkness, Jill flicked off the lamp and wandered to a nearby window where she stared into the night. What had compelled her mother to install a system of protection that proved so dangerous? What had happened to convince her it was necessary?

Those last years while Jill had lived at home, her mother refused to see Lenore and Uncle Drew, but not because she was afraid of them. She didn't even hold ill feelings toward them. She had simply grown tired of the struggle over Windtop and decided it was best they go their separate ways.

Why install this security system? The easy answer said the doctor was right. Her mother's mental health had degenerated while Jill searched for her birth father.

"Lord, is that right?" If so, her plan to find her father in order to help her mother had gone so awry, and she was too tired to think about it anymore tonight.

She turned from the window and walked through the shadowed room into the light of the entrance hall. Rest. She needed it badly, but would she ever rest again?

Murder! Murder! Murder!

Maggie's accusation rang in her tired head as she climbed the stairs. She covered her ears. *No! Lord, there has to be another answer.* Maybe an accident and she could prove it. Clay was right. She was her mother's physical likeness, definitely the same height.

Trembling, she approached the second-floor railing. What if she was wrong? What if she was simply refusing to accept the truth?

She held back, moistening her lips, and stared at the polished railing. It seemed to mock her with her distorted reflection gleaming on its surface. Her too-pale skin and widened eyes. *Please, Lord, let it be an accident.*

Slowly, she leaned against the railing and bent forward. With a sickening wrench in the pit of her stomach, she backed away. The railing was too high. Her mother's death was no accident. She would've had to climb over the railing.

Or be thrown over.

The grandfather clock tick-tocked in the silent hall below while the carpeted floor beneath her seemed to undulate until she thought she might throw up.

Then a door clicked softly behind her, raising the hairs on the back of her neck.

Chapter Seven

*A*nother moment and that stupid girl would've caught me. What was she doing haunting the hall railing at this hour?

Ha! As if I don't know. All her sweet talk about coming back to confess her lie. She didn't fool me for a minute. She knows ... or at least suspects. Either way, I'm not waiting around to find out which.

Too bad she's not more like her mother. Susannah made it easy by staying in her room. Not this one. I have debts to pay, and she could hamper me. From now on, I'll plan more carefully, and if she makes the same mistake her mother did, she'll have to go. In the meantime, I'll work on a right way to get rid of her.

A way she'll never see coming.

Jill tucked her bedspread into place, her mind utterly elsewhere. She had whirled around last night, only to find an empty hall. Yet the soft click behind her hadn't been her imagination. Someone had been watching.

Was it her mother's killer?

She would need irrefutable proof before she would believe anyone at Windtop could do such a thing. Neither would she just walk away from the truth and spend the rest of her life wondering.

Wasn't it hard enough knowing her mother's death could only be murder or suicide? She couldn't accept either, which left her with no other choice but to dig out the facts. She'd had plenty of practice in the last three years while working for Nona, but this time, she'd have to do it without alerting anyone. Not an easy task in a small town.

Adjusting her purse strap on her shoulder, Jill made a quick check of her room and spotted Clay's sweater. She picked it up from the dressing table and held its brown folds to her face, breathing in the clean, masculine scent. He had wrapped her in its warmth last night and seen her safely into the house.

As she sighed, she caught her image in the mirror. Her reflected eyes widened.

For a moment, her face had held the same wistful expression as her mother's whenever Jill had asked about her father. She couldn't be attracted to Clay this soon, could she? He was just a kind stranger, nothing more.

One thing was sure. She didn't need another Brian Caldwell in her life. She'd promised herself as much.

That didn't stop Brian's mesmerizing blue eyes and commanding presence from swimming through her memory with as much force as the day he walked into Nona Anderson's agency. The young, up-and-coming lawyer arrived on business but wouldn't leave until she agreed to have dinner with him.

How quickly they fell in love and began planning their future. To Brian's credit, he stayed with her through the shattering grief of her mother's death, but when she became a Christian, the climate changed.

"Bible study and church," he groused. "That's all you care about these days." He reached for her hands, urgency radiating from his handsome face. "If you keep this up, Jill, how can we be right for each other? I haven't changed. Please. Don't ruin it for us."

Though she tried to make him understand, every attempt ended in an argument. They strained in opposite directions until finally, they agreed. Their engagement had to end.

She had wept for days before she made up her mind. Never again would she be torn to shreds like that. From here on, any man who came into her life would have to love the Lord as much as she did.

So why this attraction to Clay Merrick—someone she hardly knew? He was kind, but if he loved God, he hadn't said so, and she wasn't ready for a relationship so soon after Brian.

Be careful, Jill.

Maybe Clay's words last night had been God's way of warning her. Was she to guard her heart against a risky entanglement with Windtop's restoration contractor?

As she laid the folds of Clay's sweater over her arm, a tug at her shoelaces demanded her attention. Button. She lifted him to eye level and kissed the top of his soft, furry head. She'd almost forgotten him.

"Okay, you little blessing. Time to hang out in the bathroom until I get back."

Hopefully, she would return soon with information leading her closer to the truth about her mother's death.

Jill slipped into the morning room. The phone on the desk only connected with the gatehouse and was powered by a generator. No good for her purposes.

Setting Clay's sweater on the spindle-legged desk, she opened a side drawer and removed this year's edition of the phone book. She found the sheriff's and the coroner's numbers and jotted them on a piece of Windtop's ivory note paper.

The temptation to use her cell phone nearly won, but the island's formation made communication spotty at best. Besides, she couldn't chance being overheard.

She tucked the phone numbers into her purse and picked up Clay's sweater. If she hurried, she might make the calls from the public phone at Williams Landing, stop for a brief visit at the cemetery, and return before the Bradwells came down for breakfast.

A flow of low conversation in the entrance hall arrested her. "I'll see to it," Clay said to Lenore, then glanced in her direction and jerked.

"See to what?" Jill asked.

Lenore startled as well, then glided toward Jill. "You're up early. Perfect. We need to talk."

The last thing Jill wanted. Likely her aunt had been watching her last night. "I was just leaving."

"So soon?" Her aunt flashed a coy smile.

The woman wearied her. "Not from the island." She stepped past her aunt to speak to Clay. "See to what?"

When he didn't respond, her heart plummeted, and she held out his sweater. "I forgot to return this to you last night. Thank you for its use."

"You're welcome." He reached out to take it, his intense gaze locked with hers.

She scrunched her eyebrows together. Well, really. As if last night had never happened, this morning he shut her out. He wasn't going to tell her anything. Maggie was right. She couldn't trust anyone at Windtop, not even Clay. If that's the way he wanted it, she could live with it. It's not as if they meant anything to one another. "I'm visiting my mother's grave this morning. Is Windtop's Jeep available?"

"I'll see to it," he said, quick to leave.

Lenore looped her arm through Jill's, pressing her back toward the morning room. "In the meantime, you do have a moment after all."

Jill extricated her arm. "What do you want, Lenore?"

"Let's get comfortable first, shall we?" She gestured toward the morning room and preceded Jill, glancing back. After seating herself behind the desk, Lenore indicated the two pink upholstered chairs facing it. "Please."

Jill chose the one nearest the door while her aunt laced her fingers together and rested her elbows on the desk. "Yesterday, you said I could use this house as I had planned. You haven't changed your mind, have you?"

Yesterday ... eons ago. If she could snatch the invitation back, she would, but she couldn't afford stirring up trouble with her aunt. Not before she knew the truth about her mother's death.

She shook her head.

Lenore smiled. "We planned to celebrate Tia's sixteenth birthday at Windtop."

She could celebrate a family birthday. "I don't see a problem."

"Excellent! We mailed the invitations months ago."

Jill blinked and swallowed. *Invitations?* This was to be one of her aunt's lavish parties? At one of them, Lenore had humiliated Jill's mother so deeply that her mother had been ill for weeks and withdrew from everyone except her daughter and Maggie.

An excited flush highlighted Lenore's cheeks as she rushed on. "It will be the social event of Tia's young life, a tradition celebrated by my side of the family for generations."

Wait a minute. Hadn't her aunt been an orphan? "I don't understand."

The woman's gaze darkened. "Don't be difficult, Jill. The party is only two weeks away, and changing arrangements this late is next to impossible. Not to mention costly."

Jill settled back into the chair and crossed her legs. Lenore hosting a party at Windtop was the last thing she wanted with the cause of her mother's death so uncertain.

Lenore tapped her ring finger on the desktop as she waited.

Jill studied her aunt. Actually, the party might work to her advantage, keeping the Bradwells distracted and less likely to notice her search. Agreeing to it now would end this interview.

She stood. "I have no objection."

"Wonderful! But wait," Lenore rushed on. "To complete preparations, we must finish Windtop's restoration."

Jill moved toward the door. "Whatever you need to do."

"Then I have your permission to bring in its historic furnishings? Drew felt you might object to replacing Susannah's things."

Jill stopped and stiffened. "Remove my mother's things?"

"I'm sorry, but your mother's furniture looks completely out of place. Of course, a few pieces belonged to the original house. They will remain."

"And the others?" She wasn't yet ready to part with reminders of her mother simply to please Lenore.

Her aunt moistened her lips. "We'll store some in the attic and the rest in town."

Jill released the tense breath she had been holding. As long as her mother's belongings wouldn't disappear, she could live with that. This disruption of the house so soon after her return would be hard to bear. Being surrounded by her mother's things, able to touch them and recall the little details of life they had shared, comforted her. Yet the transition Lenore had in mind would keep the Bradwells' attention focused away from Jill.

"All right. Do what you think is necessary."

Lenore's dark eyes widened.

"But don't get rid of Mother's things. I want every one of them." What Jill would do with them, she wasn't sure, but she should be the one to decide. "Is there anything else?"

Her aunt blinked rapidly as if unable to believe her good fortune, and then shook her head.

A soft breeze swept off Murray Bay, urging Jill up the pathway to the cemetery. At her mother's gravesite, she buried her face in the great bouquet of garden flowers she carried in her arms and breathed in the sweet fragrance of daisies, lavender, and daylilies.

How kind of Clay to leave them on the front seat of the Jeep along with a scrawled note. *For your mother.* Strange how one moment, he shut her out and the next, he displayed such thoughtfulness.

As she crouched to place the flowers on her mother's grave, a hollow sadness enveloped her. Did her mother know the Lord before she died? Had she accepted his forgiveness?

A twig snapped in the forest glade. Jill glanced around catching nothing but a fleeting shadow. Was it a passing deer or someone watching her?

Touching her fingertips to her lips, she pressed them on her mother's cold grave marker and hurried away. It was time to make those phone calls at Williams Landing.

Jill drove along the road on the island's southern shore as fast as she dared. Even so, she caught a glimpse of the cottage on Murray Bay. Her father had stayed there the summer he met her mother, and a fresh ache of longing pressed on her heart.

Cut off from her father and never again to know the touch of her mother's hand or hear her voice, she was surrounded by family who neither trusted nor wanted her. Did she belong anywhere?

Under a cloudless sky, she barreled toward Williams Landing and, hopefully, some of the answers she sought. At the public phone attached to a tree, she pulled the phone numbers from her purse and glanced across the channel. She had little time. A large flat barge had already begun its brief island-bound journey from Powell's Point.

A sheriff's deputy answered her first call. News of her return had already reached their department. On Monday, he said, she could pick up copies of the records of their investigation into her mother's death, including the coroner's report. No need to make the second call after all.

Hanging up, she pulled herself together just as the barge docked.

Thick-muscled men looped heavy mooring ropes to the pier pilings and dropped the ferry's ramp to the shore. Released from their tethers, two big trucks cranked their motors and lumbered off. *Munising Moving and Storage* stretched across their sides.

So Lenore had played her again! Why had her aunt even asked permission? She obviously already knew Windtop's historic furnishings were on their way.

Jumping into the Jeep as the trucks lumbered past, Jill turned her key in the ignition and gunned the engine to follow.

While Jill parked the Jeep outside the carriage house, the trucks pulled up in front of Windtop's main entrance. Men in striped uniforms opened the large doors at the back of the trucks and set ramps into place. She glared at her aunt. The ungrateful woman!

"You're back."

Jill whipped around. Clay smiled from the carriage house's open door, a light breeze playing with the deep waves of his dark brown hair. She pointed toward the house. "Did you know about this?"

"That they were coming today? Sure." His smile faded, and his gray eyes lit with understanding. "No one told you."

"I ... well, yes. Lenore said something before I left this morning, but she didn't say a thing until the trucks were on their way."

Opening the door to the Jeep, Clay stepped aside. "How about taking a walk? I pulled together the information about Windtop your uncle asked me to go over with you."

She'd rather give Lenore a piece of her mind, but some down time might be a good idea. It would give her a chance to gain control of herself before confronting her aunt. "Lead the way."

"My clipboard is in the gazebo. Let's drop off this hammer where it'll be handy when we finish."

Jill fell into step beside him. They skirted the house and entered the brick walkway dividing a maze of flowerbeds surrounding Windtop's gazebo. The same flowerbeds, it appeared, had provided the beautiful blossoms now lying on her mother's grave.

★★★

Sunlight glistened like precious gold in Jill's hair as she bent her head, not looking his way. "Thank you for the flowers. Mother would have loved them."

A glimmer of light pierced the wall of his heart. "My pleasure."

"And I owe you some money." She dug in her purse.

"No, you don't."

"For Button's supplies." She opened her wallet. "Is this enough?"

The amount she thrust into his hand more than covered what he had spent. He returned some and held up the rest. "This will do."

He set the hammer inside the gazebo and grabbed a clipboard from the top step. "Ready?"

Walking her through the gardens and around the grounds, he pointed out various features of the landscaping and the exterior of the house. He answered her questions and explained in detail what he had done and the cost of each renovation. Together, they sat on the back porch, going over his records and examining the photos he had taken of the progress with both the interior and exterior of the house.

Her sweet breath brushed his cheek. Their heads almost touched, and his pulse quickened. Annoyed with himself, he pulled away, forcing himself to focus on the final details of his report. "I planned to begin work on the carriage house Monday. It's in pretty good shape, so it shouldn't take long. Sam will help me rebuild the stone wall next to it. It needs a lot of work. Then, restoring the kitchen garden and the flower beds at the base of the house's wraparound porch and repairing the gazebo should about do it."

Just as before while they had walked around the house, she listened with rapt attention. He'd forgotten how good that felt. Regretfully, one of life's pleasures he would soon learn to do without. Once she knew the truth about him, she'd never see him in the same way again.

Wishing otherwise was pointless. Sometimes, a man had to do what was right for those he loved, no matter what it cost him.

Right now, he'd finish this report and hopefully get her go-ahead. "As for the house, it's finished except for a minor detail." From the clipboard, he pulled out a photo of an oval crest decorating the gable end of the roof extending over Windtop's drive. He pointed to the elaborately scrolled B. "This original feature all but disappeared."

"It's beautiful, but I don't remember ever seeing it. How did you find this photo?"

Her sincere interest warmed him. She really cared about this passion of his life. "Your aunt owns an impressive collection of old documents, pictures, and information about Windtop."

"I suppose I shouldn't be surprised." Jill nodded toward the trucks. "She's obviously been collecting an abundance of things Windtop-related."

The hurt in her voice made him pause. He knew how difficult her aunt could be. He found the woman challenging at times, but he also had to admit she had been a great help with this project. And he had her to thank for hiring him.

Jill carefully examined the photo. "It's sometimes difficult to find important information like this."

"All the work your aunt had done before I arrived sure sped up this project. Before I started, she purchased copies of the original wall coverings and the paints each room required. They matched what I discovered when I removed the layers applied since the house was built."

Jill followed him as he led the way back to the gazebo. She stopped and tilted her head to gaze up at him in a way that tempted him to let down his guard. "You really love your work, Clay, and I want you to finish this project."

Good. He still had a cover while he worked to catch a killer. He slid a glance toward the woman at his side as they came full circle to the gazebo. If only his life weren't so complicated.

"About the security system," she said. "Did Mother explain why she thought it was so important?"

He shook his head. "But her housekeeper mentioned evidence of unexplained break-ins making your mother anxious."

"What kind of evidence?"

"She didn't say, and I didn't ask." Now he wished he had. "Jill?"

Her soft gaze made his gut glitch. "I tried to warn your mother, but she wouldn't listen. Please don't make the same mistake."

She stepped back, her eyes wide.

"Leave as soon as you can."

Chapter Eight

Leave as soon as you can.

The same words Maggie had used.

His gaze flicked beyond her. "We have company."

She turned to face the house and found her aunt advancing with Tia at her heels.

"There you are!" Lenore's sharp voice called out. "I have been waiting for you."

Jill stood her ground. "I want to talk to you too."

"Never mind that. Follow me!" Her aunt spun around, returning to the house without a backward glance.

Jill stared at the back of the woman who invaded her house, tricked her, and ordered her around like a servant. Why should she be surprised? She'd never known Lenore to act otherwise.

She sighed and turned back to Clay. "I'd better see what she wants, but please, let's continue this conversation later."

His gray eyes solemn, he nodded. "I'll be around."

She hurried toward the house, still troubled by his cryptic statement. Why did he think she should leave? Why as soon as possible? She shivered as she entered the house.

Dodging six workmen carting her mother's couch and chairs from the parlor, she backed onto a small Persian rug at the foot of the stairs and refused to move one more step. "What's the emergency?"

Lenore speared her with a dark glare. "Can't you see? These rooms must be cleaned before the men unload the trucks."

Tia flipped her blonde hair behind her shoulders and grinned. "It seems Mother's temporary help didn't show up." She dipped her head toward a

65

girl in a maid's uniform who was hiding in the corner. "Elma can't finish nineteen rooms by herself."

"And our housekeeper is threatening to quit," Lenore added.

Jill gaped at her aunt. "What does this have to do with me?"

"It is your house!" her aunt asserted.

"But this"—Jill gestured to the chaos around them—"is your doing, and you didn't tell me it would be going on this soon."

Tia's brown eyes danced. "Time to pack up and go home, Mom."

"We will not!" Her aunt was never one to give up.

All right then, Jill could think of one solution, but Lenore might not like it. "We could all pitch in together and get the work done."

Tia backed up. "Not me."

Tapping her chin, Lenore appeared to consider the idea. "We will still need Mrs. Fenton. You two, come with me."

Out of curiosity, Jill followed her aunt into the morning room. Tia slipped in behind her before Lenore closed the door.

A stout woman with graying hair perched stiffly on the fragile pink chair Jill had occupied earlier. The woman lumbered to her feet and addressed Lenore. "You have my check?"

Her aunt smiled sweetly. "Now, Mrs. Fenton, we've always been fair to you, haven't we?"

The woman eyed Lenore with suspicion. "That's got nothing to do with it. My mind's made up. I ain't working in no haunted house. I'd appreciate my pay."

"I do have your check." She held it up. "But first, I would like you to meet my niece. Jill, this is our housekeeper."

Mrs. Fenton's head jerked toward her. "You ain't dead?"

"Exactly!" Lenore's satisfied smile sealed her point.

The housekeeper crossed her arms. "So what? Her mother ain't alive."

Jill's heart nearly buckled under the woman's words. How little it took. This time, just the mention of her mother in such a context pierced her. How could people believe the dead haunted places? Even if it were true— which it wasn't—who could believe her gentle mother would hurt anyone?

"Excuse me, Mrs. Fenton," Jill said, interrupting the two, "has anyone reported my mother haunting Windtop?"

The woman pursed her lips. "Well, no. But I don't aim to be the first."

Jill inhaled a bracing breath. How could she convince this woman for her own sake that she was wrong?

An idea came to her. "Mrs. Fenton, do you believe in God?"

The woman arched indignantly. "Of course!"

Now they were getting somewhere. "What about the Bible? Do you believe that it's God's Word and tells us the truth?"

Mrs. Fenton nodded decisively and then stopped to eye Jill with suspicion. "Hey, what are you getting at?"

"Well, it says, *people are destined to die once, and after that to face judgment.*"

"So?"

"It means we have one life to live. When we die, we go immediately before God, and then to wherever we will spend eternity. Our spirits don't stay on earth."

Mrs. Fenton wasn't buying it. "So you say, but what about my pa? I saw his ghost with my own eyes."

"My friend, Nona, could explain this much better than I can, but here's what she told me. What appear to be ghosts aren't. They're evil spirits who have the power to appear as people who have died."

The housekeeper slanted a narrow-eyed glance.

"Whatever you saw, Mrs. Fenton, wasn't your father. It was an illusion from God's enemy."

The woman thrust forward a stubborn chin. "Why would Satan do that?"

"He's the father of lies. I imagine he did it to deceive you. To frighten you. To take your attention away from God."

The housekeeper tilted her head to one side. She appeared to be wavering.

"You have nothing to fear, Mrs. Fenton," Jill continued. "My mother is already in her eternal home. She's nowhere near Windtop."

"You're sure the Bible says that?"

"Yes." Jill let the housekeeper chew on this truth for a few moments. "Did you know my aunt values your work? She said we can't do without your help."

"She did?" Mrs. Fenton pursed her lips, glancing first at Lenore and then back at Jill. Finally, she stuck out her hand to Jill. "Okay, I'll stay, but the minute anything funny happens, I'm outta here."

Jill shook the woman's hand. "Fair enough."

Lenore brushed past Jill. "Well, then, Mrs. Fenton. Let's get you settled in."

The woman eyed Lenore as if she might be entertaining second thoughts. "I guess."

"Tia," Lenore said, "show Mrs. Fenton to the rooms above the kitchen. She will want to choose which one suits her best."

Jill waited until her cousin left with the housekeeper before she addressed Lenore. "You knew the movers were on their way when we talked earlier this morning. Before you asked my permission."

"I did." Lenore shuffled some papers on the desk as if looking for something important.

"Then why bother to ask?"

Her aunt shrugged. "Drew insisted I get permission, so I did the best I could. After all, I had no way of contacting the company to reschedule."

"You could have said so."

"I could have, but I didn't want any fuss. My way was more"—Lenore flashed a triumphant smile—"efficient, and may I say you impressed me just now. You were quite clever in how you handled Mrs. Fenton. Your suggestion about us all helping to clean Windtop's rooms is also excellent, so hadn't we better get to work? The trucks must leave by evening, and we have much to do."

Tia poked her head in the room. "Mrs. Fenton says breakfast will be ready in fifteen minutes."

"And we will be ready." Lenore smiled sweetly. "Won't we, Jill?"

Barely nodding, Jill held her tongue. Lenore might think she had won this round, but Jill knew better. She had a good reason for giving in to her aunt. The less she rankled the woman, the more her aunt would concentrate on Windtop, and the more Jill would be free to look into her mother's death.

With only a few minutes to spare before meeting the family in the dining room, Jill hurried upstairs. Button couldn't be shut up alone in the bathroom all day. He must be hungry by now.

She opened her bathroom door, and the kitten greeted her with urgent mews. Picking him up, she gathered his food and water dishes and went down the back stairs to the kitchen.

Nearly finished with breakfast preparations, Mrs. Fenton muttered to herself as she went from refrigerator to cupboard to stove. Jill stayed out of her way and prepared Button's food.

As she placed the food dish and the kitten on the floor near the back door, a shriek rent the air. Button crouched, ready to run, and Jill looked over her shoulder.

"What is that?" her aunt screamed.

Mrs. Fenton rolled her eyes. "A kitten."

"I can see. Get it out. Get it out!" Lenore advanced as if to seize the tiny creature.

Button backed away, and Jill stood to face her aunt as the screen door creaked. Tia came in, and the kitten shot out before the door closed.

"Now you've done it!" Jill glared at her aunt. "I welcomed you into this house, and you've been nothing but trouble. I warn you. This is still my house. The kitten stays, and you'd better hope nothing happens to him before I find him."

Letting the screen door slam behind her, Jill left to find Button. She called and called, but he didn't answer. She looked under the steps and searched every other nook and cranny where he might hide.

After a while, the screen door opened and Mrs. Fenton stepped out. "Any luck?"

Jill glanced around one last time and blew a stray lock of hair away from her face. "He's disappeared."

"Don't worry," the housekeeper soothed. "He'll come back when he's ready."

"He's only been here one day." How far had he gone? Did he know his way back? Would he feel safe enough to return?

Mrs. Fenton held the screen door open. "You've missed breakfast, and Mrs. Bradwell is moving pretty fast. If I was you, I'd keep an eye on her. Oh, and if you're hungry, I can fix you something quick."

Jill took Mrs. Fenton's advice and found Lenore in the entrance hall overseeing the workmen. They had cleared the area of everything but the grandfather clock and the portrait above the fireplace. On a ladder, one workman lifted her mother's portrait down into the waiting hands of two others.

"What are you doing?" Jill advanced, ready to stop them.

Her aunt intervened. "We talked about this, remember? This portrait wasn't part of Windtop's original furnishings." Lenore waved the workmen on.

"Where are they taking it?"

"To the attic, of course."

Three other workmen set out to hang another large portrait in its place. Within minutes, the unfamiliar face of a middle-aged gentleman in late 1800s' garments had taken her mother's honored place.

She squeezed her eyes shut and clamped down on the hot words springing to her tongue. *Lord, this is going too fast. I know you want me to be patient with Lenore, but it's so hard.* Yet, like it or not, she had given her aunt permission. Now she must keep her word no matter how much she wanted to take it back.

Swallowing the hard lump in her throat, she nodded toward the men waiting with her mother's portrait. "Please be careful. Cover it well and make it easily accessible," she said.

As they carried it up the stairs, uneasiness enveloped Jill and lingered through the rest of the day under Lenore's watchful eye. Something awfully wrong was going on here, but she couldn't quite identify it.

Working alongside Tia, Elma, and Mrs. Fenton, Jill helped to dust, polish, sweep, and vacuum each empty room. By late afternoon, every muscle in her body ached. Lenore, on the other hand, seemed to possess endless energy.

How did her aunt do it? Had adrenaline super-charged the woman who had spent years preparing for this day? As the furnishings were put in place, it was obvious Lenore had invested thousands of dollars and an untold amount of time collecting them.

All those years her aunt had no hope of owning Windtop.

An ugly suspicion crossed Jill's heart with muddy footprints. *Surely my aunt would not*—Jill closed her heart against such a possibility. Lenore might be many things, but surely she was no murderer.

Yet, all day, Jill had caught glimpses of Lenore's wary glances. Clay, too, had kept an eye on her as he helped to move larger items into place.

By the day's end, they had completed Windtop's transformation into an 1890s home, and Jill made the long climb to the third floor, pained to realize her mother's version of the house was no more. In her bathroom, she gazed at Button's empty kitten bed and shut the door. Where was he? Was he safe? Would he return?

She sank into Maggie's Bentwood rocker and set it into motion. Those long-ago evenings, when their dear housekeeper would rock her before the warmth of the fire and tell her stories, came to her. Back then, nothing disturbed her that Maggie couldn't quiet with common sense and loving wisdom. Not even Windtop's dark shadows and night noises.

Her gaze wandered to the fireplace. Someone had prepared logs and kindling, ready to dispel the evening's dampness. She rose to take matches from the mantel and stooped to light the fire. It flamed to life.

In its comforting glow, she pulled back the bedspread and lay down to rest a few minutes before preparing for bed. *Please, dear Lord, bring Button back safely.*

She reached for her Bible and lay on the bed, too drowsy to read but reassured by its nearness.

Clay started down the drive toward the gatehouse, unable to get Jill out of his mind. *Please, we must talk later,* she had said. Her lovely eyes pleaded with him. Yet the day passed without a single moment to talk alone.

He glanced back to the house. It was late, but not too late. Lights blazed from the entrance hall and parlor as he knocked on the door.

Drew Bradwell opened it.

"Your niece wanted to speak to me."

"She's gone to bed," the man said. "Can't it wait 'til morning?"

Bradwell made sense, but Clay hesitated. He couldn't shake this peculiar sense of urgency.

Carver's voice boomed down the stairwell. "Fire!"

Hair raised on the back of Clay's neck. He sprinted toward the staircase. Two steps at a time, he bounded toward the second floor, passing Tia, who stood at her door, her eyes wide with alarm. Footsteps pounding behind him let him know three Bradwells scrambled to reach Carver as well.

"I smell smoke," Carver said. "Jill's door won't open."

"Is she in there?"

Carver glared at him.

Clay didn't wait for the fool to answer. Rattling the door handle, he called out, "Jill!"

His pulse racing, he pressed his hands to the door ... no unusual heat. He put his ear to the door. No crackle or hiss of flames, but he did detect a faint odor of smoke. He pounded on the door. "Jill? Can you hear me? Open the door!"

No response.

He turned on Carver and grabbed him by his collar. "Are you sure she's in there?"

Carver pushed him away. "I came from the billiards room and smelled smoke. That's all I know."

Clay put his shoulder to the door. It shuddered but wouldn't budge.

Bradwell pressed in. "If she's in there, she won't last long."

Sprinting past the family, Clay skimmed down the stairs to the second floor and raced through the tower room. Yanking open a window, he dropped to the porch roof and scrambled to gain the section of the roof beneath the balcony to Jill's room.

His lungs squeezed as he grasped the railing and swung onto the balcony. He came down outside the French doors, his heart hammering. Thick smoke pouring from the fireplace had already obscured the ceiling. Jill was sliding down the door to the hall, holding her hands over her mouth and nose.

Wrenching the handles of the French doors, he threw his strength into making them give way. Smoke billowed through the opening, clearing much of the room as he raced to Jill's slumped form. Dropping to his knees, he pulled her away from the door. The wet cloth over her mouth and nose fell away.

Thank, God! She had taken the precaution and was still breathing.

"I've got her!"

The door rattled and burst open.

Aware only of strong arms scooping her up, Jill almost sobbed as she was carried down the hall and through an open door. Cool, damp air washed over her face and arms. Ragged coughs wracked her aching lungs as she breathed in the clean, fresh air.

When her coughing subsided, she opened bleary eyes. Starlight winked above the large balcony at the end of the hall. Clay's tense face hovered over hers, his eyes searching.

Uncle Drew pressed close. "Is she all right?"

Clay clenched his jaw. "If she hasn't taken in too much carbon monoxide. She needs oxygen."

"I'll get it." Her uncle raced away, returning within minutes with a tank and mask.

"Dad has sleep apnea," Tia offered.

While Clay fit the mask to her face, her uncle prepared to feed the oxygen.

Even in her weakened state, she tried to smile to let them know she appreciated their efforts and to thank them for saving her life.

A movement behind Clay proved to be Carver joining the family. Lenore stood nearby, fanning away tiny wisps of smoke drifting from the hall. "Has the house been badly damaged?" her aunt asked.

"It'll be okay," Carver assured her. "The fire was contained in the fireplace. I put it out and closed off all the rooms. Most of the smoke is gone already."

Uncle Drew ran a hand through his thinning hair, his eyes pinched with worry. "Thank God Jill is okay."

Carver smirked. "God had nothing to do with it. She was just lucky."

Jill closed her eyes for a moment. *Poor Carver! How wrong he was.* At least her uncle had the right idea. God had sent Clay to her rescue and provided the oxygen through her uncle.

"It looks like something went wrong with the damper in the fireplace," Carver said. "It's all right now."

Clay gritted his teeth and muttered so low only she could hear, "Nothing was wrong with the damper." His hard gray eyes sought hers, their intensity sweeping her back to the gazebo and his words of warning.

Leave as soon as you can.

She tried to lick her dry lips. The new tightness invading her chest had nothing to do with anything she might have inhaled. Something was terribly wrong at Windtop.

"We have to get her to the hospital," Clay said.

Chapter Nine

The French doors stood ajar, admitting early morning sunshine while a warm breeze swept in to play with the hem of Jill's cotton nightgown. She leaned against the open door to Maggie's room, her head lolling against the frame as her gaze slowly swept the room. The faint odor of smoke tickled her nose.

Last night's surreal images rippled the edges of her memory. Coughing, she woke to a smoky haze backlit by an eerie glow from the fireplace and fear seized her. Holding a wet washcloth over her mouth and nose, she had struggled with the bedroom door. Why wouldn't it open? Just as weakness overtook her body, the French doors wrenched open, and Clay's strong arms lifted and carried her to fresh air and safety.

Most of all, she recalled his muttered words. They chilled her soul.

She shivered, shaking away their unwanted conclusion. How could he believe her near disaster was no accident? He had to be wrong.

"Miss Shepherd!"

Fists jammed on her ample hips, Mrs. Fenton stood in the hall, her kind eyes dark with disapproval. "What are you doing up here? You should be downstairs, resting in bed. You promised the doctor."

Jill squeezed her eyes shut. Oh, yes, the downstairs bedroom. With Maggie's room no longer habitable for the time being, the Bradwells had whisked her to the second floor as soon as she returned from the hospital and several hours of oxygen therapy. If Clay was right, that room nested among her enemies.

Her chin quivered.

"Ah, now. You see? You've overdone." Mrs. Fenton arranged a plump arm around her shoulder, gently urging her toward the stairs. "Come and rest. Get your strength."

Jill eased herself free and moved back toward the room. "Please. I need my Bible."

"Of course you do." Mrs. Fenton hurried to retrieve the book from the floor next to the bed. She brushed it off and put it into Jill's outstretched hands. "There ya go."

Jill held it close. *God, I need you now more than ever.* If only she could think of what to do next, but her brain felt so foggy—as if packed in cotton.

"So now." Mrs. Fenton peered into her face. "Back to bed?"

"I need … I need something … to wear to church."

"Miss Shepherd, you really shouldn't." The housekeeper held Jill's elbow as if trying to lend her support. "You don't have the strength this morning."

With a huge effort, Jill lifted her chin a bit. "I … I'm fine."

But was she? It had taken all the reserves she had to come this far. The second floor loomed before her as if miles away. Would she make it? She clenched her jaw. She must make the half hour trip to the mainland. She wouldn't find what she needed here in this house. "I'm going to church. I have to."

Mrs. Fenton squinted at her, doubt clouding her gaze, but at last she sighed. "Well, if you're sure. I aired some of your clothes last night and put them in your room this morning."

Jill tried to smile. "Thank you." Words seemed inadequate in light of the woman's thoughtfulness.

The housekeeper hovered nearby as Jill concentrated on not wobbling while she moved down the stairs. She'd have to do better than this if she hoped to go to church. Tears pressed behind her eyelids. She fought to subdue them. She wouldn't let the lingering fright of last night steal her resolve. She would *not* let it win.

As they reached the door of Jill's temporary room, Mrs. Fenton added, "So you won't worry, your kitten is in the kitchen, eating breakfast."

"You found him?" He was safe! *Oh, thank you, Lord.*

"The hungry little rascal came to the screen door this morning. Couldn't resist the milk I set out for him." The housekeeper grinned. "Should I bring him up to you? Unless, of course, you're set on going to church. In that case, I don't mind taking care of him until you return."

That did it! The tears she had fought so hard to contain slipped silently down her cheeks. In some ways, Lenore's housekeeper reminded Jill so much of Maggie. "You're a good woman, Mrs. Fenton."

The housekeeper flushed in a pleased sort of way, then grumbled as she ambled away. "I still think you should stay home and rest."

A smile tugged at the corners of Jill's mouth as she observed the woman retreat. At least Mrs. Fenton didn't wag her finger at her as Maggie would have done.

Bathing and dressing took quite an effort. Jill had even lain down for a while, but now she was almost ready, not nearly as wiped out as earlier. With slow strokes, she drew the silver-handled brush through her hair while Clay's warning chilled her heart.

He had to be wrong. For one thing, Lenore would never risk damaging Windtop and her antiques with a fire. She had a hard time passing through the rooms without a satisfied smile and reaching out to touch or adjust them. No, her aunt was not behind last night's smoke damage.

Yet if Clay was right, someone else was.

Her heart beat heavy in her chest as she lowered her brush to the dressing table. Did that someone hate her enough to want to kill her?

Maybe they only meant to scare her away.

Clay had tried to talk her into leaving. He knew how the fireplace worked and had arrived just in time to rescue her. Would he arrange such a risky accident, hoping she'd take his advice and leave?

Somehow such reasoning didn't quite make sense. Her overwrought brain must be swimming through mud this morning.

She fastened a delicate gold chain around her neck, then wrapped her fingers around the cross pendant. *Please, God, I need to know. Am I in danger?* Had someone murdered her mother and now felt she was a threat?

Fire surging through her veins, Jill reached for her Bible. If such a someone existed, that one would find Susannah Bradwell Shepherd's daughter didn't frighten easily. As God gave her strength, she'd get to the bottom of this. She would know the truth before she left Windtop.

The aroma of freshly brewed coffee and the scent of crisp Applewood bacon greeted Jill warmly as she entered the dining room. Yet it was the sweet fragrance of Mrs. Fenton's hot cinnamon rolls made her mouth water. A little breakfast should fortify her for the trip from the island.

She went straight to the buffet while Lenore and Tia seated themselves at the dining table, their breakfast plates filled with Mrs. Fenton's delicacies. Her aunt draped a linen napkin over her lap. "Don't dawdle, Tia, or we will be late."

Tia stirred sugar into her coffee. "I'm skipping this morning."

"You are not."

"I am." Tia lifted her porcelain cup to sip the steaming liquid. "The weather is too beautiful today. Besides, I hate church. It's boring."

Placing a cinnamon roll and a glass of orange juice on the table before her, Jill settled in and bowed her head in silent prayer. When she looked up, Tia was spreading strawberry preserves on buttered toast.

"Good morning, Jill." Following the abrupt greeting, the girl turned back to her mother. "Carver never goes. Dad only does when he's not busy at the office."

"All the more reason you and I should make the effort. After all, you certainly don't want people—"

"—to say we Bradwells are heathens?" Tia said. "I'm sure I don't care."

"A good reputation is everything in this small town," Lenore snapped.

"And, of course, we have such a good reputation to uphold." Tia rolled her eyes before taking another bite of her toast as her father entered the room.

He poured himself a cup of coffee. "Listen to your mother, Tia." He stopped and raised his eyebrows as he caught sight of Jill. "Good morning. I see you're feeling better."

She sipped a bit of juice. "Yes, thank you."

Lenore tipped her head, studying her. "A rather quick recovery after last night's experience, isn't it?"

Offering no answer seemed the best way to handle her disagreeable aunt at the moment.

Lenore squirmed slightly and rearranged the napkin on her lap. "Well, you *are* your own boss."

Tia huffed. "Jill is her own boss, but I'm treated like a child?"

Uncle Drew set his cup of coffee on the table and sat down. Jill couldn't help but notice how he had ignored the rest of the buffet.

"Dad, are you going?" Hope laced the girl's voice.

He gulped a swallow of the black liquid. "Not this morning, little girl. I'm needed at the mill, but I'll be back in time for dinner." He set his cup down. "Now be a good girl and go with your mother. If Jill feels well enough, maybe she'll go too."

"Wonderful idea!" Lenore gushed. "You do go to church, don't you, Jill?"

"I do." But Lenore wouldn't like what her niece had in mind. Jill pulled the slip of paper from her Bible.

Tia leaned in. "What's that?"

"The address of a church in town where my pastor's friend ministers."

Lenore snatched the paper and wrinkled her nose. "No one who is anyone goes there."

Tia craned to read the note. "Some nice people do," she offered quietly.

Lenore thrust the paper back at Jill. "Not us."

Sliding her mother a sideways glance, Tia grinned, her brown eyes gleaming with mischief. "Well, I would. You know, a change might be interesting."

Uncle Drew drained the rest of his coffee. "Tia, do as your mother says."

"All right, but I won't like it." The girl threw her napkin on the table and stomped from the room.

Jill finished her first bite of cinnamon roll and pushed the plate away. Her appetite had vanished. She'd forgotten how contentious her uncle's family could be. Even for a short time, living with them would be a challenge. Could she handle the constant bickering? She'd have to if she wanted to know what happened to her mother.

Clay stood at the helm of Bradwell's boat, stretching and fisting his fingers as the family threesome boarded ahead of Jill.

Tia pouted. "You can make me go, but you can't make me like it." She sought a place on the deck as far from her mother as possible. As usual, her mother ignored her while Bradwell cast off the lines tethering the boat to the dock. He then settled himself and opened his briefcase to shuffle through some papers.

Not looking well enough to make the trip, Jill seated herself and gazed across the bay toward town. A wistful expression graced her pale face and tugged at his heart. Strange how the feel of her in his arms had remained with him throughout the night. As if … no, God would never set Jill up for a hurt like that.

Clay tore his gaze away. If God had any such plans, Clay would make sure they failed. He had a sacred promise to keep.

"Everyone's aboard, Merrick," Bradwell called from the deck.

Clay eased the boat forward to clear the dock, then pushed from idle to full throttle, thrilling to the throb of the inboard motor's power beneath his feet. Two weeks left to nail a killer, and after last night's close call, he'd make every hour count.

Turning the boat into the bay's choppy waters, Clay aimed for City Dock.

Jill paused outside New Hope Church. The sturdy clapboard building needed paint, and its cement steps showed signs of wear, but the large sign above its double front door bravely announced "Jesus Saves" and drew her inside.

Within the paneled vestibule, a cheery atmosphere enveloped her as strangers with kind faces smiled and suspended their conversations to greet her. Their sincere welcome strengthened her, but her short walk from City Dock had left her surprisingly weak.

Taking advantage of her first opportunity, she slipped into the sanctuary and made her way down the thinly carpeted aisle to a pew near the front. Across from her, a short, silver-haired woman with a pleasant face and clear, blue eyes smiled at her before resuming her prayers.

On a green-carpeted platform stretching across the front of the sanctuary, a tall man in his late thirties arranged papers on a wooden pulpit. Near an organ at the left side of the platform, a young man with a shock of red hair sat on its round stool and softly strummed a guitar. The melody brought the hymn's familiar words to Jill's heart:

"Abide with me, soft comes the eventide,
The darkness deepens, Lord, with me abide …"

The darkness deepens at Windtop, Lord. A strange, frightening darkness. She would grab Clay's advice and beat it back to her life in Chicago if she weren't so sure the Lord had sent her to Windtop.

Folding her hands in her lap, she closed her eyes and let the hymn's words become her prayer while God's love wrapped around her like a healing balm.

"Good morning!"

Jill opened her eyes to focus on the tall man behind the pulpit. A broad grin lit his face.

"Welcome. For those of you who might not know, I'm Pastor Bill McGee, and the young man playing guitar for us today is my nephew, Leo. My wife, Helen, is still visiting her mother in Wisconsin, but should return tomorrow. Our prayer today is for God to meet you in a special way during this morning's service. Shall we worship together in song?"

About fifty people rose to their feet, their voices accompanied by the guitar's now lively beat. The service progressed with songs, prayers, and Pastor McGee's sermon giving strength to Jill's weary soul.

Looking up from her own desperate prayers near the end of the service, she noticed the elderly woman across the aisle praying fervently. *Lord, please grant that woman her heart's desire.*

With a final blessing, Pastor McGee dismissed the congregation. As the elderly woman struggled to her feet to leave, her Bible and the contents of her purse spilled on the floor. She bent down to retrieve them and winced. "Oh, dear!"

Jill hurried to her side. "Let me help you."

The woman smiled and eased back onto the pew. "Thank you."

While Jill picked up the scattered contents of the woman's purse, Pastor McGee arrived with a metal walker. "Here, you are, Mrs. Tanner. I'll be back in a few minutes to walk you home." At the back of the church, several people waited to speak to him.

The woman nodded and smiled. "Take your time, Pastor."

"I could walk Mrs. Tanner home," Jill offered.

"Is it all right with you?" he asked the older woman.

"Certainly! I would enjoy getting acquainted with this lovely young woman."

"All right, then, I'll leave you with—"

"Jill." Who remembered last names on a busy Sunday morning? "I'm glad Pastor Tim recommended your church. He said you were roommates in Bible College."

"Tim Ketter?" In response to her nod, he grinned. "Well, I'm doubly glad you came."

Someone called from the back of the church. He excused himself and hurried away.

"Are you ready, Mrs. Tanner?" Jill asked.

"Please call me Amelia." The woman rose to her feet with an effort and laughed. "This old body isn't as young as it used to be. You're sure I won't be too much bother?"

Jill glanced at her cell phone. "I have plenty of time. Where do you live?"

As they emerged from the church, Amelia pointed to a white one-and-a-half-story bungalow across the street. A picket fence enclosed a yard filled with flowers of every height and color. A cement walk marched up the center of the lawn to a broad porch with an old-fashioned swing at one side.

When they reached the front door, Amelia patted Jill's hand. "Thank you so much."

Warmth stole into Jill's heart. "My pleasure," she said, opening the screen door. "Something sure smells delicious."

"A roasting chicken. I have plenty if you'd care to join me."

The dear woman's eyes had filled with such hope that it saddened Jill to decline. "I'm so sorry, but my family is expecting me."

Amelia smiled through her disappointment. "Family comes first. Perhaps another time."

"I'd be honored." The truth was, she'd prefer dinner with this dear woman, but her family—such as it was—waited.

Sunday dinner with the Bradwells was not something Clay cared to do. Yet the promise he'd made himself regarding Jill's safety compelled him— and he might pick up on something helpful. People often let slip useful information without realizing it.

He entered the dining room to find the family already seated. "Sorry I'm late." He took the only chair available, one between Bradwell and his son and across the table from Jill, glad to note her complexion had regained its color. She had recovered quickly from the ill effects of last night's misadventure.

Carver forked three pieces of fried chicken on his plate and passed the platter to Clay. "I hear you plan to check the fireplace in Jill's room. Any ideas on what might have gone wrong?"

Certain he was right about an attempt on Jill's life, Clay chose to take care how he responded. "It's a strange case."

"How's that?" Bradwell asked.

"It operated fine on its last inspection," Clay said.

Jill passed a bowl of mashed potatoes to her younger cousin who helped herself to a generous portion.

"Lightly, Tia," her mother chided. "Your party is only two weeks away. Eat lightly, or you will never fit into your lovely dress."

The girl stared at her mother, then ducked her head and ate a forkful of potatoes.

Mrs. Bradwell let it go for the moment and addressed him. "Will you be able to manage the repairs on the third floor yourself, Mr. Merrick?"

"I'll know as soon as I inspect it more thoroughly." It would give him a chance to work inside the house. His heart leapt at the prospect.

"Might you finish before my luncheon here on Tuesday?"

"I'll do my best." For Jill's sake, he'd stretch the time as long as possible.

Bradwell poured gravy over his potatoes. "It's fortunate you arrived when you did last night."

"Yes," Carver said, scooping peas and carrots onto his plate. "We wouldn't want anything happening to our Jill. By the way, cousin, what kind of work do you do in Chicago?"

"Mostly genealogy reports on both buildings and families." She placed a small portion of mashed potatoes on her plate.

Carver's lop-sided grin held no warmth. "So this is a legitimate business, not just a hobby?"

Jill's face flushed at the man's intended insult.

Her cousin feigned interest. "So how does one get into your line of work?"

Jill looked him in the eye with a sweetness the man didn't deserve, and he squirmed. "By being in the right place at the right time, I imagine."

Clay restrained a satisfied grin. Good for her! She stood up to the worm.

"While trying to find my father, I learned how to use the same research tools Nona Anderson uses in her business, and she offered me a job."

Lenore's soft, derisive noise set Jill to blushing again and Clay's temper on edge. It wouldn't hurt the woman to treat her niece decently.

Carver speared a mouthful of meat. "So how do you prepare those reports?"

Jill returned her forkful of salad to her plate and shrugged. "I search public records, locate historical information, and interview people. I examine house features and come to conclusions. Then I write a detailed report on whatever the client requests."

How did she keep her sweet spirit? Clay couldn't help but admire her for it.

Carver sat back, grinning. "So, you're a kind of detective."

Jill paused as if digesting the idea. "I never quite thought of it that way, but I suppose you're right."

"Smaller bites, Tia," the girl's mother admonished, "and, for heaven's sake, not so much butter."

Ignoring her mother, the girl focused on Jill. "I have a question because I don't get it. Why are you so different? I mean, inviting us to live in this house when you know my mother doesn't like you. She'd take this house from you in a minute if she could."

As Jill sucked an uneasy breath, Clay darted a wary look at Mrs. Bradwell. Yet the woman made no attempt to correct her daughter.

"I'll tell you," Jill said. "But remember, you asked." She looked from one to the other. "As I said before, a few months ago, I decided to become a Christian and give my life to Jesus."

Carver snorted while Lenore uttered a soft noise of contempt.

"But why?"

"Tia," her father chided, "don't be rude."

"It's all right, Uncle Drew. It's not an easy story to tell, but I don't mind her honest question." Jill looked down as if collecting her thoughts. "For weeks after Uncle Drew told me Mother and Maggie had died, I didn't sleep well. I didn't eat much. Most days, I couldn't concentrate enough to do my work. One day, I went to my room, locked the door, and called Brian."

Tia's brown eyes lit up. "Brian?"

"We were engaged. I called to cancel our date."

The girl wrinkled her nose. "You're kidding!"

Jill paused and then forged ahead. "I sat up all night, believing my life was some terrible mistake, convinced I never should have been born."

"You're right about that one," Carver grumbled under his breath, but Jill obviously heard him.

"By morning, I …" She hesitated before going on. "I decided to correct the mistake."

Carver looked up with riveted attention, a detail she didn't seem to miss. It appeared to Clay that it actually encouraged her. "I took a knife from a kitchen drawer and returned to my room where I locked the door. A minute later, I heard my boss, Nona Anderson. She rapped on my door. 'Jill,' she said, 'don't do it.'"

Tia's eyes grew large. "How did she know?"

"Just what I thought," Jill said.

Clay couldn't wait to hear her answer.

"I tiptoed to the door and listened," she said, "hoping Nona would go away. She said she wouldn't leave until I opened the door. So I let her in. She stood there in sweats with her hair sticking out in wisps."

Tia laughed and Jill chuckled too. "I'd never seen her like that before. I checked my clock, hoping she would take the hint and go away. Instead, she babbled on about how she had been praying and she knew she had to find me right away."

Carver rolled his eyes. "A religious nut case."

Jill nodded. "I thought so, too. So I said, 'I suppose you're going to tell me God sent you.' She said she knew I didn't want to hear that, and she was right. Then she saw the knife. 'Oh, Jill, don't,' she said, 'Please let me help you.'"

"I told Nona she couldn't help me, but I still let her take the knife from my hand. Maybe she'd think the crisis was over and go away. She didn't. She told me I was right. She couldn't help me, but she knew Someone who could."

Carver snorted again and resumed eating.

Jill went on. "Nona didn't leave me alone for a moment. We talked for hours. Around morning light, we knelt in my room, and I turned my life over to Jesus."

Tia rolled her eyes. "Oh, right! Just like that."

"Not exactly," Jill said. "For two years, Nona handled some pretty sticky problems with prayer and the Word. You know, the Bible."

"I'm not stupid!" Tia snapped.

"I never thought you were," Jill said. "The point is, what I observed in Nona's life gave me hope for a better life with Jesus and it's the best thing I've ever done."

If Jill expected a hallelujah from her family, it didn't come, and her obvious disappointment cut Clay to the quick.

Mrs. Bradwell smirked and turned to her husband. "Drew, you remember Kitty Wentworth, don't you?"

Bradwell wrinkled his forehead.

"You know, my college roommate. She's coming to help with Tia's party and bringing her son and his friends. Suitable young men to round out the guest list." She smiled at her daughter. "You are so fortunate, Tia. The Wentworths are one of the finest families out East."

The girl's lips quivered. "Mom, I told you. No party."

The Bradwells were back to bickering, and Clay had about all he could take. It was time he left. How did Jill cope with this chaos?

"The party is all set so let's not go over all this again," Tia's mother said.

Tears formed in the girl's eyes. "Dad, don't make me do this."

Mrs. Bradwell sat ramrod straight, frowning. "Drew, tell your daughter to be reasonable."

Bradwell spoke gently. "It's only a party, Tia."

The stricken girl's face reddened and she jumped up. "Only a party? You know it's more than that! Go ahead if you want to, but I won't have a thing to do with it! I won't—"

Her eyes widened, and with a hoarse cry, she crumpled to the carpet.

Chapter Ten

Jill dropped to the floor beside Tia as her cousin's body stiffened. "Somebody do something!"

Within moments, Uncle Drew and Carver yanked the dining chairs away from the girl and searched the area—for what? Jill wasn't sure. Clay rounded the other end of the table, stripping off his suit jacket. He folded it and knelt beside Tia.

Cool as ever, Lenore rose from her chair and checked her watch as Elma rushed into the room. Lenore held out her hand. "My notebook please."

They all seemed to know the drill. Each worked with calm determination.

Clay placed his jacket beneath Tia's head like a pillow and gently turned the girl on her side.

"Excellent, Merrick." Lenore nodded her approval. "You have experience."

"A close friend," he said, his face grim.

Jill couldn't help but stare at him, still not sure what was going on.

Touching his jacket, he lowered his voice. "It protects her head and keeps her airway clear during the seizure."

Seizure?

Tia's body began to jerk, and Jill instinctively reached out.

"Don't touch her," Lenore warned.

Jill snatched her hand back. "She's turning blue!"

Incredible! As if Tia's seizure were nothing unusual, her aunt stood there writing something in the small leather book the maid had given her. She made no attempt to touch her daughter, no attempt to reassure or comfort her.

Anger burned in Jill's heart. Growing up, she might not have had a father, but she had been blessed with a far more loving mother than her cousin.

Clay took Jill's hand, enclosing it in the warmth of his own. "She'll be all right," he said, helping her up. "We've done all we can for her comfort and safety. Now we stand back and give her room."

Jill allowed him to lead her a few feet away to observe beside Uncle Drew and Carver. Her uncle touched her shoulder. "Don't worry, Jill. Tia's seizures only last about two minutes. See? The muscle spasms are beginning to slow. She's already starting to breathe normally."

Tia's jerking slowed to a stop. She groaned and opened glazed eyes as Uncle Drew knelt beside her and gently took her hand. "You're all right, Tia. You had another seizure, but you're all right."

Observing Uncle Drew's tender care of his daughter, Jill released a shuddering sigh. Clay squeezed her hand and released it.

Lenore jotted a last note in her book. "Two minutes and two seconds." She closed the book. "Elma, clear the table. We are done in here."

Jill's attention slid back to Tia, who could hardly keep her eyes open. "So sleepy, Dad."

"I know." Uncle Drew patted his daughter's hand. "We'll get you to your room. You'll be fine after you rest."

"Don't you dare lift her, Drew," his wife snapped. "Your back is bad enough." She looked around. "Carver?"

Jill searched, too, but he was nowhere to be seen. How sad. A cold-hearted mother and a brother who couldn't care less. Tia deserved better.

Clay crouched beside her uncle. "Let me carry her."

Her uncle nodded and wiped his beaded forehead with a monogrammed handkerchief. "Thank you, Merrick."

Jill breathed a sigh of relief. Clay wore kindness like a garment and lifted her young cousin.

Along with her aunt and uncle, Jill followed him up the stairs to Tia's room.

Her aunt moved efficiently, preparing Tia for bed and allowing Jill to help her. When they finished, Lenore turned toward the door.

Jill couldn't believe it. "You're not leaving, are you?" Neither Mother nor Maggie would have abandoned her at a time like this.

"Tia will be fine," the girl's mother said, opening the door. "We will check on her every half hour. Are you coming?"

Jill clamped her mouth shut and refused to move.

Lenore huffed. "She won't know you're here."

"I'd rather stay if you don't mind." Even if her aunt did mind, Jill had no intention of leaving.

"Do as you please." Lenore moved into the hall and paused beside her husband. "Drew, tell her what she needs to know, then join me downstairs."

How could a mother be so cold? Didn't her aunt realize she still had precious time to spend with her daughter? Time she would never get back. Mother and daughter time she might one day regret losing.

As—too late—Jill did now.

Uncle Drew bent over Tia and stroked his daughter's hair as he gazed on her sleeping face. "My sweet girl."

He turned to Jill. "I wish I could stay." He brushed the back of his fingers over his daughter's pale cheek. "Wake Tia every half hour to make sure she's all right. She'll go back to sleep." He turned to leave.

"You're not staying either?"

"Jill, when you observe my wife, you see a strong woman. The truth is she's more fragile than our daughter right now."

The door clicked softly as he left.

Clay pulled back from crouching inside the fireplace in Jill's room. After re-examining the throat, damper, smoke shelf and part of the smoke chamber above, he had no doubt.

Nothing was wrong with it. Someone had rigged last night's *accident*. That someone had already removed the evidence.

While he washed the soot from his hands in the adjoining bathroom, Jill's door opened. He grabbed a hand towel and peered into the room. A bedspread snapped above the sheets.

He entered on the housekeeper's blind side. "Mrs. Fenton."

She jumped and put her hands to her heart, breathing hard. "Mr. Merrick!" The bedspread floated down askew. "What can I do for you?"

"Do you know who cleaned the fireplace?"

She pursed her lips and wrinkled her brow. "Why, Mr. Bradwell and his son took care of it last night. I finished what cleaning I could do this morning."

"Did you notice anyone else come up here yesterday?"

"Other than Miss Shepherd, only the movers who brought furniture to the attic."

He studied her clear-eyed gaze. If she was lying, she was good at it.

"Most of the time, Mrs. Bradwell kept me busy," she said. "She didn't leave any of us a moment's rest."

Clay left the room, rubbing the back of his neck. Someone had tampered with the fireplace. For all he knew, the whole family was in on it, but he suspected otherwise.

He trotted down the stairs to the second floor and paused outside the half-open door to the tower room. Dim lamplight picked out the golden highlights of Jill's hair as she rested on a chaise lounge, reading.

He moved toward her and then stopped. Windtop's walls had ears. What he had to say, no one but Jill should hear. Someone had viciously taken her mother from Windtop. The threat had now passed to Jill, and it pained him to realize he couldn't protect her every moment.

From Tia's room, Jill glanced through the open door into the hall. Was it her imagination, or had someone been observing her from its shadows? But nothing moved out there.

She shifted her gaze to Tia. Every half hour, she had awakened the girl. In between, she passed the time by reading her Bible, fascinated by its words and the comfort they gave her.

Resting the book on her chest, she closed her eyes. In this house, she could use every scrap of comfort offered. Both Clay and Maggie seemed to think she was in danger. Were they right? If so, would God continue to watch her back as he had last night?

Smiling, she recalled how he had sent Clay just in time.

She stretched out her arms and then looked about the room. It no longer resembled the one she knew while growing up. Lenore had transformed it into a rose garden, but new decorations couldn't block the memories embedded in Windtop, including her childhood memories of Lenore doting on Carver and the bewildered hurt in Tia's toddler eyes.

Tia must hunger to know her mother's love as much as Jill hungered to know her unknown father's. Both dreams seemed so hopeless.

But at least, Lord, I have your love to fill the aching void. If only Tia knew your love too.

The clock on the dressing table indicated it was time to wake her cousin again. She went to the girl's side and shook her gently. When Tia didn't respond, Jill's heart sped up. She shook the girl harder.

Tia groaned and turned her head heavily. Her eyelids fluttered as if she could hardly open them. When at last her gaze focused on Jill, a groggy surprise registered. "J-Jill, why ...?" Her words were labored and slurred.

Jill adjusted the girl's summer blanket. "I'm staying until you feel better, Tia."

Her eyebrows lifted above barely focusing eyes. "Sure?"

"Yes. Now go back to sleep."

Tia closed her eyes and soon was sound asleep again.

A soft knocking at the door alerted Jill before Mrs. Fenton entered. "How's she doing?"

"All right, I think."

The housekeeper set a tray on the table beside the chaise lounge. "You hafta be hungry by now. Oh, and your room upstairs is clean. Your kitten's sleeping on his bed in the bathroom. I changed the litter and filled his bowls."

"Thank you so much, Mrs. Fenton. You're so kind."

"Not all in this house thinks so." She bobbed her head and scooted out.

The evening wore on as Jill continued her vigil. How lost Tia looked in that big bed.

Not long before midnight, Uncle Drew entered the room. "Lenore's asleep," he said before brushing a kiss on his daughter's forehead.

Jill looked on, longing to know such fatherly love.

Uncle Drew pulled out the dressing table bench and sat near the chaise lounge. "I know I said it before, but thank you for staying with Tia."

"She's been sleeping, just as Lenore said," Jill admitted.

He glanced at the Bible on her lap, a wan smile on his lips. "I've often wanted to stay with Tia, but Lenore wouldn't hear of it."

Jill snorted. "I'm sure!"

"Don't be hard on your aunt, Jill. She made a lot of mistakes with you and your mother, but she's also given Tia excellent care since her epilepsy began."

I should hope so. "When did Tia have her first seizure?"

"About three years ago. Not long after you left."

That's why she hadn't known. "So how did it happen?"

Uncle Drew's round face showed signs of fatigue. "Tia and I were in the park, talking about her last year in middle school. All of a sudden, she collapsed and went into a seizure. It scared me half to death. I rushed her to the hospital, calling Lenore as I drove. The minute the doctors told us what we were dealing with, she threw herself into becoming an expert on Tia's care."

"Really?" Maybe her aunt wasn't as cold about her daughter as she seemed.

"At first, Tia had several seizures a day," Uncle Drew continued. "Now, they only occur occasionally."

Hope rose in Jill's heart. "So she's getting better?"

He shook his head. "She'll be on medication the rest of her life. Missing a dose even for a few hours could put her in a non-stop seizure or a coma."

Jill sat up sharply. "Does anyone know what causes her seizures?"

"Doctors tell us her brain's electrical system passes too much energy through its cells. The sudden overload triggers a seizure."

"Awful!"

"Yes, but what makes Tia's situation harder is coping with people who act as if epilepsy is contagious. It isn't. One in every hundred people has it. Some don't even know. By the way, you handled yourself very well for a first-time helper."

Jill sighed. "I'm afraid I just made Lenore angry."

"Lenore is angry with anyone who doesn't have to live with this problem. You saw how unpleasant Tia can become before a seizure, and when she has one, most people shrink back. You didn't. You did well."

"But I didn't do anything." How could she? She didn't know what to do.

"You cared. You cooperated. That's more than most."

"She's my cousin."

"Yes, of course." He glanced over to the bed where Tia slept. "You know, as much as I wish Tia were free of this thing, I do see a positive side."

Jill couldn't imagine what that might be.

"She gets more attention from her mother. Lenore handles all of her medical regimens and takes her to her doctor appointments."

Jill quashed a smirk. Taken by itself, not exactly her idea of great mother love, but at least her aunt didn't ignore Tia altogether.

One question still troubled her. "Does anyone know what started Tia's epilepsy?"

Her uncle nodded. "We think we do. You were very young, so I'm not sure you remember, but Lenore fell at Windtop when she was pregnant. Tia's doctors think our baby girl suffered brain damage in the womb then. It showed up as epilepsy when she entered puberty."

He lapsed into a faraway look. "The truth is, Lenore's fall was my fault. If I hadn't argued with her, none of this would have happened to our baby girl."

"That can't be true."

"But it is. Your aunt was so blind with anger she missed the first step and fell down the stairs. We're lucky both she and Tia survived." He rubbed his face with both of his hands and then looked up. "Well, Jill, you're tired. You've been here long enough. You'd better go to bed and get some rest. I'll stay with Tia."

When her uncle insisted, Jill bid him good night.

Up in her room, she lay in bed, haunted by his sad story. As she stared into the darkness, an unbidden memory surfaced along with Maggie's words. *If you stay, trust no one. Especially that one who tried to end her baby's life by falling down the stairs.*

Jill sucked in a staggering breath.

Chapter Eleven

Jill stirred in her bed and groaned before sinking back into a dream that dragged her through yet another loop. Seven years old, she hid in a shadowed corner on the padded bench just inside Windtop's main door. Swinging her feet, she clutched her doll for comfort. The muffled screams upstairs behind closed doors had frightened her.

Her aunt's and uncle's fight was really bad this time. She hummed to drown out the noise. A door banged open on the second floor, and she stopped humming.

"I'll never forgive you!" her aunt screamed. "Never!"

Jill snatched up her feet and wriggled into the deepest shadows, her heart pounding in her thin chest. She blinked and looked up.

Her aunt hesitated at the head of the stairs. One hand touched her swollen belly while her face turned red and her eyes scary. A slight smile curved her lips.

Jill's throat went dry. She tried not to breathe. At any moment, as in dream after sickening dream this night, her aunt would deliberately miss that first step and tumble down the stairs to the first landing.

Only this time, Lenore's piercing gaze pinned her. She cried out and turned away.

Silence.

When she dared to look again, her mother stood at the second-floor railing, smiling at her with such tenderness.

She scrambled to her feet. "Mama?"

Maniacal laughter raised goose bumps on Jill's little arms and back.

From behind, a grotesque figure rushed at her mother. It struck, and her mother fell from the second-floor railing, screaming and arms flailing.

Jill woke and leapt from her bed.

Run! Somewhere. Far away. Somewhere her aunt would never find her. Somewhere ... but there was nowhere to go.

Her knees buckled. She eased herself to the floor and clenched her teeth. She would not cry. Not even if Maggie was right.

"God, help me." She could barely breathe the words.

I have not given you a spirit of fear, but of power, love and a sound mind.

A spear of morning sun touched her through the window as the words wrapped her in comforting peace. She needn't be afraid. God would surely see her through this strange mission to the end.

She pushed up onto unsteady legs and made it to the bathroom where she splashed her face with cool water. While she washed and dressed, she forged a plan to grab a ride to the city and dig out every available scrap of information on her mother's death. She would find what she needed to put her torment to rest.

Hurrying down the back stairs to the kitchen, Jill arranged for Mrs. Fenton to care for Button. Sprinting through the house, she burst out the front door in time to catch Clay and Uncle Drew climbing into the Jeep.

"Wait!"

Clay searched the store fronts up and down the street. Jill's flushed, determined face as she caught a ride with him to Munising hours earlier still left him uneasy. In a town this small, she should be easy to spot, so where had she gone?

He crossed the street and glanced through the café's expanse of windows as he was about to pass by. In the crush of noontime patrons, she sat alone against one wall at a table for two, her laptop open. Whatever she had ordered remained untouched as she studied the screen. Her brow crinkled.

He opened the café door and made his way through the crowd, hoping to reach her before she spotted him. No such luck.

Clicking her wireless mouse, she closed the laptop and slipped it into its case, carefully lowering it to the floor between her chair and the wall. She pulled her salad and milk toward her.

"Do you mind if I join you?" he asked.

"Please." She indicated the lone vacant chair.

He sat down facing her. "I think you should know. Someone rigged the fireplace to malfunction."

She paled, searching his face. "You're sure? How?"

He couldn't blame her for hoping he was wrong. "My guess is by tampering with the damper to make it appear to work at first, then setting it up to fail as the heat increased." He locked into her shocked gaze.

"You're certain."

"The fireplace was in good working order before and after. I checked it both times." He propped his forearms on the table and leaned forward, lowering his voice further. "Jill, you're not safe at Windtop."

"How do I know you didn't rig it yourself?"

He hadn't seen that one coming. "First of all, it's too dangerous. Too much could go wrong, and I would never risk harming you. Only by dumb luck was I in the house when Carver called for help."

Blushing, she looked down at her hands. "I'm … sorry. I didn't really believe it. You've been too kind. But I had to ask. I don't know you." She looked up again, her incredible eyes searching his. "Who are you, Clay? Why are you here?"

He itched to reach for her hands and reassure her, but he'd stay with the facts. "I *am* a renovation contractor, but you're right. That's only part of the story." A story he still couldn't reveal to her.

"You—" Her voice caught and turned so soft he barely heard the words. "You know something about my mother's death, don't you?"

All right, he'd tell her as much as he dared. "I have strong suspicions but can't be sure. I'm missing a crucial piece of evidence."

Without blinking, her beautiful wide eyes stared. "Tell me! I'll help you find it."

Slowly, he shook his head. He still couldn't risk it, for her sake as much as his. The hurt in her gaze weighed on his heart like a molten lead.

She leaned toward him. "Then tell the police. Let them deal with it."

He clenched his jaw and then sat back as the waitress arrived to take his to-go order. When she left, he continued. "Without that evidence, they'd never listen. In the meantime, you would do me a favor if you returned to Chicago where you'd be safe."

She stared at him unblinking. "You don't know my family."

"I didn't say anything about your family."

"You didn't have to. But if I'm in danger as you say, we should work on this together, help each other."

"You can help me best by going home and letting me handle it."

"That's not happening, Clay. I have too much at stake." She grabbed her purse and laptop and hurried away.

He sighed and sank back. At least she hadn't fired him yet.

Jill paid her bill and left the restaurant. Standing out on the sidewalk, she fumed. Her morning had vanished, and what had she accomplished? The sheriff's and coroner's records proved as useless as the brief news articles she had downloaded to her laptop. No matter how closely she scrutinized those documents, nothing came close to supporting Maggie's accusation.

Now, this encounter with Clay left her with more questions. Why did he refuse to tell her what he knew? What crucial evidence was he looking for?

She combed the fingers of her free hand through her hair. She couldn't return to the island yet and wasn't in the mood to shop. *Lord, what do you want me to do?*

Amelia Tanner's sweet face came to mind, along with a pang of regret. How disappointed the dear woman had been when Jill declined her dinner invitation yesterday. Maybe a visit this afternoon would make up for it.

Pink hollyhocks and yellow sunflowers peeped over Amelia's picket fence as Jill approached the open gate. Juggling two pots of mums along with her purse and laptop, she walked up the porch steps and knocked on the screen door.

A shuffling sound came from within before Amelia's silver-haired head popped around the edge of the door. "Jill! What a nice surprise." She unhooked the door. "Come in, come in!"

Peace wrapped around Jill as she entered the homey combination living and dining room.

Amelia nodded toward the potted mums. "What's all this?"

Jill smiled. "For you."

The elder woman glowed with pleasure. "Whatever for?"

"To say thank you for inviting me to Sunday dinner even though I wasn't able to accept. I hope you like them."

"They're beautiful," Amelia crooned.

Jill glanced around the room. "Where should I put them?"

"The foot of the stairs would be fine."

While Jill arranged the potted flowers to one side of the bottom two steps, Amelia continued, "Do you have time to visit?"

"I'd love to."

"Have you had lunch?"

"I had a salad at the café." Those few bites would have to hold her.

"You need more than that, and I was about to eat a little beef stew. It's hot on the stove, and I made fresh lemonade." She grinned, her eyebrows arched. "What do you think?"

Her stomach growling on cue, Jill laughed. "Sounds heavenly."

Amelia pushed her walker toward the kitchen. "It's good to have company." She stopped to catch her breath.

"How about letting me get the stew and lemonade," Jill offered.

The older woman smiled. "That would be nice."

In the galley kitchen, Jill poured lemonade into two tall glasses and dished up two bowls of savory stew while Amelia added another setting of napkin and silverware to the dining room table. Jill joined her to enjoy the best stew she had tasted in years.

After their meal, Jill washed the few dishes and straightened the kitchen before returning to the living room where Amelia sat at a large, rectangular, wooden structure.

"My quilting frame," she explained. "I nearly have ten queen-sized quilts ready to sell at the church booth during the Fourth of July picnic."

Jill bent closer to inspect the two layers of cotton fabric in a tiny flowered print. They were separated by a middle layer of soft, white batting stretched across the horizontal frame. "Is it hard to do?"

"Not at all." Amelia threaded a large-eyed needle with a short length of dark green yarn. She poked it down through the layers and up again about a quarter-inch away. Tying a double knot with the yarn, she clipped the ends to a one-inch length. "See? Nothing to it. Do you want to try?"

"May I?"

"Of course." Amelia threaded another needle and grimaced. "Oh bother. I'm almost out of this color. I have extra skeins upstairs. Would you mind getting them for me?"

Jill headed toward the stairs. "Where do I look?"

"The bottom dresser drawer." Amelia returned to work with the remaining yarn.

At the head of the stairs, Jill entered the only bedroom and found the dresser. A white cotton scarf edged in hand-crocheted lace covered the top, setting off the framed picture of a warm-eyed young woman.

Jill opened the bottom drawer and carried the four dark green skeins downstairs.

"Thank you," Amelia said. "This will keep me busy for a while. With four quilts to finish before Friday, I don't have a moment to spare."

"I'd love to help," Jill offered. She could use a welcome break from the tension at Windtop.

Amelia kicked up her heels and laughed. "Was I that obvious?"

Jill pulled up a dining room chair on the opposite side of the frame. With a needle in hand, she pierced the three layers every few inches, tied a double knot, and trimmed the ends.

"Your granddaughter takes a lovely picture," she remarked.

Amelia blinked and cocked her head.

"The picture on the dresser upstairs."

"Oh, you mean Janice, my grandson's fiancée. She was a lovely girl." Amelia tied another knot and trimmed the ends. "She died two years ago."

At the sadness lacing her new friend's voice, Jill murmured, "I'm sorry."

"A hit-and-run." Amelia poked her needle through the layers. "Maybe that's why Sonny hasn't gotten over it though I pray for him every day." She smiled ruefully and cut a few more lengths of yarn. "Are you interested in someone?"

Clay's kind eyes and tender heart immediately came to mind, along with his exasperating ways. "I doubt it will work out."

Amelia's gentle eyes held a question.

"I don't think he's a Christian." Another reason her new friend would understand.

"You're wise, Jill. I wish my grandson would learn to love someone like you, someone to draw him back to Jesus." Dampness appeared on her lashes, and she pulled a tissue from her apron pocket.

Jill sighed. No one lived for long without some heartache. "Would you like me to pray with you?"

Amelia blotted her tears and nodded.

Jill went to the woman's side and took her thin hand. "Lord, thank you for Sonny and your faithful love for him. Please heal his broken heart and send the right person to love and draw him back to you."

"Yes, Lord," Amelia agreed, "and thank you for Jill. Bless her with a young man who loves you."

The screen door rattled. "Amelia? May I come in?"

Jill's new friend quickly tucked the tissue in her apron pocket. "Please do."

A slightly plump woman in her thirties entered with a bulging shopping bag. "Here's the yarn you need for those last quilts." She paused as she noticed Jill. "Oh, you have company."

"Helen, this is a friend I met at church on Sunday. Jill, this is Pastor McGee's wife."

"I'm so glad to meet you," Helen said, putting the shopping bag down. "Amelia, are you sure all this isn't too much for you?" She indicated the quilt on the frame and the two others folded in the corner waiting to be tied and hemmed.

"I'm fine. Just pray they sell at the booth this weekend. How is the auction coming along?"

"Auction?" Jill asked.

"Amelia's idea," Helen said. "Our church is sponsoring a craft booth on the Fourth of July and an auction on the following Saturday to raise funds for a new organ and to paint the church." She smiled sweetly. "Though it's true, we could use a few more items for the auction."

"Between the all-school class reunion and the Fourth of July celebration this week," Amelia went on, "we should find enough interested buyers. If the Lord blesses, we might even have money left over for missions, too."

"What can I do to help, Mrs. McGee?"

"Oh, please call me Helen," the woman said. "Tying quilts is a big help already. I feel better knowing Amelia isn't doing this alone. Every church woman is already working hard on some craft, including me."

"But I wish I could do more," Jill said. "Ah ... the furnishings!"

"What?" Amelia and Helen chorused.

"I have some lovely old furnishings in the attic that I don't need. Could I donate them to your auction?"

"Well ..." Helen hesitated. "How many pieces are you thinking of?"

"I think a truckload, and I believe I have a perfectly good organ, too. If you think it's good enough, you are welcome to it."

Helen looked doubtful. "That's very generous, Jill, but are you sure?"

"Absolutely, on both counts, but can your auctioneer handle it on such short notice?"

"I could ask him," Helen said, "but please don't act in haste. You might regret it. Think it over and let me know. No matter what your decision, Jill, we certainly appreciate your offer."

As Helen departed on her next errand, Jill noticed the time on Amelia's mantle clock. After tying off a final piece of yarn and trimming it, she looked with satisfaction over the work she had accomplished. At least something in her life was turning out all right.

"I'm having so much fun, Amelia, I'm sorry I have to leave." She gathered the needle and scissors to put them away. "But my ride will be waiting."

Amelia insisted on walking her to the door. "Thank you for visiting and for the lovely flowers." She paused as if trying to decide. "I wonder. Would you mind if I gave one of the pots to my friend? She can't get out like she used to."

Jill kissed Amelia's thin cheek. "Please do that."

With a lighter heart, she returned to City Dock and the trip back to Windtop.

Lord, you were so right. My visiting Amelia was just what we both needed. Thank you for giving me this loving place to rest—far from the troubles at Windtop.

At Windtop, Jill ran up the porch steps. Her aunt and Mrs. Fenton were studying the arrangement of wicker tables set up on the veranda's wide expanse.

"I think they're evenly spaced now," Lenore said. "Make sure each table seats four."

As Jill tried to skim past unnoticed, her aunt whirled about. "We certainly could have used your help to get ready for the historical society's luncheon tomorrow. I am exhausted."

Exhausted? If anything, Lenore appeared exhilarated and primed for an argument.

"You will attend, won't you?" It was more a command than a question.

No hovered on her tongue. More important things demanded her attention, but a little nudge in her heart made her think again. What if the Lord wanted her there? "I'll arrange it."

Lenore scrutinized her. When her aunt turned away, Jill slipped into the house, glad to escape without further confrontation. The less she was forced to contend with her aunt, the better.

Jill stopped short of Elma. The small Persian rug at the foot of the grand staircase had been pushed to one side, and the frenzied girl scrubbed the floor with all her might. A strand of limp, brown hair escaped her maid's cap.

She looked up at Jill and pointed to the stain on the parquet floor embedded in the wood pieces. "It won't come out." Her chin quivered. "Mrs. Bradwell won't like it. She sure won't."

Jill stared at the stain, and a terrible knowing spread like fire in her chest. Trembling overtook her limbs. The stain resembled ... a pooled liquid.

Her mother's blood!

The fire in her chest threatened to explode and her stomach revolted. Clapping a hand over her mouth, she lurched forward to skirt Elma and race up the stairs.

Chapter Twelve

Jill slammed her bedroom door and pressed her hot forehead against its cool surface. Her temples throbbing, she pushed away and paced, unable to dislodge the image of her mother's blood embedded in Windtop's floor.

Tears flooded her eyes. What was she doing in this hateful place? She had come to find peace. Peace to go on with her life without regret. Yet everywhere she turned, reminders of her mother's pain and her own failures assaulted her.

If she were smart, she'd do what Clay begged of her. She'd pack her bags and get out. But if she did that, she'd be buckling to her old habit of running when things got tough. This time ... this time ... *Lord, please help me stay and face whatever lies ahead. No matter how much I want to run.*

Run from what? Even Clay had only suspicions. Now she had them too. They crawled within her and gave her no peace. Yet neither of them had any proof. So with God's help, she had to stay until she knew one way or the other.

As she palmed the tears from her cheeks, something warm and fuzzy rubbed her ankles. She looked down to find Button, her little bundle of comfort. She picked him up and sank into Maggie's rocker. No more full-fledged bawling sessions. She was done with tears. She'd dig until she found the truth.

As Button nuzzled her neck, Jill's gaze found the fireplace. Clay believed someone deliberately set it to malfunction. Yet she'd spent the entire morning looking for some piece of information to settle her doubts about her mother's death and came up with nothing. "Lord, we need more than dead ends."

The truth might be somewhere right here in front of her. If only she knew what her mother had been thinking those last days of her life, but only God, her mother, and her mother's journals … her mother's journals! Why hadn't she thought of them before?

Mother kept them for years, but where were they now? Jill had seen one a month before she left to find her father. When she burst into her mother's room without knocking, her mother looked up, closed the leather-bound volume, and locked it in a sturdy box. Did that box still exist? Or had someone already disposed of it?

The kitten leapt from her lap as Jill jumped up. More likely, the box was hidden somewhere in this house.

As Jill came down the grand staircase the next morning, exquisite music floated up through the heart of the house. She followed the haunting melody into the parlor where Tia sat at the grand piano, the last notes of an intricate Rachmaninoff concerto fading.

In spite of her weary heart, Jill managed a weak smile. "You're feeling better today."

Tia closed her sheet music and rested her hands on her lap. "Why did you stay with me Sunday after … well, you know?"

Jill studied her young cousin's somber face. "I didn't want you to be alone."

Tia closed the keyboard. "Dad used to stay with me until Mom put a stop to it. She said I had to learn to be strong, and it wouldn't happen if they babied me."

Her trembling voice trampled Jill's heart. "Uncle Drew said your mother takes excellent care of you."

"If you count giving me pills, talking to doctors, and studying all that clinical stuff." Bitterness laced Tia's words. "Dad talks to me. He listens, and sometimes he cries."

Jill nodded, wishing she had more to offer.

"My teachers and a few of the kids in my classes seem to understand. Some even try to help, but …" She clenched her fists. "I'm so tired of these seizures. They make me feel like some ugly monster. Why, Jill? Why me?"

Jill reached out to touch her cousin's arm. What could she say to comfort her? "Everyone has some kind of problem."

The moment the words left her mouth, her cousin's eyes flashed. "Problem? Do you know what a seizure is like?"

Sorry she had failed to help Tia, Jill shook her head.

The girl's eyes glittered with pain. "It's time all mixed up. Like being lost in some spooky forest where I can't hear. My body feels like it's coming apart, and when it's over, I'm so exhausted I have to sleep for hours. What kind of life is that?"

How could Jill answer her cousin's question? All she knew of Tia's suffering was what she had witnessed. She scrambled for the positive angle her uncle had offered. "You have fewer seizures these days, right?"

Tia eyed puddled. "You don't understand. I want to be like any other girl, but just when I think the seizures are under control, something happens. A little too much confusion. A little too much excitement. Too much or too little medication, and—another seizure." She rubbed away her tears. "Anytime … any place."

"Tia, I …"

The girl jumped up and fisted her hands. "You know so much about God, so tell me. Why did he let this happen? What did I ever do for him to hate me like this?" Her voice choked.

Jill's chest hurt. How was she supposed to answer?

"Well?"

"Tia, I'm so new at being a Christian. I don't know all about God, but I know this much. He doesn't hate you. He loves you."

"This is love?" The girl spat the bitter words.

Jill could only stand and gaze at her cousin, empathizing with her. "I don't know why you have epilepsy, any more than I know why my mother died as she did. I only know God loves you and me."

The anger in Tia's brown eyes faltered. "How do you know that?"

"From what I've read in my Bible. From the tender ways he answers my prayers."

The girl folded her arms. "You don't really believe what an old book says, do you?"

"Yes. This one. Because it's God's Word."

Tia huffed. "Now you sound like that girl in my class."

So God was already at work in Tia. Then what held her back? A notion popped into her head. "Tia, are you afraid of God?"

"Shouldn't I be?"

Sadness pooled in Jill's heart. What a terrible place for her cousin to be, feeling alone and unloved.

Jill moved to the couch and sat down. "Would you let me tell you about the God I've come to know in these last few months?"

Tia drew back, but she didn't say no.

Jill patted the place beside her and her cousin, still wary, joined her.

"Imagine a God who loved you so much, he was willing to die so you could be his very own. Fully accepted, fully loved, and part of his family. A God who did everything possible so one day, you could be with him forever in his beautiful heaven. Does he sound like someone who wants to harm you?"

Tia pursed her lips, and then slowly let them relax. "Even if you're right, I'm still stuck with epilepsy and Mother's awful party."

Jill had forgotten the party. "I don't understand. Why is it such a problem?"

A heavy sigh escaped the girl's nostrils. She looked into her lap. "It's not so much the party. I might even like it if it weren't for the seizures."

"Do you think your mother is really out to hurt you?" Jill didn't want to believe it.

"I don't think she gives me a thought one way or the other. Her life is all about this house and Carver. I never mattered and I never will."

"Tia, I can hardly believe—"

"You don't believe me? Come on!" She shot up and raced ahead, pausing at the doorway to look back.

Jill stood and followed her up the stairs.

In her room, Tia flung open her closet doors and snatched a long white gown from the clothing rod. "See?"

The flowing gossamer skirt with hand-stitched lace panels had a tiny waist and a bodice intricately decorated in a style reminiscent of the early 1900s. Jill touched the soft skirt. "It's old-fashioned but lovely."

"Look again. Does this look like my size?" Tia threw the dress in a heap on the bed. "It's way too small, but Mother insists I wear it."

"Why would she do that?"

"Family tradition." The girl grimaced.

"What tradition?"

"I don't know. She had costumes made for all four of us. Old-fashioned stuff, copies from some old photo she found."

Jill retrieved the dress and held its delicate fabric against Tia. "I still don't understand why she would insist you wear a dress too small for you."

"Get a clue, Jill!" Tia bit out the words. "The party isn't about me. It's about Mom. If she were sixteen, she'd wear the thing herself. Instead, she's forcing me to live her crazy fantasy. It's the one thing Carver can't do for her." She pushed the dress away. "Mother's using me to get what she wants. Welcome to life in what's left of the Bradwell family."

If Tia was right, how pitiful this whole family was. Jill shook out the dress and hung it in the closet.

"Someone has to stop her," the girl said. "Do you really want to be my friend? Then stop this party!"

"I can't do that."

"Why not? You own the house. She can't do anything here unless you let her, and I know she won't hold the party anywhere else."

"I'm sorry, Tia, I wish I hadn't, but I've already given your mother permission."

"Tell her you've changed your mind."

"Breaking a promise wouldn't be right."

"Can you at least talk to her?"

Jill sighed. Such hope lit her cousin's eyes she didn't have the heart to quash it. "I can try."

"Right now?"

A sudden dryness seized Jill's throat. "Uh … as soon as possible."

Fat chance she had of success. When Lenore made up her mind, even Uncle Drew couldn't change it.

In the flower bed below the porch railing, Clay stretched to relieve his cramped muscles just as Jill walked from the house. Her forehead puckered in an adorable way, stopping him mid-motion. Something was bothering her. "Good morning."

She blinked, her fine-boned features softening into a smile that ramped his heartbeat. She leaned on the railing. "What are you doing?"

He stooped to toss another clump of weeds and a handful of stones in an old metal bucket. "Giving these new plants a chance to grow."

"But isn't … I mean, doesn't Sam do that?"

He lifted up his hands encased in dirt-smudged gloves and grinned. "You've discovered my deep dark secret. I can't resist any part of the restoration process and don't even mind getting my hands dirty, when necessary." He tossed another couple of rocks in the bucket. "By the way, your mother did a first-rate job caring for this rosebush."

Jill cupped a newly opened crimson blossom and breathed in its fragrance, her expression suddenly wistful.

He combed the soil with his gloved fingers, checking for any rocks he might have missed. "Can I ask what's bothering you?"

She released the blossom and sat on the top porch step. "So little of the reminders of my mother remain here anymore. I guess it's just as well I'm donating some of her things to charity. They'll do a lot more good than gathering dust in the attic."

Her deep sigh tugged at his heart. "Maybe you should give yourself more time before you let them go."

"No, the time is right. I just didn't realize I'd feel this overwhelmed, especially since I only have a couple of days to inventory them."

"Would you like some help?"

She shook her head, sunlight dancing among the loose curls cascading to her slender shoulders. "You have enough to do."

"I could spare a few hours."

Her wan smile nestled against his heart. "You're sure?"

He shooed a fly away from his forehead. "When would you like to start?"

A soft blush stole across her face. "Would this afternoon be too soon?"

"See you after lunch." As he crouched and tossed a few more rocks into the bucket, she reentered the house. He sat back on his heels. No doubt about it. Jill had the power to steal a man's heart. Sadly enough, it couldn't be his heart.

With one dilemma solved, Jill headed for the library to confront Lenore on Tia's behalf. Not that it would do any good. Yet Tia's stormy melody at the piano in the parlor pushed her across the entrance hall. She stopped within the library's doorway.

"Look at all these responses to our invitations, Drew," her aunt gushed, holding up the list. "Nearly everyone is coming."

Uncle Drew peered over the collapsed corner of his newspaper. "How nice, dear." He went back to reading.

Lenore waved an envelope. "And Kitty Wentworth arrives next Thursday. Thank goodness, as soon as today's historical society luncheon is over, I can turn my full attention to the final details of Tia's party."

Her aunt stopped, suddenly aware of Jill's presence. "What do you want?"

A dark piano arpeggio pushed Jill forward. She might as well get it over with. "Tia asked me to talk to you. She's really unhappy about the party and doesn't feel ready."

Lenore's eyes narrowed. "Are you suggesting we cancel?"

"Not cancel, but perhaps postpone." Did the woman have no pity?

"Two hundred guests will arrive in less than two weeks." Her aunt's eyes smoldered. "Months of planning and thousands of dollars invested, and you want us to postpone?"

"For Tia's sake." Surely the woman's daughter meant more to her than any party.

"You feel you know what is best for our daughter." Lenore stomped her foot. "Have you cared for her all these years? Have you coped with her disorder?"

"It's only that—"

The crashing chords and crescendos of Tia's music escalated. Her uncle cringed.

"Lenore, dear," he ventured, "maybe we should postpone."

Her aunt's face reddened. "Absolutely not! We cannot allow her to hide in this house and crawl into some corner. She must get out and make the right friends."

Jill sucked a surprised breath. Were right friends what the party was all about?

"But she's so upset," Jill said. "Can't this stress bring on another seizure?"

Lenore smirked. "Don't be so easily duped, Jill. Our daughter is quite the little actress. She's using you to get her way."

Jill gaped at her aunt. If true, Tia had learned at the knees of the best.

The woman lifted her chin and lowered her voice. "Tia needs to believe epilepsy is only part of her life. Not who she is."

Tia didn't already know that?

"She needs to feel good about herself," Lenore went on. "We urge her to leave the house, volunteer, develop friendships, but what does she do? Plays piano until my nerves fray." Lenore squeezed her eyes shut and pinched the bridge of her nose. "Drew, please tell her to stop that racket. I'm getting a headache."

Uncle Drew put his newspaper aside and left the room.

"You don't know our daughter, Jill. Drew offered her a part-time job in his office at the mill. Would she take it? No! We talked to her about going to college after high school. Will she consider it? No!" Lenore retreated behind the library's desk. "Tia is far from easy to handle, leaving us with no choice but to force her do what is best for her. If we make her participate in life, it is because we want her to enjoy a full life. Do you understand?"

Warmth crept up Jill's neck as she nodded. Perhaps her aunt did care about Tia. More than Jill thought.

"In the future," Lenore said as Uncle Drew reentered the room, "let us handle our daughter."

Her uncle put his warm hand on her shoulder. "I'm sorry Tia dragged you into this, Jill. We appreciate your concern, but Lenore really does know what's best for her."

"We are not heartless," her aunt said. "I consulted her doctor, and he encouraged us to hold this party."

"I didn't know." Jill backed away, suddenly aware her cousin had duped her.

Lenore smiled sweetly, her eyes as cold as ever. "Don't forget the luncheon this noon. You are coming, aren't you?"

Jill nodded and escaped to the carriage house, grateful she had promised to help Amelia with the quilts this morning. Windtop was becoming less and less a place she cared to be.

Now, she couldn't even trust her teenage cousin.

Chapter Thirteen

Seated at Amelia's quilting frame, Jill poked the needle with a short length of yellow yarn through the layers of a fall leaf-patterned quilt. She could barely keep her hand steady.

"You're so quiet," her friend said. "Is something wrong?"

Jill knotted the yarn. "I was thinking about my mother."

"She's all right, I hope."

Shaking her head, Jill busied herself threading another length of yarn through the eye of her needle. "She died two years ago."

"I'm so sorry." Amelia's voice grew soft with sympathy. "Was she a Christian?"

Jill nibbled at her lower lip. "I wish I knew. I could accept her death so much easier if I knew she was safe in heaven."

Tilting her head, Amelia paused mid-stitch. "If only my grandson felt as you do. We know Janice is in heaven, but he can't seem to let go."

Weighty matters troubled her friend's heart too. "Would it help if we prayed for him?"

Amelia bowed her head. "Please."

Following Amelia's lead, Jill bowed her head too. "Father in heaven," she said, groping for the right words, "please help Sonny accept Janice's death. Help him place his hurt in your healing hands and go on with his life according to your will."

"Amen, Lord!" Amelia said.

Jill went on, "And, Lord, please give Amelia the assurance you are working in her grandson's life. Thank you. Amen."

Amelia rummaged in her apron pocket, pulled out a tissue, and blew her nose. "Thank you, Jill." She bowed her head again. "And, Lord, thank you for Jill. Please give her the peace she needs about her mother's death."

Raising her chin, Jill gazed at the ceiling, blinking rapidly. With so many unanswered questions at Windtop, would she ever know peace?

"Jill." Amelia picked up a spool of scarlet thread and prepared to hand-stitch the edge of the quilt. "Sonny is coming for dinner tonight. Could you join us? I would like you to meet him."

Quickly ducking her head, Jill tried to look as if she were concentrating on the quilt. Meet Sonny? Her life was complicated enough.

"Thank you for asking." She stopped to swallow the ache in her throat. "But I … uh … I don't think so." She glanced up to make sure she hadn't hurt the dear woman's feelings.

Her friend bent her silver-haired head not quite fast enough to hide her disappointment.

How she hated to see Amelia so sad but, no matter how much hope loomed in the dear woman's eyes, she doubted Sonny would appreciate an obvious attempt at matchmaking any more than she did. Still, she had hurt her new friend. "Maybe some other time," she hedged.

Amelia's eyes brightened.

Before the morning disappeared, they had finished the quilt. Amelia leaned on her walker near the front door. "If you change your mind about tonight, you don't have to let me know. Just come."

"Sure." As much as Jill appreciated Amelia's friendship, she would not change her mind.

Jill hardly reached the sidewalk when Helen McGee hailed her from across the street. She came running. "I'm so glad I caught you. Have you decided what to do about your furnishings?"

"Can your auctioneer accept them at this late date?"

Helen grinned. "Yes, but he needs to see what you have, and soon."

"Is tomorrow afternoon convenient?"

The woman checked the slip of paper in her hand. "I have just enough time to tell him. If you give me your address, I'll pass it on."

Jill pulled a pen from her purse and wrote the address on the back of one of her Chicago business cards. "I look forward to seeing him."

As she read the card, Helen's eyes grew large. "Windtop? Jill *Shepherd*? Oh, are you sure you're not being too generous?"

A smile tugged at the corners of her mouth. "I'm sure."

Clay surveyed the flower bed that followed the curve of Windtop's veranda. Bright splashes of red from newly planted petunias added a cheerful note. He hoisted the last bucket of rocks and weeds into a wheelbarrow and headed for a discreet dumping station in the woods behind the carriage house. He glanced back along the drive that led to the gatehouse. Where was Jill? Why hadn't she returned?

His insides squeezed as he continued on into the woods and dumped the bucket's contents. Doing his job and keeping an eye on her wasn't as easy as he had hoped.

Coming back around the carriage house, he stopped short of bumping into the parked Jeep. Jill hopped down inches from him. "Hi, there."

His pulse kicked up a notch. "Hi, there, yourself. Where have you been?"

"Helping a friend." She held up a card. "And I bought a pass for the ferry so I won't tie up the family boat or your time when I go to town."

Without realizing it, she was always one step ahead of him, complicating his resolve to watch over her, but what could he do?

"I'm glad you're back," he said, surprised at how deeply he meant it.

Her smile nearly knocked him over. She gazed into his eyes, her own lit with happiness. "See you this afternoon about two o'clock?"

What was he doing, grinning at her retreating figure like a love-sick kid? *Get a hold of yourself, Merrick.* Yet he couldn't tear his gaze away.

When she finally disappeared, he snatched up a garden hose to wash out the wheelbarrow and bucket. If only it were as easy to hose away the rebellion of his heart.

The sweet fragrance of honeysuckle wafted on a warm breeze as Jill took her place near the porch steps. She glanced around. The luncheon tables were beautifully set and the guests would soon arrive. Where was Lenore?

Mrs. Fenton came to stand beside her as several cars approached along the drive.

"My aunt had better hurry."

The housekeeper pursed her lips. "She said she changed her mind. You're to greet these women and Elma will seat them. A lot of to-do about nothing, if you ask me," she grumbled before ambling back into the house.

In a starched maid's uniform of the late 1800s with its long gray skirt reaching to the toes of her black shoes, Elma waited among the round wicker tables spread with damask linen. She smoothed her white apron and danced from one foot to the other, wringing her hands. Her eyes darted nervously, inspecting the tables.

Each held four place settings of bone china, polished silverware, and crystal goblets arranged around a gold bud vase with a single red rose cradled in greens.

Jill gasped and turned to her mother's rose bush. Every blossom had been snipped.

How dare Lenore! *How dare she rob Windtop of the last vestige of my mother? Lord, what is the matter with my aunt?*

Gritting her teeth, she glanced about. The dreadful woman was nowhere in sight and a good thing. Jill wanted to make her sorry!

At the little catch in her heart, she slowly released her pent-up breath. She had offended God much more than her aunt ever offended her. But each time, God had forgiven her and given her another chance. Should she do less? She wanted to do right, but she'd need God's help because she still wanted to throttle that woman.

The first car pulled up before the house. Others parked behind it, and Lenore's guests began to emerge. With an excited chatter, they moved toward the porch.

Plastering on her warmest smile, Jill extended her hand to the first woman. While she continued as hostess, Elma stiffly seated each of them. Before long, pleasant conversations flowed in a low, appreciative buzz.

Elma served the salad course with hot, butter flake rolls. Then Mrs. Fenton appeared with their exquisitely garnished baked whitefish on a bed of flavored wild rice.

The ladies dined happily enough, but Jill soon heard whispers of "Where's Lenore?" Picking at her food, she wondered the same. The woman was nothing but a constant irritation.

The main course finished, Elma removed the plates, refreshed the glasses of sweetened iced tea, and served each guest a small dish of homemade apple ice cream.

As if on cue, Lenore made her grand entrance. Smiling graciously, she stepped into view garbed in a white 1890s lawn shirtwaist with leg-of-mutton sleeves and a long, embroidered, lace-embellished skirt. Her audience murmured appreciatively.

Elma hurried to Lenore's side. "May I present Madame Madeleine Antoinette Beaupre, first mistress of Windtop?" She gestured toward her employer, curtsied awkwardly, and scuttled into the house.

As her aunt moved gracefully among her guests, Jill watched with fascination.

"Welcome to Windtop." Lenore's dark brown eyes glowed with the promise of secrets to be revealed. "My husband, Philippe, sends regrets he could not be with you this day. However, he bid me to offer his greetings and to tell you about our lovely home."

Jill sat back in her wicker chair, ignoring her ice cream. Her aunt played the role quite expertly.

"My beloved husband," Lenore went on, "had this beautiful home built in the East and shipped to this island in sections. He oversaw every detail before bringing me here as his bride in 1876. Of course, we came at the gracious invitation of Abraham Williams, the first white settler to make a home for his family on Grand Island."

Elma returned, holding a large book with an ornate cover and brass clasp. Lenore held it up for all to see. "This lovely photograph album tells the story of our family which I shall now relate to you."

Beginning with Madeleine's arrival, Lenore told, in elaborate detail, one story after another about the Beaupres.

In the early afternoon heat, Jill soon found it hard to concentrate. Only Lenore's sly looks in her direction prevented her from quietly slipping away.

Bees droned among the honeysuckle, ignoring her mother's now blossomless rose bush. With Lenore's story droning in the background, Jill hugged her waist. If only her aunt would stop that endless chatter about people Jill never knew and, at the moment, didn't care about. She'd much rather listen to the truth about her mother's death, however hard it would be.

As Lenore glanced in her direction, Jill held her chin stiffly. A whisper of annoyance crossed the woman's face before she continued her story.

"Then in 1898, Thomas Bradwell arrived in Munising. Philippe invited this stranger to our home, telling me in private how the well-dressed young man was from a good family he had met out East. Much impressed by our humble home, this man often enjoyed our hospitality.

"One day Philippe felt need of amusement. My dear husband had been drinking when he happened on Monsieur Bradwell. The man knew of Philippe's weakness for the game of cards. While I waited through the long night at home, Philippe played hand after hand.

"When morning dawned, my sweet husband appeared at our door, supported by Monsieur Bradwell. Strangely enough, this man excused himself and left. I soon learned the reason for his hasty departure. Philippe had done well enough early in the game, but as the long night progressed, and his friend—" Lenore spat out this last word. "—plied him with more drink, Philippe began to lose. On the last hand, he lost our beautiful home to this despicable rogue."

Lenore's face had turned dark with a controlled rage. "Much to our distress, the man who had put his feet under our table made himself our enemy. I wept many tears, but nothing could dissuade Monsieur Bradwell. We and our only daughter were dismissed from our home and its years of precious memories."

In Lenore's brown eyes, tears pooled.

How she played her role to the hilt. It would seem Tia was not the only accomplished actress in the family.

"Now, before I leave you, let me show you our beautiful home as we knew it." Lenore bid her guests rise.

As the women followed her into the house, Jill remained on the porch. Across the lawn, Clay conversed with one of the men hired to help landscape the grounds. It was nearly two o'clock. She had just enough time to hurry upstairs and change into jeans and a summer tee before he arrived to help her with the attic inventory.

Jill made it as far as the second floor when a breathless Tia pulled her into the octagon room. "What happened? Was Mother angry? Did she throw a fit when you insisted she call off the party?"

"I talked to both of your parents. They—"

"Yes?" Tia urged Jill on.

"—refused."

The girl's narrow face froze in disbelief. She whirled away and slammed a hairbrush on her dressing table. "I counted on you. You and your God, who answers prayer." She turned back to Jill. "Well, maybe he answers your prayers, but he doesn't answer mine." She threw herself on the bed and wept.

"You shouldn't have given her false hopes, you know." At the unexpected sound of Carver's voice, Jill turned to find him leaning against the door frame, a sardonic grin marring his face.

She shooed him into the hall and shut the door before returning to Tia.

The girl moaned on her bed. "I wish I'd never been born!"

"I hope you don't mean that," Jill soothed.

"I do!" The girl sat up, her reddened eyes smoldering. "I thought you were different. I thought you could help me, but you can't. You're as afraid of Mother as we are."

Jill sat on the bed to be near Tia, but the girl jumped up.

"I'm not surprised," she vented. "No one dares stand in my mother's way. When you stood up to her about the kitten, I thought you might be the one person she couldn't dominate. I thought your faith in God made you strong, but I was wrong."

She speared Jill with stormy brown eyes. "You made a big mistake bringing us into this house. You made another when you let Mother win about the party. You'll be sorry! Just like your mother."

"Like my mother?" Jill's skin prickled. "What do you mean?"

"Now that my mother knows how weak you are, you had better watch out."

Jill held her young cousin's wild gaze. Either the girl knew something, or her hateful words were a bluff.

"Don't you see?" Tia's eyes sparked. "We're both Mother's helpless pawns."

Did Tia really feel this way? Jill didn't feel helpless. She knew she could face anything if she did her best and refused to quit. Maybe she could help Tia do the same.

She reached out to her hurting cousin, but Tia pulled back.

The girl's eyes narrowed. "You don't get it, do you? You are all that stands between Mother and this house."

Chapter Fourteen

A chill slithered down Jill's spine. How much truth fueled the teen's passion? How much mere vengeance?

Tia threw herself on the bed again, her shoulders heaving as she wept.

Jill quietly withdrew. Closing the door behind her, she wandered to the second-floor railing and gazed below. Since that first day when she arrived, she had been drawn back to this spot where Lenore's upturned face had paled the first moment she saw Jill.

Her hands flew to her mouth. Had her aunt believed for a moment Jill was the woman whose life she had snuffed out?

"You know, Jill—"

Lenore's throaty voice startled her. She whirled around.

Her aunt's cold gaze lingered. "You would fare much better if you ceased your unhealthy musings about your mother's death. Don't you think it's time you moved on?"

A soft gasp clogged Jill's throat. She stared at the woman who, because of her anger, had dared to risk her own life and the life of her unborn child. Would such a woman also kill for an unfulfilled dream?

Her aunt left her gaping and entered the master bedroom. As the door clicked softly behind Lenore, Tia slipped into the hall, her young face dripping with triumphant disdain. "See what I mean?"

No, she didn't. At least she didn't want to. It was too awful to believe.

Jill turned away and gripped the railing just as Clay strode across the entrance hall. He couldn't have timed it better. She released a heavy breath as he bounded up the stairs, grinning.

"Here to help as promised," he said, apparently not noting anything amiss. "Show me what you have in mind. I'm all yours for two hours."

"Give me a minute to change," she said. "I'll meet you in the attic."

She raced up the stairs to the third floor, aware of Tia's eyes boring into her back. She shook the eerie sensation away.

Clay released each lock of the attic windows and pushed them open. Fresh air swept in, carrying the clean scent of Lake Superior while displacing the attic's smothering heat.

He turned to survey the attic's accumulation of her mother's discarded furnishings. Most of them had been piled into the small space the day after Jill arrived. Pieces this good would bring a good price. Surely some had sentimental value.

Pushing dust off the top of a fine tallboy dresser, he shook his head. What was Jill thinking when only this morning, she had been sad about the house being stripped of nearly everything that reminded her of her mother? It was none of his business, but he sure hoped that some snake wasn't trying to take advantage of her. In the meantime, working at her side gave him the opportunity to keep an eye on her.

He glanced at the attic doorway as the gray kitten dashed through it. Jill darted in after it, and his pulse quickened, every nerve in his body pleasantly aware of her presence.

She scrambled after the kitten, failing to catch him as he slipped behind a box. "Button, we don't have time to play."

The kitten poked his head around the corner of the box but backed out of reach.

She sat on her heels and giggled. "Okay. Explore, you little dickens, but don't get lost."

Clay caught himself smiling. "He won't."

He reached out a hand to help her up.

"I suppose you're right," she said.

The moment her soft hand nestled in his, an electric warmth traveled up his arm. As she stood, the fresh fragrance of her hair teased his nose, and her eyes sparkled with mirth, stealing his breath. He released her hand and widened the gap between them. "What's the plan?"

She handed him a clipboard, held up a fist full of tags, and pulled a slim digital camera from a pocket in her jeans. "We'll tag each item with a number, take a picture, and list it with the corresponding number on these papers. That should give us an accurate record."

"Where do you want to start?"

Her gaze swept the jumbled collection. "How about this highboy dresser?"

She looped a tag through a drawer pull and arranged the number to show. After stepping back to snap a picture, she leaned in to show him the result. "Good enough, right?"

"Should do." He jotted the item next to its number on the clipboard paper while she tagged a gate-leg table.

"We'll list these out-in-the-open pieces first," she said, snapping the next picture. "Then I'll need your help to untangle the rest."

From what he could see, this was no two-hour job, but they'd have to do what they could in the little time available. He began listing the items, doing his best to keep up as she tagged and snapped their photos.

Finally, she took a breather and looked around her. "I suppose we'll have to untangle the rest."

His curiosity got the best of him. "Why are you doing this?"

She smiled, her eyes filled with delight. "I'm giving them to charity."

"Everything?" He knew enough about their quality and the bucks each piece would command to wonder if she had thought this through. "Couldn't you use the money these things would bring?"

A faraway look invaded her eyes. "I guess we can always use extra money, but no. Along with the house, my inheritance includes an annual income. I also have my job. I'll be fine."

"There's nothing you want to keep?" A woman with a tender heart like hers must have an emotional attachment to some of these pieces.

She paused a bit. "I may keep some, but the rest—well, I want Mother's things to make a difference in this world and could never put all this to good use any other way. Why let them rot in the attic when they could do so much good elsewhere?"

He grunted, hoping that one day, she wouldn't regret her decision. "Are we ready to get back to work then?"

Together, they untangled the four-poster bedroom set that had been moved from the octagon room. She caressed the rich wood of each piece as if saying goodbye. This parting wasn't as easy for her as she wanted him to believe, yet she forged ahead.

They continued working their way through mounds of furniture and storage boxes—all part of her yesterdays. Yesterdays he knew nothing about but was beginning to wish he did.

An hour passed, and they had barely touched the assemblage of decades when she sat down on a dusty trunk. He pushed a drawer back into its place in an oak buffet. "Are you having second thoughts?"

"I keep telling myself it doesn't matter, but it does in here." She rested a hand over her heart.

"Did you sign a contract?"

"No."

"Then leave it, Jill. When you marry, you may want some of these things."

She appeared to turn the idea over in her mind, and then shook her head. "Let's keep working."

He pulled the covering from a large portrait, the one of her mother that had hung above the entrance hall fireplace. "What about this?"

Coming near, she touched the frame tenderly. "I'll have it crated and sent to my place in Chicago."

"Let me take care of that." He moved the portrait through the door and into the hall.

When he returned, he found her kneeling on the floor before a humpback trunk. With her right index finger, she traced the three initials on its large brass plate. She gazed up at him with soulful eyes.

"S.B.S." Her voice quavered. "Mother's keepsake trunk."

He crouched beside her, wanting to put an arm around her and let her rest her head on his shoulder, but it wouldn't be right. "Do you have the key?"

Jill examined the lock. "Uncle Drew gave me a box with two keys in it. One might fit. Anyway, I'll keep this trunk too."

"Where should I put it?"

"At the foot of the bed in my room, if you would please."

Her soft smile and hurting gaze tied his heart in knots. "The foot of the bed it is."

He reached for the trunk's handles, and in the cramped quarters, his right hand brushed against hers. How warm and soft it was.

She shot to her feet and stumbled back, falling into a jumble of oak kitchen chairs. One of the legs jabbed her in her side. "Ugh!"

Abandoning the trunk, he snatched her from the tangled mass and set her back on her feet. "Are you hurt?"

In the awkward silence, he realized he had an arm around her, holding her steady as he checked her over.

Staring at him with widened eyes, she eased his hands away. "I … I'm fine."

He wiped his suddenly sweaty palms on his jeans. "Sorry. I … uh … I'll get that trunk to your room." Gripping its handles, he swung it to his left shoulder and strode from the attic.

He needed breathing space and maybe more.

Jill rubbed her arms, trying to still the tingling sensations his touch had caused. She wasn't falling for Clay, was she? All right, he was attractive, but he wasn't for her. For Pete's sake, she hardly knew anything about him. He could be married for all she knew—though she hadn't seen any sign of a ring, and no one mentioned a wife. She couldn't allow another Brian into her life.

When Clay returned, they went back to work. It seemed he was as careful as she to keep an adequate distance between them. As comforting as that was, shaking off his powerful attraction proved impossible. Each time he glanced her way, she struggled to catch her next breath. This couldn't go on.

Footsteps pounded down the hall.

"Tia, come back here!" her aunt called.

Jill took a bracing breath as her cousin stopped outside the attic door.

"I won't help with that party. You can't make me."

"Yes, you will. Your father and I feel it is best for you."

The girl crossed her arms. "Don't drag Dad into this, Mother. He wouldn't insist if you didn't make him." She burst into the attic. "Jill, get some backbone and tell Mother the party is off!"

Lenore stormed in right behind her daughter as Jill stood up beside a corrugated box of odds and ends and brushed the dust from her jeans.

Ignoring her, Lenore speared her daughter with a piercing stare. "It is a lovely tradition. Most girls your age would kill for all it offers."

"Well, I won't!" Tia scowled at her mother and turned to Jill with eyes pleading for help.

Jill held her breath, not wanting to be dragged into another of their mother-daughter squabbles. "You two need to settle this yourselves. I can't help you."

"You mean you won't." The girl screamed and stomped from the attic.

Lenore glowered. "Well, Jill, thank you for your less than stellar support. I suppose you also have no intention of helping with the party."

Without bending to her aunt's manipulation, Jill met the woman's challenge. "I will help when I have the time."

"What could possibly stand in your way?" Lenore stopped as Clay moved into sight from the back of the attic. She looked from him to Jill. "What are you two doing in here?"

"We're making an inventory," he said.

Her aunt's eyes narrowed. "What in the world for?"

"I'm donating these things to charity," Jill added quietly.

"What?" Lenore's voice grew shrill. "Jill Bradwell Shepherd, if you get rid of them, it's this house that should benefit from the proceeds, not some dubious charity."

Closing her eyes briefly, Jill took a deep breath. She could take no more of her aunt's greedy preoccupation with Windtop. "My grandparents' will provides for the annual upkeep of this house from the mill's profits each year. I doubt it needs more than that."

"It wouldn't if your mother hadn't let it fall into disrepair during her last years," Lenore countered. "It's only right that the sale of these things makes up for that loss."

"She had her reasons, as you well know," Jill said.

The obvious reference to Lenore's disastrous garden party, where she had publically humiliated Jill's mother, was not lost on her aunt. After that, her mother never ventured out again. Eventually, she also agonized over allowing repair people in, and then stopped doing so.

"Then you intend to dump the entire burden on your uncle. Well, he will hear of this before you have the chance do anything foolish." Her aunt whirled about and left.

In the sudden silence, Jill combed her fingers through her hair and let it fall around her shoulders. What should have remained a simple act of kindness had quickly turned into a power struggle with her aunt. The last thing she expected, but she would not back down. She was no longer the child Lenore used to intimidate.

Clay stood beside her. "We still have a little time left. Should we get back to work?"

He was right, of course.

A half hour later, he checked his watch. "I have to go, but I can free up some time tomorrow to help you finish."

"In the morning?"

"No problem." As he handed the clipboard to her, their fingertips touched.

For a breathless moment, Jill didn't move. She gazed into his eyes, part of her longing to linger, another part horrified that her heart had again overruled reason.

Clearing his throat, Clay broke away. "I'll … uh … see you in the morning then."

Watching him retreat, Jill fought a longing that made no sense. He was a good man, but he'd never indicated any interest in God, and she couldn't take less than a man who loved God. Why this pull, then? Why did it seem so right when she knew it was wrong? "Lord, I'm in trouble."

As she locked the attic windows one by one, she thought again about Amelia's invitation. Maybe meeting her friend's grandson would distract her from her runaway attraction to Clay. Escaping Lenore for an evening wouldn't hurt either.

"Me-ew."

Jill picked up Button and headed back to her room to get ready. For one evening at least, she would push Clay out of her mind.

129

At the foot of Maggie's bed, she found her mother's trunk where Clay had placed it. If only ... but, no, she wouldn't think about him. The trick was to focus on something else.

Like those keys Uncle Drew had given her. Maybe the larger one would open this trunk.

Minutes later, she pushed back the trunk's heavy lid, revealing those things her mother had collected as treasures worth saving. In the wooden compartment that stretched across the top, she found a pair of baby shoes, yellowed with age, ones she recognized from her baby pictures. A satin-covered baby book with photos of her growing up, her long, lacy baptismal dress and bonnet, and a collection of her school report cards and awards spoke of her mother's love. News clippings about her achievements, her few attempts at poetry, and her high school graduation cap expressed her mother's pride in her.

Jill lifted the wooden compartment and set it aside. Here was the dress her mother had worn in the portrait. Beneath it, layers of tissue protected the folds of a wedding dress, a gossamer creation embellished with delicate, hand-crocheted lace. How lovely her mother must have been while beside her father as they took their vows of undying love.

Why had they ever separated?

If only her mother were alive. Jill had so many questions. Questions her mother might finally feel free to answer. Now only her mother's journals could tell her what she longed to know, if she could find them.

She turned the smaller key over in her hand. Did it belong to her mother's journal box? Her heart beating rapidly, she placed the wedding dress on the bed and continued digging through the trunk. When she finally reached its bottom, she sat back on her heels. No diary box. Yet her mother never went anywhere without it, and since she had spent her last days in this house, the box was somewhere within its walls. Where?

"Me-ew?"

Jill stroked the kitten's head. "You're right, Button." She had just enough time to repack the trunk, take care of him, and get ready for Amelia's dinner.

Jill hesitated on Amelia's porch. This could be an awful mistake. Her new friend hoped a romance would develop from this meeting, a romance to help Sonny get over Janice's death.

Wrapped in the fragrant evening air, she prayed that Amelia would have a sensible heart. This was, after all, just one dinner.

She rapped on the screen door.

Within moments, Amelia pushed it wide. "Jill, I'm so pleased you came. Sonny isn't here yet. I hope you won't mind waiting."

"Not at all. I'm early. I had to take the ferry. Could you use some help?"

"Everything's almost ready, but I guess we'll need another place setting now, won't we?" She smiled and headed for the corner cupboard near the dining table. "You will like Sonny."

Jill couldn't have cared less, but at least her new friend wasn't trying to hide her intentions.

Amelia arranged the additional plate, napkin, and silverware. "There! Now I'll fill the water glasses."

Jill followed her into the kitchen. "Let me do that."

"The pitcher is in the refrigerator," the older woman said as she took the glasses from the cupboard. "While you're doing that, I'll check the roast." She opened the oven door.

The savory aromas of roast beef with onions, potatoes, and carrots filled the small kitchen. Jill left the kitchen with the water glasses, realizing how truly hungry she was. At the very least, she would get a good meal from this evening.

"Goodness!"

Jill rushed back into the kitchen. "What's the matter?"

Amelia straightened up from the refrigerator. "I forgot to make the salad." She pulled an array of fresh vegetables out and placed them on the cupboard countertop beside the cutting board.

"I'll have it done in a minute," Jill said. "You just relax. You've done more than enough." Getting right to work, she chopped tomatoes and cucumbers, adding them to frilly lettuce already arranged in a large glass bowl.

Amelia smiled gratefully. "Did I tell you Sonny is a Christian?"

"Yes." *As if that made any difference.* The man was still in love with someone else, and Jill had no desire for the complications that would bring to her life. Besides, she wasn't all that good at attracting terrific love relationships.

However, there was no stopping Amelia. "He was five years old when we knelt together in my living room. He asked Jesus to forgive his sins, come into his heart, and be his Savior. I'll never forget it. The minute he finished praying, he looked so surprised. 'Grandma,' he said, 'I feel so clean!'"

Jill glanced at her friend who grinned and went on. "I couldn't imagine what sins a little boy might commit to make him feel unclean, but I knew then that his experience was real."

Dumping the vegetable scraps into the sink, Jill turned on the water and ran the garbage disposal.

"Years later," Amelia continued, "his grandpa and I were so happy when he asked Janice to marry him. A sweet girl who truly loved the Lord and our Sonny. Then she died." Her eyes misted, and she shrugged. "Who knows why God allows such things?"

Jill's heart went straight to her mother. *Yes, who knew?* "Salad's done," she said.

"Good. Let's start dishing up."

Arranging the roast beef in the center of a large china platter, Jill surrounded it with roasted carrots and potatoes while Amelia poured buttered garden beans into a bowl.

Clay's smiling face invaded Jill's memory. She pushed it away. The least she could do was give Sonny a fair chance and concentrate on enjoying the evening.

"Let's leave the hot food in the warming oven while we get everything else ready," Amelia said. "Would you slice the bread while I put the salad on the table?"

Jill took the clean dish towel off a loaf of fragrant, freshly baked bread and picked up a knife.

"Sonny!" Amelia exclaimed from the living room.

During the ensuing moments of silence, Jill imagined Amelia hugging her grandson. Her own heart beat faster. This was a mistake. She never should have come. She should grab her purse from the counter and slip out the back door.

No, Amelia might be trying to fix her grandson up with a stranger, but Jill could not abandon her new friend. She finished cutting and arranging the bread in its basket.

"I have a wonderful surprise for you," she heard Amelia say. "Jill, come out and meet my Sonny!"

Her stomach fluttered. Showtime! She brushed the last bread crumbs from her skirt and stepped into the dining area.

She stared as she felt the color drain from her face.

Chapter Fifteen

Clay's stomach knotted as he eyed the unsuspecting Jill. She had obviously been caught as off-guard as he. His dear grandmother ... what was he to do with her? She meant well but had no idea of the disastrous complications her matchmaking plan might unleash.

She scrunched her brow, looking from him to Jill and back. "You two know each other?"

"Windtop belongs to your new friend, Grandma." He hadn't meant the words to come out quite so cold, and the puzzlement in Jill's eyes made him feel lower than dirt.

She grabbed her purse from the counter inside the kitchen door. "I'm sorry, Amelia. I think I should go. Maybe some other time."

As she hurried past, the hurt in her eyes cut him to the core.

"Don't, Jill," he blurted. He couldn't let her leave like this. "You've both gone to a lot of trouble. Let's enjoy the meal. Then I'll take you home."

While she weighed her options, he waited with a lump in his throat. He wouldn't have her alone and unprotected in the night while he dined with his grandmother.

"I'll get our dinner from the warming oven, Amelia," Jill said.

As she returned to the kitchen, he released a tense breath. Spending this evening with her, he'd at least know she was all right until he could get her back to Windtop. In the meantime, he'd have to scramble to protect the plan that brought him to Windtop.

"Let me help you, Grandma." Clay moved around the table to seat her while Jill carried the platter of pot roast to the dining table. She returned to bring in the bowl of beans and then slipped into the chair opposite him. As he seated himself, she glanced his way, confusion swimming in her gaze.

In a heartbeat, he'd tell her everything to save her from any suffering because of him, but what he'd have to say could hurt her more. If what he suspected was true, he couldn't allow this psychopathic killer get away to murder again.

He opened his napkin and dropped it on his lap.

Right now, he needed to know how much his grandmother had told Jill about him and Janice. One loose word to the wrong person would scuttle all he had accomplished so far. If she already knew too much—even if she didn't realize it—how could he convince her to say nothing until he found that final piece of condemning evidence?

His grandmother smiled at him. "Sonny, would you please ask the Lord to bless our food?"

He hated to disappoint her, but since he and God no longer saw eye to eye, he wouldn't play the hypocrite. He slowly shook his head, and his grandmother's sweet smile faded. He sat in silence while she prayed.

As always, her food was delicious, but this time their meal progressed painfully. It was his fault. He watched Jill pick at the bounty on her plate, seldom looking up. He didn't do much better. His grandmother fussed, urging each of them to eat.

Maybe a change of subject would help. "How are your quilts coming along, Grandma?"

Her faded eyes brightened a little. "Much better since Jill started helping me. We're on the last one."

With a stab of regret, Clay glanced across the table. If only he and Jill had met at another time, in another place.

His grandmother's forced cheer broke the thick silence that had fallen on them again. "How was your day, Sonny?"

"Fine." A lie, of course. He was hurting the ones he loved. *Ones. As in the plural?* Had his feelings for Jill progressed that far? He liked her, admired her, but surely he didn't love her. He couldn't. He wouldn't.

"Clay's helping me inventory the furnishings," Jill said. "If everything goes well, we should finish before Ed Drummond arrives tomorrow."

"So Ed can handle your pieces along with the rest. Wonderful!" His grandmother turned to him. "Did Jill tell you she's donating those things to our church auction?"

"She said something about a charity." Nothing about his grandmother's church.

A bright smile lit his grandmother's face. "That's where we met."

"And you didn't connect her with Windtop."

"Well …" His grandmother blinked. "I don't think Jill ever offered her last name, and I never thought to ask."

Jill looked up. "And Amelia always called you 'Sonny.'"

Of course she would. She had never called him anything else.

He sat back in his chair and pushed his empty plate away. So that's how they wound up in this precarious triangle. Had that Someone he tried to avoid masterminded the situation?

But why? An all-knowing God should realize that he was anything but right for Jill.

Jill had to admit she couldn't eat another bite of Amelia's delicious dinner. The strained atmosphere had stolen her appetite. She laid her fork across her plate, still trying to fathom the evening's surprise.

Clay was the little boy who had given his life to Jesus in Amelia's living room. He was also a Christian and unattached. The barriers she had imagined between them never existed. Her heart had been trying to tell her this. No wonder she was so easily drawn to him, and why it all seemed so right.

Yet the scowl that darkened Clay's face the moment he saw her tonight and his gray eyes quickly appearing guarded made it clear. He didn't want her in his grandmother's house or in their lives. Sonny was no more ready for a new romantic relationship than she was. How disappointed Amelia would be.

Jill glanced at her friend, wanting to comfort her but knowing this was not the time. The truth was she felt a little disappointed herself. The tender look in Clay's eyes when they were together over the last few days had vanished tonight. It was just as well. If she were ever ready for romance, she would want a hardworking and kind man like Clay. *He won't always be estranged from you, will he, Lord?*

Realizing she was staring at him, she blinked. Was she right? Was what she saw in his eyes now more like fear?

"Excuse me." He rose from the table and took his dishes to the kitchen. A minute later, he disappeared up the stairs.

Amelia stared at the ceiling as if she could see him through it. "I hate it when he sits alone in that room with Janice's picture. Why can't he put all that behind him?"

Jill busied herself clearing the table, understanding the grief that held such power over Clay. Janice hadn't simply died. Someone had taken her life. The killer was still at large. It wasn't right, any more than the circumstances surrounding her mother's death. Clay needed time to heal. She did too.

So this was Clay's secret that stood between them. Make that *who*.

Jill started the dishwater in the sink and went to collect the last dirty dishes from the table. She smiled for Amelia's sake as her friend joined her in the kitchen. "Do you want me to wash, Amelia, or dry?"

Clay wiped his hands on his slacks and paced back and forth alongside the bed. He stopped at the dresser, picked up Janice's picture, and then put it down again. It didn't quite fuel his resolve as it once had.

What was the matter with him? Had so much changed in the short time since Jill arrived at Windtop? Every day, his thoughts centered more and more on her. The depths of her violet eyes captivated him, promising a future that beckoned him. A future he would have no right to claim if he followed through with his plan.

He punched his right fist into the palm of his other hand and resumed pacing, faster than before. It's not that he wanted to follow through. He had to. If he was right, the killer had not stopped with one or two victims. If he didn't move fast enough, Jill might be next.

He picked up Janice's picture and cradled it in his hands. What a wonderful love they had known, planning their future, putting the pieces together with care until someone brutally ran her down.

Why God? Why did you let it happen? Why when I was serving overseas? When I wasn't here to protect her?

What puzzled him most was why the killer targeted her. Janice was the one person in the world who had a heart of kindness toward everyone who came into her life.

Jill was so much like her.

He stopped pacing. Was that why he found Jill so attractive and looked forward to every moment with her? Not just because of her soft curves and sweet ways.

He set Janice's picture back on the dresser. He would stop her killer.

If he could count on the law, he would. Jill was right. In most circumstances, that was the way to go. But the law failed when his father died in a convenience store hold-up. It failed when his sister was killed in a drive-by shooting at her school, and again when Janice was murdered. This time—as soon as he found that last piece of evidence—he would hold this one killer accountable. No more innocents would die.

At the sound of Clay's footsteps coming down the stairs, Jill looked up from her work on the quilt.

He entered the room, his gaze shrouded in a firm purpose and his jaw tight. "Are you ready?"

She put her needle and yarn away and collected her purse while he hugged his grandmother and kissed the woman's upturned cheek. Jill hugged Amelia, too, but didn't miss the concern for her grandson in the older woman's eyes.

"We've gotten enough done," she said, leaning on her walker near the door. "I should be able to finish this quilt myself, but thank you for helping and for coming."

Jill slipped her purse strap over her shoulder and followed Clay into the night.

He drove in silence. At the marina, its metal dock echoed with their footsteps. The evening's dark sky hovered above, alive with tiny, bright stars. She shivered. Their light seemed so cold.

As they reached the boat, Clay pulled her gently around to face him. "Jill?"

Was she crazy, or he had uttered her name in tender anguish? She stared at their shoes, unwilling to let him glimpse her confusion.

With his finger beneath her chin, he urged her gaze up. His own held an astonishing hunger. Only a breath away, he brushed a strand of hair from her cheek. She trembled as the back of his fingers caressed her face, but this was no invitation. This was something far different.

He opened his mouth, then sighed heavily and backed away. An aching distance gaped between them. Jill swallowed hard, unable to move. She could do nothing but stare. He cared for her but not as much as for Janice.

She stumbled toward the boat, and just that fast, his hand caught her elbow, steadying her. She tried to ease away, but he wouldn't release her until she stood safely on the deck. Refusing her heart's urge to glance back at him, she sought a cushioned seat as far as possible from where he would man the helm.

The boat roared to life and headed for the island, leaving a frothy wake. Jill looked out across the dark waters on the first leg of their lonely ride back to Windtop.

God, I didn't come here looking for love. Certainly not a love that would cause this much pain.

A palpable silence reigned, even as they left the boat and drove to Windtop. It was just as well. One minute he revealed he cared, the next he backed away. At least now she knew why. She also knew that, once again, she had fallen in love too fast.

Instead of going on to Windtop, Clay parked the Jeep outside the gatehouse and turned off the ignition. He stared ahead, not making eye contact. "I wish I could, Jill, but I can't."

"You don't have to explain." She didn't want to hear it anyway. Wasn't it enough that he had made his choice, and it wasn't her?

"All right, but you do know my grandmother rigged tonight's dinner to bring us together, don't you?"

She nodded. Nothing she had planned or even wanted, but that didn't matter. Sagging back in her seat, she looked out her window into a darkness she could almost feel.

"I'm sorry," he continued. "She believed she was helping me. Probably both of us. But it won't work. It can't. I wish circumstances were different."

She turned back and stared at him. Did he wish things were different? Her foolish heart wrapped itself around his soft words as he gripped the steering wheel.

"When I finish what I came here to do, I'll leave. You won't see me again."

His resigned sadness echoed hers. No mere words would change what must be. He had made up his mind, and she had no choice but to respect his decision except for one thing.

"What about Amelia?"

"What about her?"

"Do you expect me to stay away from her?" She sincerely hoped not.

"I don't expect you to stay away from either of us. I just want you to know where things stand with me. As for Grandma, I'm glad she has a friend like you, but I am curious."

"About what?"

He looked worried. "What did she tell you about me?"

She stared at him. *Why was that so important?*

"Humor me, Jill," he said.

"She said you're still having a hard time about Janice's death."

"True, but that's something I have to work out for myself. What else?"

She cringed but, since he wanted to know, she would tell him. "That, since then, your relationship with God hasn't been the same."

His lips pressed into a grim line. "Also true, and also something I have to work out for myself. Anything else?"

Jill shook her head. Funny how life held out a shining promise, then snatched it away. "I didn't know that you were her grandson."

"I believe you."

He took her hand, sending shock waves through her. She didn't pull away, even when he put his other hand over it. "Would you do me a favor?"

"If I can."

"Don't mention Janice to anyone. *Not anyone.* Will you do that for me, Jill? It's important."

"Yes." Who better than she would understand how difficult it was to come to terms with the violent death of someone you love?

The intensity of his gaze held her breathless.

"Thank you."

She longed to soothe the pain in his heart. If circumstances were different, he might have let her. They might have been a comfort to one another, might have found a way out of their pain together.

He eased his hands from hers. "Don't, Jill. Don't love me. You'll only get hurt, and I don't want to hurt you."

Not love him? Couldn't he see it was already too late? As for not getting hurt, it was too late for that too.

She turned away, grieving for their love that would never be. He might have given his heart and life to Jesus at one time, and one day he might return. But right now, he not only loved another, but he was letting Janice's death wound his relationship with God.

Please, Lord, heal his hurting heart. And mine too.

Chapter Sixteen

Sunlight filtered through the attic windows, sending crosshatched patterns among the stored furnishings. Dust motes danced in the air as Jill wrestled with opening the last window and setting its brace. She leaned on the sill and gazed across the lawn toward the gatehouse.

Clay was late, and she was on her own with more than she could hope to accomplish. She picked up the clipboard and a handful of tags from an end table next to a heavy, brass floor lamp. Numbering a tag, she slipped it on the lamp, snapped a picture, and listed the item. As she crouched to attach another numbered tag to the end table, a long shadow fell across the floor from the brightly lit hallway.

Clay's silhouette filled the doorway.

Her heart tripped with happiness, yet she reined in her sudden urge to throw her arms around his neck in welcome.

"You're surprised," he said.

"After last night, I ..." She pushed up from the floor to face him. "I wondered."

"No matter what happened last night, Jill, I'm still your friend." He reached out with an open hand. "How about giving me those tags?"

She placed them in his hand, and while he tagged a large, ornate mirror, she took a picture of the end table and listed it.

Warmth seeped into her traitorous heart. He was here only as her friend, but he was here. And he cared deeply, whether he was willing to admit it or not.

Jill's proximity was more of a challenge than Clay had expected. When she bent her head over the clipboard to add an item, sunlight nestled in her hair, begging him to touch those silken waves. When she gazed into his eyes as she answered his questions or gave him directions on the next piece to be listed, he could hardly tear away and return to work. Every innocent move of her slender form flowed like music into the deepest recesses of his being.

He couldn't go on like this much longer. Yet, they had to finish this inventory before Drummond showed up this afternoon, and he wouldn't abandon her to cope alone.

Approaching footsteps arrested his gut-churning musings. In unison, he and Jill looked toward the attic door. Her aunt swept in wearing some vintage dress that covered her from neck to high-buttoned shoes. Its long sleeves ballooned in huge puffs at her shoulders. Her gaze raked the attic. "I see you are still at work."

The acid words could have etched brass, yet Jill greeted her aunt with a cheerful good morning.

"Good morning, nothing!" The woman jammed fists on her hips. "You failed to show for supper last night and breakfast this morning. Don't think you can escape us so easily. Your uncle will join us for lunch today and we expect you in the dining room promptly at noon." She whirled about on her heels. "Don't forget or I'll be back."

Clay's jaw twitched. "Why do you let her talk to you that way?"

She shrugged, a sad smile tugging at the corners of her mouth and he realized his gaze lingered on her soft lips. "She's a difficult woman, but she is my aunt. I'm trying my best to understand what drives her, even if I'm not having much success."

He tagged a sofa. "That dress she's wearing. What's that all about?"

"She says it helps her to get a feel for Windtop in its early days while she prepares for Tia's party." Jill aimed the camera and snapped the sofa's picture, then listed it. "But I keep wondering if there's more to it than she says."

Jill entered the dining room precisely at noon. Elma's hands shook as she placed a chilled salad before her. Just as quickly, the maid disappeared into the butler's pantry.

Bowing her head, Jill silently asked God's blessing on the food and His hand on the matter to follow. When she looked up, Carver regarded her with a thinly disguised contempt while Tia gazed at her with open curiosity.

"Tell her, Drew," Lenore said.

Her uncle's eyelids flickered rapidly. "At your aunt's request, Jill, I discussed the matter of your selling Windtop's furnishings with our attorneys this morning."

Lenore flashed a fleeting smile, her dark brown eyes gleaming.

A heavy rock dropped in Jill's heart. Had she and Clay gone through all that work for nothing? Would she have to turn Mr. Drummond away and withdraw her contributions to the church's benefit auction?

Her uncle cleared his throat and glanced from his wife to her. "And … uh … you are free to do with those things as you please. Your grandparents only specified that Windtop remain in your possession as long as you live."

Lenore shrieked. "No!"

Carver leaned back in his chair, appearing to digest the information.

"Then I can give them to the church?" What an absolute relief.

"Yes." His stout bulk squirmed in his chair at the head of the table.

"Are you going to let her get away with this?" Her aunt nearly choked on the words.

"We have no choice, dear." A tight resignation laced her uncle's voice.

Was that sadness in his eyes? Of course it was. What had she been thinking? She should have discussed the idea with him before going ahead with it. He had a lifetime of memories tied to Windtop. Many more than she did.

"I'm sorry I didn't think of this before, Uncle Drew. But is there anything you would like before I send the rest away?"

His brown eyes softened. "If it's not too late, I would like the library's red leather chairs. I have fond memories of them connected with my father."

"Done."

Carver snorted.

"And don't worry, Lenore." Her uncle spoke with concern for his wife. "I will use them in my office at the mill."

Fuming, her aunt looked away.

Uncle Drew shrugged. "What about you, Jill? What do you intend to keep?"

"My mother's portrait, a trunk of her mementos, and the desk she kept in her room as soon as I find it."

Lenore sniffed. "That desk is an original piece and belongs right where it is—in the master bedroom."

Jill's fingers dug into the linen napkin on her lap. No matter what, she wouldn't argue. "Mother's desk can stay where it is." *For now.* "It's just that I don't want to lose it."

Lenore thrust her chin in the air. "You don't have to sell anything."

"No, but I try to keep my promises." *Which is why you are still in this house.*

Lenore's eyes narrowed. "Tell them you have changed your mind."

"No." Why did that woman's demands prod her to dig in her heels in?

With a lazy grin, Carver gazed at her. "At least be practical, cousin. Sell those things and keep the money. You'll make a bundle." As she opened her mouth in protest, he raised his hands palms out. "Don't tell me. It's something like love others the way you want to be loved."

Jill blinked. He knew something about Scripture.

Lenore waved away Uncle Drew's warning look. "Well, if this is your idea of Christian love, you are failing with your own family's needs."

Carver laughed. "Don't kid yourself, Mother. She just thinks that little run-down church has greater need. Am I right, Jill?"

Tia pushed her chair back and stood. "Maybe she's right."

Lenore frowned at her daughter.

Jill held her breath. What was the girl up to now?

Tia grinned at her mother. "I think I'll go with her tonight and check it out."

"You will not." Lenore pressed her lips together and glared at her daughter.

Tia eyed her mother, a slight smile on her lips. "What time do we leave, Jill?"

Lord, is this your plan or Tia's?

"It can't do any harm, dear," Uncle Drew said.

"As long as it's all right with your father," Jill said, "it's all right with me. I'm leaving right after supper."

"See you then." Her young cousin smiled sweetly and left the room.

Lenore pursed her lips. "You were no help, Drew. Must I do everything myself?"

He shrugged and kissed his wife's cheek. "It's time I get back to work. Carver, are you coming?"

Jill rose to leave as well, but Lenore stopped her. "I'm not sure what I dislike more about you—your insane obsession with Susannah's death or your revolting fascination with religion." She shook her shoulders as if dislodging something loathsome. "Why can't you be satisfied with the real world? Who even knows if the other exists?"

"But it does!" Did her aunt really think otherwise?

Lenore's gaze pinned her as if she were some deluded fool. "Even if you're right, I will concern myself with that when I'm too old for anything else."

"Mother was your age when she died."

"I don't plan to kill myself," Lenore said through clenched teeth. She snatched the napkin from her lap and dropped it on the table. "In the meantime, you will forgive me if I have better things to do than chat with you."

As her aunt walked away, Jill sagged back in her chair. She could give to charity what she had planned, but at what cost? Both Lenore and Carver despised her more than ever, and her uncle wrestled with greater family conflict. As for Tia, Jill wasn't sure what the girl's newest maneuver was all about, but it didn't feel right.

"Ready to get back to work?"

Jill looked up to find Clay in the large doorway to the library.

She sprang from her chair. They had little time left to get ready for the auctioneer.

Ed Drummond arrived a bit earlier than Jill had expected. Fortunately, her aunt never made an appearance as the man's crew prepared the tagged items for transport to his auction barn in Munising. By mid-afternoon, they had loaded his truck. He offered to return in the morning for the rest.

With Clay by her side at the attic windows, she viewed the truck pulling away. Was she doing the right thing? Or only causing more trouble?

"Mew! Mew!" The distressed cry came from behind a trunk of old photos.

Clay reached into the narrow space. "I can't quite grab him." He pulled the trunk away, and the kitten shot out as a board in the wall dislodged and clattered against the trunk.

He removed the board. "Look here, Jill."

With Button in her arms, she peered over his shoulder. Stacked between the wall's studs were many little books. Putting the kitten down, she reached for the volume Clay held out to her. She opened its pages and gasped. Her mother's journals! She would never have found them if not for this charity project, if not for Button and Clay.

He grabbed an empty box and pulled book after book from the hiding place. "There sure are a lot of them."

"My father gave Mother the first one. As far as I know, she kept up the habit until the day she died." Turning the tiny book over in her hands, she quivered with excitement. Now, at last, she had what she had been looking for. Now she might find the answers to her questions, and all it had cost was giving away things of sentimental value that she no longer needed. Her charitable impulse had been right on.

She added the volume in her hands to the others in the cardboard box. Button stretched up and hooked his paws on the edge of the box to peer inside. She picked him up and kissed the top of his head. "You have no idea what a great help you've been."

Standing beside Clay, she reached out to touch his forearm. "Thank you."

He stepped away, and she snatched her hand back. That's right. He'd made himself clear last night. They were friends and nothing more.

Clay picked up the box of books. "Should we quit for the day? I have other work to do."

She led the way to her room where he deposited the carton of books next to the trunk before he left. Sitting on the floor beside the box, she gazed at the open doorway.

Lord, will I ever get it right? First, she had fallen in love with Brian, who didn't love God. Now, she loved Clay, who had somehow lost his way.

Please, Lord, show Clay the way back to you even if he and I have no future.

She picked up one of her mother's journals. Hopefully, these small volumes would help her discover her mother's state of mind before her death. Maybe even the name of her mysterious father, the man her mother had quietly loved all those years.

Unfortunately, checking that out would have to wait until later tonight. She stacked them in her mother's trunk and locked it for safekeeping while she and Tia were away at church.

"Mother was right," Tia remarked as they mounted New Hope's concrete steps. "This building is nothing to brag about." She pulled a piece of cracked paint from the wood siding near the door and dropped it. "What a wreck."

Jill led her cousin inside to the third pew from the front and introduced her to Amelia.

"How nice to meet you, Tia."

"We're not sitting so close, are we?" the girl whispered.

"Don't you worry about me," Amelia said, smiling at Jill. "I'll be fine."

Another teen about Tia's age waved as Jill followed her cousin to the back of the church.

"Someone you know?"

"A girl from school."

"Would you rather sit with her?"

"No! She's nice and all …" Her gaze strayed to the girl. "But all she can talk about is getting right with God and how much fun her church youth group is. Spare me!"

Tia dropped into the pew closest to the door. "Good grief, do you see that?" she said, as Jill sat down beside her. "It's the most broken-down organ I've ever seen."

The words barely left her mouth when a muscular, red-haired boy approached the old organ and seated himself on its stool. He ran his fingertips lightly across the strings of his guitar.

Tia sat tall and strained forward. "Hey! Who's that?" she whispered.

"The pastor's nephew, Leo McGee." Jill unzipped her Bible cover to prepare for class.

"He's cute! What's he doing here?"

"Visiting for the summer."

Tia's attention remained riveted on Leo during the opening worship song.

Jill smiled to herself. God had found an interesting way to snag her cousin's reluctant attention. She paged to the section of her Bible Pastor McGee referenced as he started the class.

Tia squirmed in the wooden pew and then fussed with her nails. "Boy, how do you stand this stuff?" she whispered. "I'd be outta here in a minute if it weren't for that good-looking guy. Can you introduce me?"

"I don't really know him, Tia."

Scowling, the girl slouched in the pew.

"Being good doesn't get a person into heaven," Pastor McGee said.

Tia leaned over and grinned. "That leaves you out with the rest of us sinners, Jill."

She let her cousin's jibe pass, praying the girl would catch enough of the lesson to make a difference in her young life.

"Ephesians 2:8-9 tells us: *For it is by grace you have been saved, through faith—and this not from yourselves, it is the gift of God—not by works, so that no one can boast.* So you see, heaven cannot be earned. It's a gift from the Father through his Son, Jesus, if we are willing to receive it."

Jill glanced at Tia. The girl stopped fidgeting and appeared to be listening. *Please, God, reach Tia's troubled heart.* She even dared to hope her cousin would ask questions, but Tia jumped up the minute the class ended.

"Let's get out of here."

They reached the sidewalk before anyone else, and on the way home, Tia fell quiet. Jill let her cousin be. Maybe silence was what God needed to work in the girl's heart.

Yet when they reached Windtop, Jill's curiosity took over. "What did you think?" she blurted.

"About what?"

"Church tonight." *As if Tia needed reminding.*

"Boring. Hey, I only went to irritate Mother."

Jill wilted. So that was what Tia's interest in going to her church had been about. Again, she had unwittingly let a Bradwell use her. Yet Tia couldn't weasel out of one thing. "You were listening," Jill insisted.

"Okay, a little. But really, heaven a free gift? Nothing's free. Anyway, I'm sure Mother's plenty upset by now, and that's all that matters. Thanks for the help." She ran up the porch steps and into the house.

★★★

In her room, Jill slipped into her soft blue pajamas, unable to shake her concern for Tia and Lenore. How sad they were missing out on the special love a daughter and her mother should know. They needed one another yet were playing games and throwing away these last years before Tia would make her own life.

Just as I wasted those last years of my mother's life on a fruitless search for my father, Lord. Years she would never get back. Now, all she had left were memories, a restored house, and the few things in this trunk.

Sitting on the floor before her mother's collection of precious memorabilia, Jill unlocked the trunk and raised its cover. She could touch the satiny baby shoes and hold the folds of her mother's wedding dress, but she would never again know the warmth of her mother's hand. She would never again enjoy the comfort of her mother's loving arms around her. Worse, she faced a lifetime of not knowing if they would one day see one another in heaven.

Button pounced playfully around Jill's feet while she pulled her mother's journals from the depths of the trunk and organized them by the years in which they were written. She picked up the first. Her fingers tingled as she opened it. *New Year's Day. My baby and I begin this new year safe with Mom and Dad. I can hardly believe they have forgiven me for the pain I caused them and made us so welcome in their home. We never speak of you, my Dear One, but I miss you more every day. My one comfort is our sweet daughter. My greatest pain is that we will never raise her together.*

My Dear One. If only her mother had mentioned her father's name.

Well, this wasn't the journal her mother kept the year she met Jill's father. Neither was it the one written the year when Jill was born. She skimmed each of the volumes she did have, working far into the night. *Lord, why is there no mention of Mother's spiritual life or my father's name?*

With a heavy heart, she returned them to the trunk.

Another fruitless search like the one in Chicago where every candidate had been a long shot and her quest narrowed to a final possibility. Waiting in the lawyer's office for his return, she noticed a picture on his desk that told her the man and his daughters were much too old. Her last slim hope of finding her father vanished, and she fled the man's office to avoid embarrassing them both.

Now, she faced another dead end. Without her mother's first two journals, she would never know her father's name. Without the most recent, she could never be sure about her mother's state of mind near the time of her death. She needed the three most important journals. Still missing, they had to be hidden somewhere in this house.

She reached for the chain around her neck and the smaller of the two keys her uncle had given her. Would the smaller one open her mother's journal box?

If she could find that box, would it hold the answers to her questions?

Likely, her mother had hidden the box in the master bedroom. She could ask her aunt for permission to look in there, but that might only make it easier for those journals to disappear forever.

No, she would have to grab the first opportunity to search the room without getting caught.

Chapter Seventeen

As Ed Drummond's men loaded the last piece of her mother's furniture into the truck, Jill held back a sigh. Saying goodbye to that part of her life left her a bit shell-shocked. Yet the prospect of their sale doing so much good gave her a deep satisfaction.

The auctioneer shook his head, frown lines deepening in his bronzed forehead. He held out the inventory pages she had given to him. "We couldn't find some of the smaller items you listed here."

Jill skimmed the starred items before passing the papers to Clay. "Do you remember where we put these? In a bureau drawer? Or a box they might have overlooked?"

She inhaled his woodsy scent as he drew near to skim the list. He shook his head. "We worked so fast yesterday, I'm not sure, but they were definitely in the attic when we finished. Those pictures you took should prove that."

Yes, they would. Yet, was it strange that these items were missing? Lenore might have taken them out of spite—an ugly thought, but she knew her aunt would not be above petty vengeance.

"I'm sorry, Mr. Drummond. I don't know what to tell you, but I will look into it." She would definitely do that.

The man adjusted his sports cap with the company logo. "I hope you find them, Miss Shepherd. They're valuable."

He had to be kidding. She thought they were nothing more than interesting trinkets. Yet he didn't act as if he were kidding.

"If you do find them, you might want to keep them. We have enough inventory here to prepare for the auction. It'll be hard enough to do justice to all this on such short notice, so I'm personally contacting several buyers who should be quite interested. I'll email them the digital photos you took, and we'll do our best to give you a better profit." He climbed into the truck and shut the door.

Jill approached the driver's side window. "You will deliver the organ to the church today, won't you?"

"Sure thing."

As the truck lumbered down the driveway, Jill remembered something else. "You know, Clay, I don't think those are the only things of value that have turned up as missing from Windtop."

He scowled. "What do you mean?"

"Last night, I skimmed through the journals we found. During the last few years, Mother now and then mentioned missing trinkets. I'm going to take a closer look."

"Do you need help?"

"Thanks, but I think I can handle it myself. Besides, you must be anxious to get back to your work."

"You'll let me know what you find?"

"If I find anything." She hurried into the house.

A thief may have been operating at Windtop all along. If so, that thief might still be among them and have enough motivation for murder.

She shivered as the ugly conclusion fully registered.

Seated on the floor of her bedroom, Jill paged through the journals her mother had written during the two years before her death and noted the several times when small but valuable items had mysteriously disappeared. A queasy uneasiness enveloped her.

"Well, I hope you're satisfied! You've given away a fortune."

She looked up to find her aunt standing in the doorway.

Lenore stepped inside the room. Her sharp eyes spied the trunk. "What mischief are you up to now?"

"Attempting to solve a puzzle." Jill held up her inventory sheets. "We seem to be missing two decorative scent bottles, an egg-shaped glass paperweight, and a tortoiseshell playing card case."

Her aunt's eyes narrowed to slits. "Are you accusing me?"

"No." *Not yet, anyway. Not without proof.*

"Good, because I know nothing about them."

Her aunt had too good an eye for valuable antiques for that to be true. "You must have seen them around the house."

"But I did not take them."

Not sure why, Jill believed her. *This time.*

"What are those?" The woman indicated the pile of small volumes on the floor.

"Clay and I found Mother's journals behind a loose board in the attic."

Lenore smirked. "So that's where she hid them, and you've been reading them." It was an accusation. "I wonder what she would think of your invading her privacy."

Warmth rose in Jill's face. She hadn't considered her search through them in that way.

A vindictive smile settled on her aunt's lips. "You run away to find your father against your mother's wishes. When you don't succeed, you return to Windtop and search through Susannah's private journals. Isn't it time that you left the past alone and your mother to rest in peace?"

Jill set her jaw. She didn't have to explain herself to this woman, and the less Lenore knew while Jill straightened out the crooked places of their past, the better.

"Stubborn as always, I see. Some things never change." In a swish of long skirts, her aunt left.

Lenore was right though. Some things never did change, and her aunt's arrival in her room by chance wasn't likely. She had been surprised to find Jill. What had she been after?

Only one thing could interest her if she knew about it.

Jill scrambled to the wardrobe. Standing on tiptoe, she reached into the darkness at the back of the top shelf. Her hand swept through empty air.

A sudden weakness washed over her. The puzzle was missing.

"Miss Shepherd, is something the matter?"

Jill spun around and sagged with relief. "Mrs. Fenton!" For all of her size, the woman moved like a cat.

"I put a puzzle on this shelf. It's missing. Did you see it?"

The housekeeper nodded. "When I aired your clothes after the fire."

"Where is it now?"

"It's not there?" She peered at the empty shelf. "Acht! Well, it's only a child's toy. It'll show up. You'll see."

Jill rubbed her temples. The woman had no idea how much trouble that puzzle could cause.

"You missed lunch," Mrs. Fenton said before she left the room. "I thought you should know that dinner is ready."

Who needed dinner? She had to find that puzzle. A box didn't just walk off by itself.

She locked her mother's journals safely in the trunk and went downstairs.

Jill froze in place as Tia pointed at the center of the dining room table. The puzzle lay upside down on the dining room table, Maggie's accusations exposed for all to see.

"Is this true, Mother?"

Lenore stared at the puzzle. "Where did you get that?"

Tia's brown eyes glistened with tears. Her chin quivered. "Is it true? When you fell down those stairs, were you trying to kill me?"

Jill's stomach roiled. She should have destroyed the puzzle. She should never have let it come to this.

Lenore lifted her chin. "I'd had a very traumatic day and didn't know what I was doing."

"This says you deliberately threw yourself down those stairs."

Lenore's face reddened. "I had just found out that your grandparents had given this house to Susannah and Jill when it rightfully belonged to us. I was angry because your father had agreed to that wretched plan without first discussing it with me. I wanted to hurt him and wasn't thinking straight."

Carver put an arm around his mother's shoulders. "Let it go, Tia. It's all in the past."

Tears slipped down the girl's cheeks. "It's not all in the past. Because of her, I have epilepsy. Jill is right. God didn't do this to me. Mother did."

Jill gasped. How could her young cousin twist her words so horribly?

"All this time, Mother, I believed I embarrassed you. The truth is you never loved me." Tia dropped into a chair and sobbed.

Lenore glared at Jill. "How dare you tell my daughter that I am to blame?"

The hatred gleaming in her aunt's eyes pierced Jill. "I told Tia that God didn't give her epilepsy. I never said you did."

Uncle Drew walked in. "What's going on here?"

Carver nodded toward the table.

Positioning himself, her uncle read the words. His face darkened. "Where did this come from?"

Tia looked up, sniffling. "I found it in Jill's room."

"So, cousin, you think we killed your mother." Contempt dripped from Carver's mouth.

"Is this true?" her uncle asked, his brown eyes soft with hurt.

"Of course not."

Lenore pointed to the puzzle. "Then what was this doing in your room?"

"I found it the day I arrived."

"And you didn't tell us?" Her uncle's voice was barely audible.

Carver grinned. "Of course not. She believes it."

"I don't know what to believe." Jill bit her lip. "But what if Maggie's right? What if someone did kill Mother? I'm not saying it was any of you. But someone."

"Right, cousin, and who might that mythical person be if not one of us?"

"I don't know. All I want is the truth."

Carver snorted.

"It's not easy, Jill," her uncle said with a kindness that surprised her under the circumstances, "but we all have to accept the fact that Susannah took her life. The security system was on. She was alone in the house. What more do you need to be convinced?"

Tears stung the back of Jill's eyes. "It would help if I knew where each of you were when Mother died."

"See?" Carver said. "She thinks we killed her mother."

Couldn't they understand? "I just need the whole picture."

Lenore huffed. "Why should we humor you?"

Uncle Drew took his wife's hands. "Dear, Jill was kind enough to let us live in this house that you love so much. The least we can do is help her put this all behind her. We have nothing to hide, so what's the harm?"

Lenore pressed her lips together and shot Jill a venomous look. "All right, if you must know, I drove to Escanaba early that morning and stayed until four o'clock to bid on the last piece I needed for Windtop."

"Did anyone go with you?"

"So unless I have a witness, I'm a liar?" Her aunt's dark eyes narrowed. "I went alone, as I always do. Plenty of people saw me."

"Carver?" Uncle Drew prompted.

Her cousin's lips curled in disdain. "I was nowhere near this place."

"He was taking a college exam for Psychology 411 out east," Uncle Drew added before turning to his daughter. "Tia?"

The girl lowered her eyelids and bent her head.

"She was at home, recovering from a seizure," Lenore snapped.

Her uncle sat down and laced his short fingers. "And I was at the mill all day, dealing with an equipment failure until the police arrived to tell me of Susannah's death."

Jill's strength drained from her. Everyone had a solid alibi. No wonder the sheriff and the coroner declared her mother's death a suicide.

"There's no other explanation for Susannah's death, Jill." Her uncle's voice grew hoarse at the end.

"Your mother was a sick woman," Lenore said, "and whatever you may think, we had nothing to do with her death."

Tia looked up, her brown eyes pleading. "Honest, Jill, I didn't do it," she whispered. "Aunt Susannah was always kind to me. I'm so sorry she died."

Jill's chest constricted. What had she done, letting her doubts carry her so far afield?

"Enough!" Lenore took her place at the dining table. "Jill, stop obsessing about your mother's death. It's annoying." She shook out a linen napkin and placed it on her lap. "Mrs. Fenton, take your ear from the door and serve dinner. Someone get that puzzle off the table. The rest of you sit down."

Jill and Tia reached for the puzzle. When Tia retreated, Jill scooped the pieces into the box, her heart heavy. Her doubts had now made her more of an enemy in the eyes of her family.

Fitting the lid on the box, she picked it up and paused. She should at least apologize. "I never meant to hurt any of you. I simply wanted to know. Please forgive me."

No one responded.

Maybe she should reassure them. "I did search but found nothing to suggest that any of you were responsible for Mother's death."

No one moved.

"I … I'm not hungry. Please excuse me." Clutching the puzzle, she fled the dining room.

Leaning her back against her bedroom door, Jill squeezed out the hot tears. "I failed, God. I tried so hard to prove Mother's death was no suicide, and all I've done is alienate what little family I have."

Worse, she had ruined any chance of God using her to draw the Bradwells to himself. She no longer had any reason to remain at Windtop.

She pulled her suitcases from beneath the bed and began to pack. It would be a long night, but this way, she'd be ready to leave in the morning. When she finished, she sank into Maggie's rocker, a pad of blank paper on her lap.

Her brow furrowed and her heart lay in shards as she sighed. Why did she always push so hard for what she wanted? Once again, she had plowed headlong into disaster. She could never repair the damage now. All she could do was leave this place where she would never fit in. Leave this place of sorrow. If only she had taken Clay's advice days ago.

Gripping the pad of paper on her lap, she wrote a farewell letter, signed it, and sat back. The words stared up at her.

Dear Uncle Drew, Aunt Lenore, Carver, and Tia,
I had such dreams that one day we might truly be a family, but once again I've messed up. I'm so sorry. Please believe me when I say

that I never meant to hurt you, either by returning to Windtop or by trying to understand my mother's death. I see now that, as hard as it is, I simply have to accept her suicide.

It's too late to disturb you tonight with my decision, and by the time you find this letter, I'll be gone. Don't worry. I'll never trouble you again.

Goodbye,
Jill

She clutched the letter. Was this what God wanted? Or just something she believed was best? "Lord, please. I need to hear from you."

She retrieved her Bible from her bedside table and opened it. Her gaze fell on the words of Isaiah, "I, the Lord, have called you to demonstrate my righteousness. I will guard and support you."

What did that mean?

A timid knocking at the door arrested her attention. "Jill, I … may I come in?"

Tia. What did she want?

Folding the letter, she tucked it in her Bible and opened the door.

The girl slipped in, careful to close the door behind her. "I'm so sorry, so ashamed. You've been better to me than anyone, even when I haven't been good to you." Her large brown eyes swam with tears. "Can you ever forgive me?"

Jill stared at her young cousin. Was this another act? Was the girl setting her up again? She'd had her fill of trouble from Tia. "You had no right to go through my things."

"I didn't, but please, Jill, please forgive me."

For a long minute, Jill studied the girl. If she were acting, her mother should pack her on the next plane to Hollywood.

Her cousin's gaze went to the bed where the suitcases lay. "You're not leaving! You can't. Not now. In my room, I just asked Jesus to forgive me and gave my life to him, just like Karen kept saying I should."

"Karen?"

"You know. The girl at church. She was always telling me that inviting Jesus into my life was the best thing I could do. And you know what? She was right. I feel so clean inside."

Tia's eyes shone with more than tears. She grabbed Jill's hands before Jill could pull them away. "You have to stay. I need you," she said. "I don't know the first thing about being the kind of Christian you are. Please stay, Jill. Please help me."

As much as Jill wanted to believe her cousin, could she? Still, it was hard to ignore her pleading as the girl's eyes searched hers. They reminded her of her own desperate desire just six months ago. Maybe God was accomplishing his purpose at Windtop in spite of all the mistakes Jill had made.

"All right, Tia, I don't know that much myself, but I'll stay. For a while."

The girl threw herself into Jill's arms and hugged her so hard she couldn't breathe. Startled, Jill put her arms uncertainly around her cousin.

When Tia pulled away again, her face was wet but full of joy. Jill offered her a tissue from the box on the dressing table.

Tia blotted her tears. "Can you help me pray for the rest of the family?"

This was all too fast for Jill's sensibilities to take in, but she knelt beside her cousin on the braided rug. They took turns asking God to work in Drew's, Lenore's, and Carver's hearts.

When they finished, Tia stood up. "Thank you, Jill. I think I can sleep now." She glanced at the suitcases. "Will I really see you in the morning?"

Jill stood too, still startled by the quick turn of events. "I'll be here."

With a smile, the girl left, closing the door softly.

God, is this real? Or was Tia pretending for some reason? Yet, her young cousin's clear eyes and her words *I feel so clean* seemed sincere. Until she knew for sure, she would not abandon her.

Pulling the farewell letter from her Bible, she dropped it into the wastebasket.

Chapter Eighteen

The rapping on her bedroom door dragged Jill from a deep sleep. Groaning, she burrowed under her pillows.

Whoever you are, please go away. Hadn't last night been enough?

When the noise persisted, she pushed the pillows away. "Yes?"

Mrs. Fenton entered with a cheerful wink. "Happy Fourth of July!"

Fourth of July? Her plans to leave today wouldn't have worked even if she had gone ahead with them.

"Mr. Merrick is waiting downstairs."

"Clay?" Jill sat upright in bed. "Whatever for?"

"The Bradwells went over early with friends. He waited especially for you. He says to tell you his grandma is expecting you."

"Oh, my goodness, I promised to help Amelia with the church craft booth." She threw back the covers. "Tell him I'll be down in fifteen minutes."

A quick shower later, she searched through the clothing in her closet and dresser drawers, pulling together the red, white and blue motif the townsfolk favored. She slipped into her red T-shirt, white capris with the blue stars on the pockets, and a blue cardigan. Oh, and her gold necklace and earrings that sported American flag designs. That should do it.

Her gaze strayed to the wastebasket.

Mere hours ago she had planned to leave Windtop and all its problems. But now, Tia was counting on her, and maybe this was God's way of saying it was not yet time to leave.

Yet a certain uneasiness crept around the edges of her mind.

By the time Jill and Clay arrived with Amelia at Bayshore Park, its amphitheater-like shape echoed with the sounds of booth construction. Men no sooner hammered long boards into square frameworks than the women festooned those booths with red, white, and blue bunting. Metal pipes clanged as burly men set up the children's train and Ferris wheel rides. Up the hill in the shade of a cluster of trees, a chainsaw burr-upped with short bursts in the hands of the local stump artist as he tested his equipment.

Little had changed. Nor was change needed. The familiar sights and sounds evoked memories of previous Fourth of July celebrations, and her heart squeezed with longing. Yet, after last evening's disaster, she could hold no more delusions about gaining a warm place in the hearts of her family.

Tia might be the exception. Had the girl truly changed?

A few yards away, Lenore ordered Uncle Drew around the Historical Society booth, never once looking her way though she was sure her aunt knew of her presence. The woman never missed a detail. Yet neither glanced her way. If they were deliberately ignoring her, she couldn't blame them.

She turned back to the patch of grass where Pastor McGee and Leo were erecting a large dome tent near the park's entrance. Helen handed her husband the last tent stake which he drove into the ground.

"We're all set, Amelia," Helen said. "How do you want the quilts and crafts displayed?"

Clay opened a lawn chair. "Sit here, Grandma, while I bring your quilts from the truck."

Jill steadied Amelia as she sat in the chair while Pastor McGee fell into step behind Clay and motioned to his nephew.

"Let's give him a hand, Leo."

Safely in the chair, Amelia gripped Jill's hand and winked. "My Sonny likes you."

Whatever gave her that impossible impression?

The dear woman's faded blue eyes twinkled. "You two can't fool an old woman. I've been around the block a time or two. You like my grandson, and he likes you."

Jill couldn't deny her part, but surely Amelia wasn't right about Clay. Even if she were, as long as he distanced himself from the Lord, they had no hope of a future together. Her heart ached at the loss.

Wood clacking against wood warned of Pastor McGee and Clay's return with the card tables and quilt racks. Leo followed with a stack of colorful quilts. While Amelia supervised from her chair and the men returned to the truck, Jill helped Helen arrange craft displays on the tables and the quilts on their racks.

Tia ran toward them from the Historical Society's booth. "Hi, everyone!"

In the distance, Lenore paused to check on her daughter. When Jill offered a tremulous smile, her aunt scowled and busied herself. Jill took a steadying breath.

Unaware and all grins, Tia halted beside her. "Let me help, Jill. Tell me what to do."

"Ah ... sure." Was the girl trying to get another rise out of her mother? Tia's expectant attitude didn't seem to support that idea. "Pastor McGee, Helen, Leo, this is my cousin Tia."

Amelia nodded and smiled. "How nice to see you again."

"Glad to meet you," Pastor McGee said as Helen reached out to take her cousin's hand.

Leo grinned. "Didn't I see you at the service Wednesday night?"

Tia's cheeks pinked. "I ... ah ... yes. I'm afraid I wasn't very friendly. But a lot has changed since then. Right, Jill?"

Jill smiled quietly and nodded. She certainly hoped so.

Leo's eyes brightened. "How about cluing me in while I get the rest of the quilts from Mr. Merrick's truck?"

Tia tagged along, she and Leo talking earnestly.

Was it Jill's imagination, or was Tia really so happy? Maybe ... no, it was too early to tell whether her cousin's claims were sincere.

Once the crafts and quilts had been properly displayed, Amelia reminded everyone of the cookout at her house. "In about a half hour, shall we say?"

"I'll bring my frosted apple pie squares," Helen said.

"They're the best," Leo confided to Tia with a grin.

Pastor McGee zipped the tent shut. "See you folks soon."

At Leo's invitation, a delighted Tia left with the McGees, taking a moment to check in with her parents. Studying the young people's retreating forms, Jill couldn't help but notice that Leo actually believed Tia had given her heart to the Lord.

If only Jill were as sure.

Jill helped Clay position the picnic table in Amelia's backyard. While he fired up the grill, she went inside to see what help her friend might need in the kitchen. The spicy aroma of brats and burgers soon drifted through the open window and her stomach growled. She and Amelia burst into laughter.

"It's been so long since my last cookout," Jill said, pulling a large bowl of homemade potato salad from the refrigerator while Amelia cut the brat and burger buns.

Making two runs, Jill carried the potato salad and then a crockpot of slow-cooked baked beans to the picnic table. She returned to bring out thick slices of chilled watermelon and had just placed them on the table, along with a pitcher of iced tea, when she heard Tia call out, "We're here!"

Leo eyed the laden table while Pastor McGee made room for Helen's dessert. "Looks great! Anything we can do to help?"

"Check with Amelia in the kitchen," Helen suggested.

The two teens were off in a shot while Jill began pouring the tea. "I guess they're hungry."

Leo came back toting a large platter of brat and burger buns while Tia trailed with the ketchup, mustard, pickles, and diced onion.

She giggled, her glow reminding Jill of those first months after she had invited Jesus into her life. Hopefully, Leo's attention wasn't the only reason for her cousin's obvious happiness.

With a long-handled spatula, Clay flipped the last of the burgers. "I could use a platter here," he said, and Jill hurried to hold the dish while he piled on the grilled meat. She covered the meat with aluminum foil. His gaze caught hers before he quickly busied himself scraping the grill.

Amelia was wrong. For all of her friend's fond hopes, nothing had changed.

Jill joined the others, setting the meat platter on the table as Pastor McGee asked Leo to pray.

Without a moment's pause, the young man bowed his head. "Lord, thank you for your many blessings, for this country where we are free to worship you, for loved ones around this table, for your precious blood that paid for our sins. Please bless this food to the health of our bodies and those who prepared it. And Lord, thank you for the new lamb in your fold. Help her to grow strong in you. Amen."

A faint blush tinged Tia's cheeks.

"You don't mind my saying that, do you?" Leo asked.

Tia picked up a paper napkin. "Your prayer was beautiful."

Jill's breath caught in her throat. Maybe her coming to Windtop had been less about her finding peace from her grief and more about Tia's need. If so, she was satisfied. Though she still wished for the answers to her questions and prayed that Clay would find his way back to God.

Both seemed impossible.

Shortly after their picnic lunch, the McGees and Tia left while Clay's grandmother waved a blue-veined hand and called out to them, "We'll see you at the park after the parade."

Clay gathered up three lawn chairs and set them up at the curb in front of the house. "Grandma, sit right here in the middle." He helped her before settling in the chair to her left.

Already, a crowd had lined the street on both sides in anticipation of the parade. Nearly everything and everyone was decked out in red, white, and blue. Flags fluttered from porches, and the hum of happy conversation filled the air. Out of sight on another street, marching bands tuned up. Their disjointed practice notes had already stirred the crowd's anticipation by the time Jill finally arrived.

"The kitchen is clean, Amelia," she said, resting in the remaining lawn chair. "We're all set to leave for the park when the parade is over."

He couldn't help it. Her smile captivated him. He looked away, hoping to distract himself with all the activity around them. Why couldn't he stop wondering what life might be like with her? Sadly enough, he'd never know.

It didn't help that here he was, alone with his grandmother and Jill again. That is, if you didn't count the crowd several rows deep lining the parade route on both sides of the street as far as you could see.

While her presence tortured him, he also found it as refreshing as clean summer air. But why crave what would never be his?

Jill tried to enjoy the parade with Amelia. Her few glances at Clay revealed how uncomfortable he was. Could it be because she had joined them?

She forced herself to focus on the smartly dressed marching bands filling the air with tunes that made her toes tap on the grass. Colorful clowns gave balloons to the children along the route who wiggled like puppies from the attention. Political figures waved from fancy cars while passengers in the business trucks tossed wrapped candy to the children. They scrambled to fill their bags just as she had when she was a child.

A ripple of laughter drew her curiosity as a huge, shiny milk truck lumbered by. Hastily slapped on its back end with duct tape, a sign with a big black arrow pointed to the crumpled metal dent. It all but shouted *a deer committed suicide here!*

The crowd laughed, but Jill blinked rapidly. *Suicide.*

Even at a parade and in the midst of celebration, she couldn't avoid reminders of her mother's death.

A thin hand grasped hers and she offered Amelia a weak smile as Clay leaned forward to look her way. His gray eyes softened just as an icy blast of water hit her square in the chest. She gasped and leapt to her feet.

From a long flatbed float crowded with alumni seated on folding chairs, Carver grinned and waved. He flicked his hand off his forehead in a salute and, just as quickly, joined his classmates to surprise other unsuspecting parade watchers.

Amelia chuckled and pointed down the street. "I think he and his classmates are about to get a dose of their own medicine."

Barely visible, a water hose hung in a tree. As Carver and his classmates opened fire again, the hose drenched them from above. They sputtered and laughed along with the crowd.

Jill shook her shirt. The summer heat had already begun to dry the wet spot, evidence of the most attention in fun Carver had paid her in a long time.

Clay clenched his teeth. For two cents, he'd knock Carver's block off for shocking Jill like that. He scanned the park for any sign of Jill's cousin while she and the McGees helped Amelia with potential shoppers at the quilt and craft tent. Within three hours, his grandmother had placed the last of the quilt money in the cash box and locked it.

She grinned at him, a twinkle in her eyes, and he knew she was up to something again. "You and Jill might as well take advantage of the free ice cream bars and enjoy some of the other activities," she said. "I'm going to visit Ruth at the nursing home for a couple of hours."

When he attempted to help her, she shooed him away. "I can walk that half-block myself," she insisted. He doubted she was right, but she did appear to manage just fine.

He shook his head and turned to Jill. "That grandmother of mine sure is something else. It looks as if she's thrown us together. For her sake, should we make the best of it?"

Jill appeared uncertain, but he had no intention of leaving her on her own. He scanned the park again. Something didn't feel right. "Are you interested in that free ice cream?"

She smiled and his stomach flip-flopped. He was probably just hungry.

Less than ten minutes later, he had polished off the last of the cold, creamy treat and pitched the stick in a refuse can. While he pretty much wolfed his down, Jill had a delightfully demure way of consuming hers.

She had barely finished when the wail of a siren pierced the park in waves. Like something out of a science fiction movie, everyone around them stopped what they were doing and moved in unison toward the center of town.

Jill's eyes sparkled. "Let's go, Clay."

"Sure." He fell into step with her eager pace and, not for the first time today, the hair stood up on the back of his neck. He scanned the crowd for anything suspicious. As they walked to the top of the hill, he couldn't shake the creepy notion that someone was watching them.

Two red fire engines rounded the corner. Children chosen to ride on the tops of the trucks waved excitedly to family and friends below. As soon as the vehicles parked near the post office, the children scrambled down to join their families.

"I rode the firetrucks one year," Jill said, her face aglow.

Didn't she feel anything amiss? He glanced through the crowd and almost put an arm around her to keep her near.

Firemen in shorts and t-shirts donned their yellow hats and slickers. After pulling on their black boots, they rolled out heavy fire hoses at each end of the short city block.

Clay had seen the annual water fight a couple of summers as a kid. It was about to begin. He edged Jill into the crowd lining the block where he could get a good view while the firefighters divided into teams and positioned themselves.

Alternating with training powerful hoses on each other's team, the men waved them overhead, raining a refreshing spray on the crowd who squealed with delight.

Jill smiled up at him.

For a long moment, he stared into the depths of her eyes. He not only enjoyed it but realized that he would like to get used to the privilege. Yet one day soon, she would no longer smile at him.

He tore his gaze away, and it stopped by chance across the street, down about a half block, and set him on instant alert. His shoulder muscles bunched as he grasped Jill's nearest hand. He pulled it through the crook of his arm and covered it with his other hand. In his peripheral vision, he caught her looking up at him and sensed her confusion, but he continued to stare grimly into the crowd across the way.

She swiveled in that direction. In that split second, did she catch three men looking at them? One pointed behind a thick veil of spray.

He nodded his head in their direction. "Do you know them?"

"Well … maybe. No, I don't think so. Why?"

The men disappeared before he could get a good look at them. But he could have sworn they had been studying them. He didn't like it.

The water fight ended and the firemen began gathering up their gear.

"It's almost supper time," he said. "Let's go on back. Are you hungry?"

As they waited in line at the American Legion booth to order their food, Jill couldn't help but wonder why Clay was so worried. The uneasy feeling she experienced earlier crept back. She shook it off, determined to enjoy what was left of the celebration and the warmth of her hand in his. She might never get another chance.

Spicy hot dogs and nose-tickling sodas added a certain ambiance as they witnessed first, the pie-eating contest and later, the chainsaw artist turning chunks of tree trunks into squirrels, rabbits, and hawks. She leaned into Clay, relishing the quiet comfort of his presence. For a while, she wouldn't think of Janice, of what his murdered fiancée meant to him.

Music throbbed through the park as they strolled near the bay's edge and came to a quiet wooded area where others rested in the shade. They paused on a wooden bridge arching over a narrow creek that trickled to the bay. Clay leaned on its railing.

Their being together seemed so right that it hurt. She sighed. Better to content herself with whatever fleeting hours the Lord allowed.

"It's been a good day," he said, his gaze on the creek's flow. He reached over and covered her hand on the railing beside his.

Jill's pulse raced. *Oh, Lord, if only he loved you more than what's troubling him. If only he would come back to you.* She might be long gone from his life before that ever happened.

She forced her thoughts to safer ground. "Tia and Leo were so funny competing in the pie eating contest. I've never seen two faces covered with so much blueberry."

"Or cherry," Clay added.

"And I've never seen Tia laugh as much."

His mood quieted. "I guess Leo makes the difference."

"I think it's more than that, Clay."

"How so?"

His gaze mesmerized her. She longed to stay lost in the bright gray depths of his eyes. How would he take her news? "Tia invited Jesus into her life last night."

Tearing his gaze away, he checked his watch and tensed. "Oh! I'll be late."

"For what?"

"My ballgame," he said. "I have to drive Grandma home first."

"I could do that," Jill said.

"You would, wouldn't you?" he said as if it were something special.

"I don't think she'd mind. So if you don't ..."

He trailed his fingers over her cheek and gazed so deeply into her eyes that every nerve in her body came alive.

"I'm sure she wouldn't," he said. He squeezed her hand affectionately. "Let's go."

Racing up a grassy slope through the trees, they gained the nursing home parking lot where Clay unlocked his truck and pulled out his sports bag. He placed his keys in her hand and curled her fingers gently around them. "Thanks."

"I could drop you off at the ballpark first."

Clay shook his head. "I'll make it all right on foot." He backed away at a fast trot. "See you at the game. Park in the lot above the marina where we picked it up this morning." He turned to run.

She couldn't tear her gaze away until he was out of sight. *A part of him might always love Janice, Lord, but he also cares for me.* If only his love for her were stronger than whatever trapped him in the past. Whatever it was had to be deeper than his issues regarding Janice.

The plate glass door of the brick nursing home opened and Amelia gestured for her to come quickly.

"I've stumbled on news about your mother, Jill. Something I think you'll want to hear firsthand."

Chapter Nineteen

Their discordant footsteps echoed on the tile floor as Jill followed Amelia down the nursing home's wide, empty hall.

Her heart beat against her ribcage. What information could Amelia have found in a place like this? Her mother hadn't known anyone here in years.

Her stomach swam with anxiety as they entered a resident's room and approached the single bed near a large window with a bayside view of Grand Island. A white-haired woman lay there, her thin body barely visible beneath the white cotton blanket draped over her.

This frail woman knew something about her mother?

"Ruth, this is Jill Shepherd."

Ruth blinked her faded brown eyes. Her smile radiated a peace that amazed Jill. "Thank you for those lovely flowers to brighten my room." She gestured weakly toward the pot of russet mums on the window sill. Against pale ivory walls and drapes like sunshine, they made a spirited statement.

Amelia took her friend's frail hand. "Ruth wasn't always confined to a bed. Were you, dear?" She patted her friend's thin hand gently. "She traveled the world as a missionary nurse, going wherever God sent her. Ruth, tell Jill what you told me. You know, about her mother on the island."

The woman crinkled her forehead. "Oh, yes. You mean about a year ago when I still got around quite well."

Jill settled into a chair near the bed, her gaze never leaving the woman. She waited as Ruth corralled her memories.

"I was praying that morning—actually it was my eightieth birthday—and the Lord told me ..." She stopped as if undecided about going on with her story. "I'm sorry," she said. "Some folks are bothered when I say, 'The

Lord told me.' Does it bother you? I don't mean to suggest that he talks to me out loud."

Jill tilted her head and smiled to encourage Ruth. "It doesn't bother me. God has a way of letting me know what he wants me to understand too."

The frail woman nodded. "Exactly."

"I came back to Grand Island," Jill said, "because I believed the Lord wanted me to." But had she been right about God's reasons?

Ruth sat up, a momentary strength seeming to seize her. She gripped the white coverlet with both hands. "Don't you doubt it. God *did* send you. He will accomplish much through you if you give him the chance. You have grave and dark days ahead, but don't leave until you complete all the Lord has sent you to do." She sank back against her pillows and closed her eyes. Her breathing came in shallow gasps.

Alarmed at the woman's weakened condition, Jill turned to Amelia, who put a finger to her lips. "Wait," she whispered.

Ruth's breathing returned to normal. She opened her eyes and sought Jill's. "Now where were we? Oh, yes, the day of my eightieth birthday. That's the morning the Lord told me to go to the island and take my Bible along. Do you know Henry Lattern?"

Jill shook her head, wishing Amelia's friend wouldn't take such a leisurely pace while telling her story.

"Well, he drove me from Williams' Landing as far as the gate of a big brick house with brown wood trim."

Something like electricity ran over Jill's skin. She clasped her hands together and leaned forward.

"'You stay here,' I told Henry. Then I walked along a tree-lined driveway. Just as I came to where the trees stopped, a woman with pretty blonde hair came out of the house."

"Mother?"

Ruth nodded. "I waited in the shadows. When she looked around but didn't see me, she came down from the porch with a pail and a gardening trowel."

"You're sure she was my mother."

"Do you look like her?"

"People say I do, but Mother rarely went outside and never without our housekeeper."

Ruth smiled broadly. "If that's true—and I don't doubt it—then you can be sure this was God's doing. As soon as I saw your mother, I knew God had sent me to tell her how much he loved her and wanted her to be his child."

Jill's heart pounded. Could this be true? It was almost more than she could hope for.

"With her back to me, your mother worked in the dirt around that rosebush by the porch steps. Apparently, she didn't hear me come up the drive and seemed quite content until she sensed me behind her. Then she jumped to her feet and backed away.

"'Missus,' I said to her, 'I didn't mean to startle you,' but she scrambled up the steps and ran for the door. 'Please don't go,' I called after her, but she slammed the door and locked it."

Jill closed her eyes and swallowed again. How could her mother come so close to news that would change her life, and yet miss it?

Amelia reached for Jill's hand.

"I stood near the bottom porch step," Ruth went on. "'Lord,' I prayed, 'what have I done? You sent me to tell this dear woman you love her, and I frightened her away.' Tears tumbled from these old eyes. I couldn't stop them, so I just stood there and cried. Then the Lord told me to look up. There she was, observing me from the long window next to the door. *Take the booklet from your Bible,* the Lord said in my heart. Your mother watched as I put it on the porch near the rosebush and weighted it down with her trowel. I left, praying that God would use that booklet to help your mother understand how much he loved her."

"Did he?" Jill held her breath.

Ruth sighed. "I don't know. When I reached the trees, I looked back to see if she had come out of the house. As far as I know, she didn't. I prayed for her all through the night. Three days later, I heard she had died."

Amelia patted Jill's back. "At least you know God sent someone to tell your mother about the way to heaven."

Jill bowed her head. "Yes. At least she had a chance and I have hope." She rose to go. "Thank you, Ruth. Thank you for going to see my mother when you did."

"I'll be praying for you," the frail woman promised. "Maybe you will find out what I could not tell you."

Ruth closed her eyes. Amelia motioned to Jill, and they left the room.

"That was the last time Ruth was able to go out and tell anyone about Jesus," Amelia confided. "That evening she fell sick, was taken to the hospital, and has been in this nursing home ever since. She often wondered what choice your mother made."

Jill did, too. Had her mother read the little booklet or turned her back on it?

Whatever the case, when Ruth said not to leave Windtop until she had done all God sent her here to do, the words burned in her heart. Now, more than ever, she had to find the whole truth about her mother's death.

By the time Jill had driven Amelia home, parked the truck, and arrived at the ballpark, Clay's game was in the top of the seventh inning. She found a seat halfway up the metal bleachers, her heart still full with the wonderful possibility that she might not be separated from her mother for eternity after all.

Lights flooded the ball diamond as day faded into deep twilight. She had no trouble spotting Clay in centerfield.

She smiled to herself. That old saying about a woman's attraction to a man in uniform must be true. Except that her attraction had made itself known long before she saw Clay in uniform.

He ran for the center field fence, his back to the fast approaching ball. Thrusting his glove-covered hand in the air, he made a blind catch, ending the opposing team's streak of runs.

Amid the cheers and chatter of fans, two young women sat one row down from Jill. They laughed raucously, and she found them hard to ignore.

"Let me have some of that popcorn," the tall brunette demanded.

Her red-haired companion shoved the bag at her. "Take it all. I have better fish to fry."

"Oh, yeah?"

The redhead leaned forward. "That guy in centerfield."

The brunette followed the direction of her friend's long-nailed finger. "Clay Merrick?"

Jill pricked up her ears.

The redhead purred. "I see I've been missing something."

"You're wasting your time, Phyllis. He's not much for girls."

"You don't mean—"

"Not that. He just keeps to himself. Softball once a week. That's it."

"So that's all, is it?" The redhead took a mirror from her purse and applied a generous portion of moist, red lipstick. "He's about to make a change and will never know what hit him. I know what pleases a guy."

Her friend squealed. "Oh, Phyllis, you wouldn't!"

Jill squirmed, her stomach turning queasy.

Phyllis released a large hair clasp and tossed her long red hair until the curls bounced to her slim waist. "He doesn't know it yet, but tonight's his night. Are you with me?"

"If you say so."

The two girls put their heads together, whispering and laughing. Then the redhead said, "Don't be silly. All jocks are the same. They like the game and they like the girls. This will be so-o-o easy. Just follow my lead."

Jill's cheeks burned. For two cents, she'd … she wasn't sure what she'd do, but if Clay was anybody's, he was hers. Yet, that wasn't strictly true. If he belonged to anyone, he still belonged to Janice. That made one thing sure. He wouldn't fall for that redhead's scheme.

Would he?

Clay stepped up to home plate with two runners on base. His bat pinged, driving the ball over the leftfield fence. The crowd leapt to their feet, cheering as the runners crossed home plate to win the game.

Jill remained in the stands, waiting while Clay packed his sports bag and accepted his teammates' congratulations. When it looked as if he were ready to leave, she went down to meet him.

Before she had covered half the distance, Phyllis and her friend rushed up to him, gushing about his winning hit. Clay gave them his attention and Jill's heart fell.

A few feet away with the crowd milling between them, she waited. He glanced her way but didn't extricate himself from the conversation. After a few minutes, she returned to wait at the bleachers.

Several more minutes passed. Each time Clay looked as if he were about to end the conversation, they bombarded him with another question. Finally, he appeared to give up.

Maybe Phyllis was right. Maybe she knew something other girls didn't. Jill left the stands. She would wait on the boat.

Balmy night air caressed her as she passed two guys leaning against a convertible parked with other cars lining the narrow, shady street leading away from the ballpark. They glanced her way and returned to their low-key conversation.

A thick ground fog swallowed her as she walked down the sandy, tree-lined drive that dropped to the marina where she and Clay had left the boat. She paused halfway to the dock and turned sharply. Were those footsteps behind her? She squinted into the fog. Nothing but the lapping of the bay waters disturbed the quiet.

She again moved toward the dock and the footsteps behind her quickened.

Her heart squeezed. "Clay?"

Two men emerged, grinning, and Jill caught the flash of a knife blade.

She backed away, wildly grasping for some plan of escape. Even if she were fast enough, the docks and the rocky shoreline back to the ballpark would turn into traps. The boats in dry dock behind her were her best, and maybe only, chance.

She burst into a dead run, throwing herself to the ground and rolling under the first boat. Coming up on the other side, she found herself trapped between two boats. The men had divided, one coming around the first boat's bow, the other around its stern. They grinned and edged toward her. She dropped to roll back under the boat, hoping to break for the street, but rough hands caught her arms and jerked her up.

She screamed as much from rage as from fright. Struggling fiercely, she sank her teeth into the nearest hairy hand.

The owner swore and released her.

The other let out a low chuckle. "It's no use, girlie, so stop it, or Poke here will hafta hurt you."

Poke flashed his knife near Jill's face while the other man's hot breath reeked of alcohol close behind her. Her stomach churned.

Ignoring their low laughter, she stretched to her full height. If she couldn't outrun them, she'd outwit them. She relaxed as if she had given up the fight. "All right then. What's this all about?"

"We have a little surprise for ya," the one with the reeking breath whispered. "So just come along,"

They sandwiched her between them with Poke in the lead.

Jill's flesh crawled. She dug her toes into the sand. "Not until you tell me where you're taking me and why."

"Where you can't do no more mischief."

That scream … Jill! Clay sped down the incline at a dead run. Mumbled threats of male origin slammed his heart against his rib cage. Still hidden in the fog, he lowered his sports bag to the sand and crept forward, bat in hand.

Jill's demand to know where they were taking her gave him a fix on them. Enraged by their chilling reply, he charged from the fog, swinging his bat. With a swish and a thud, he cracked one man's midsection. The guy's knife popped into the air and clattered against the dry dock boat while he fell to the sand, grasping his stomach and gasping for air.

Clay turned on the other whose eyes widened. His grip on Jill loosened and she tore away, diving for the knife. Clay brought the bat around for a swing, but the man sprinted away.

His companion scrambled after him, and the two disappeared into the fog. Clay sprinted after them. As he emerged from the fog, a car engine roared across the street. Tires squealed, and a convertible peeled into the darkness. The car turned left at the end of the block and its red tail lights disappeared. It all happened too fast for Clay to catch the license plate number.

He stood in the shadowed street, shaking with rage. After all the warnings this afternoon, he should never have left Jill alone. He'd never do it again. This was no happenstance. The killer had escalated efforts. No telling what would happen now that this one failed.

Clutching his bat, he trotted back down to the marina, aware that a minute longer, and history would have repeated itself. This time, he would clearly have been at fault, and Jill would have paid the price.

He found her sitting in the sand. She trembled as she pushed to her feet, brushing the sand from her skin and clothing. She gazed at him, her eyes still wide with lingering fright.

Dropping his bat, he took off his warm-up jacket and wrapped it around her, gazing intently into her eyes. He would never have forgiven himself if anything had happened to her.

"I … I'm okay," she said, her voice shaking. "It's always this way. I … I'm fine in a crisis but fall apart the minute it's over."

She broke into sobs, wrenching his heart. His brave woman had fought those brutal men and earned the right to cope with that horror any way she chose.

He opened his arms, and she walked into them, her warm tears falling on his sweat-soaked uniform. How could this feel so right when he knew it was wrong?

After a while, he pulled a big, white handkerchief from his jacket pocket and handed it to her.

"I … I didn't know guys still used these things." She dabbed her eyes, wiped her nose, and lay back against his chest.

He stroked her silky curls, recalling her tremulous lips and trusting eyes. They proved what he already knew in his heart. He needed her as much as she needed him.

While the night held its breath, he cradled her until her trembling ceased. She made no move to pull away.

"Jill," he whispered, his voice husky.

She looked up, and he brushed the backs of his fingers slowly across her soft cheek.

How close he had come to losing his brave, beautiful Jill, but what mattered now was that she was safe. For that, he was thankful.

Fireworks popped in spectacular display, flaring over Munising Bay and keeping time with the upheaval in his heart. He lowered his head and brushed his lips across the full softness of hers. She groaned in response. Hesitating a moment, he moved in, deepening their kiss as his pulse throbbed.

In the sweetness of those moments, he knew he had lost his battle. His heart would never again belong to him alone.

Chapter Twenty

Jill stretched beneath her bedcovers, the lingering memory of Clay's tender kiss bringing a soft smile to her lips.

Lord, Amelia was right. Clay definitely likes me. Not only likes, he loves me.

A scampering of little paws on the bed quickly turned to a tiny wet nose pressed against hers. When she seized the kitten in a hug, she apparently applied a little too much enthusiasm.

Button wriggled free and leapt to the floor. Skittering to a halt under the glass top table, he spun to face her with accusing eyes.

Giggling, Jill threw back the covers and slipped into her terry robe before running barefoot to the billiard room. She opened a window and leaned out, savoring the morning's fresh air. Had the sun ever shone so magnificently?

Her gaze quickly found Clay working on the stone wall near the carriage house. Sunlight glistened on his dark hair as he struggled to release a heavy stone from its stubborn perch among the rubble of what had once been a sturdy wall.

His strong arms wielded the same wonderful strength that had helped her escape those despicable men last night. The same arms that had wrapped around her ever so gently while his heart beat rapidly where she rested her head against his broad chest. How safe she had felt then. How she longed to nestle there this very moment.

Sudden awareness of her nightgown and open robe brought a heat that crept up her neck and burned her cheeks. Well ... uh ... maybe not this exact moment.

She hurried away to get dressed.

181

Laptop in hand and Button scampering after her, Jill moved through the entrance hall, anxious to settle on the veranda. What a perfect place to work on the Rogers' project for Nona while she enjoyed the pleasure of feasting her eyes on Clay without getting in his way.

Voices in the morning room arrested her progress. She paused at its open door, taking in Tia's worried frown.

"You must be roasting in that long-sleeved dress, Mother."

Lenore caressed the folds of the Victorian gown. "Of course not. It is perfect …" Her voice trailed away. "Good morning, Jill."

Her aunt seated herself behind the desk and arranged her long skirts. She flicked a glance at her, and then at Tia. "If you two will excuse me, I have much to do."

She removed some papers from the central desk drawer. "The party is next week, you know."

Tia drew a shaky breath. "Can I help you, Mother?"

Lenore's head jerked up. "What did you say?"

"I … want to help," Tia mumbled.

Jill raised her eyebrows. Had she heard right?

"You were right, Mother. I should help you." Tia hurried through words obviously rehearsed. She paused uncertainly. "I'm sorry I fought you. Please forgive me."

Lenore pursed her lips. "You are beginning to sound like Jill." She turned to Jill. "Did you put her up to this?"

"This is my idea, not's Jill's," Tia insisted.

"Well, then." Lenore folded her hands in her lap and turned back to her daughter. "I suppose your sudden change of heart has something to do with that minister's son you ran around with in the park yesterday."

"Minister's nephew, Mother. Leo is not Pastor McGee's son." Tia's voice held just a bit of an edge. "And, yes, he did help me see that"—she stopped to eye her mother warily—"that God wants me to trust him and obey you."

Lenore arched her eyebrows. "I see. I now have God and this boy to thank for your change of heart." She didn't appear to enjoy the idea. "Does this mean you will no longer oppose my wishes?"

Tia shot Jill a panicky look. "I …" Her shoulders slumped. "About the party, yes."

Her young cousin's uncharacteristic response didn't make sense. How had Tia managed to grow from a rebellious teen to a submissive daughter practically overnight?

"Excellent." Her aunt turned a cold gaze toward Jill. "I see you also have work to do, so unless you have further business with us, you may go."

Jill's inward hackles reared up. She opened her mouth to put her aunt in her place but encountered Lenore's strangely glittering eyes, and the words froze in her throat. Now was no time to hold her aunt accountable for tactless behavior.

Forcing herself to breathe slowly and evenly, she withdrew to the veranda where she placed her laptop on the wicker coffee table. Button rubbed up against her ankle. She picked him up and settled him beside her on the loveseat's thick cushion.

Lenore's glittering eyes haunted her. Something was wrong with her aunt. When Uncle Drew mentioned she wasn't well, had he been hinting at his wife's mental state? Had the strain of the past years taken such a toll on her? Jill shivered.

Within the fragrance of the porch's honeysuckle shade, Jill prayed for her afflicted family and herself. Coming back to Windtop had dropped her in the middle of more problems than she had anticipated, and these problems were too big for her to handle alone.

When she looked up from her prayer, her gaze rested on Clay still working on the stone wall beside the carriage house. Other than Tia's blossoming relationship with Christ, the handsome contractor was the one factor that made returning to Windtop worthwhile.

If only they could walk away from this house and all the problems here. If only they could start over fresh somewhere else. But that wouldn't work. She'd already learned she couldn't walk away from problems. They had a habit of catching up with her wherever she went.

She sighed and opened her laptop.

Clay strained to dislodge yet another heavy stone from the tumble-down wall. After Jill came out on the porch, he had a hard time concentrating. His traitorous heart tugged at him.

He frowned. He was hopelessly in love with her. He wanted her more than he had a right to and more than he should ever have let on last night. What a mess he'd made in a moment of weakness. How was he supposed to protect her when he had become part of the problem?

The sweet warmth of her lips lingered in his memory. With a growl of frustration and muscle-straining effort, he pulled the huge stone loose.

Jill hit the save key. She had conquered the worst part of editing her rough draft in the Rogers' house history document and deserved a stretch break.

Clay glanced her way, wiping the glistening sweat from his brow, and her stomach fluttered. She smiled shyly. He nodded and turned back to dismantling the wall.

Was something wrong? Maybe it was just the backbreaking work of removing each basketball-sized boulder in this awful heat. Wasn't Sam supposed to help?

The morning wore on and the day's heat intensified. Clay's white shirt grew more and more sweat-soaked while her struggle with the Rogers' document slowed. They both could use a tall, cold glass of something. She shut down her laptop.

"How about it, Button?" The kitten's head popped up as Jill stood. "Time for a drink?"

Button jumped down from the wicker love seat and followed her into the house and the depths of the kitchen.

"Here you go." She set a shallow bowl of water in front of him before she pulled a large pitcher of lemonade from the refrigerator. She filled two tall glasses and carried them out the back door and across the lawn, ice cubes clinking.

"Hey, Clay." Smiling, she held out a glass to him.

A sheen of sweat gleamed on his face, neck and arms. He reached for the glass and gulped the cold liquid. Returning the glass, he nodded curtly.

She held his gaze.

He shook his head slowly, pain in his eyes.

"It's no good, Jill. I have no right to love anyone. Least of all you. Let's not make more of last night than we should. It was a gesture of comfort, of friendship."

Her cheeks flamed. That had been his idea of a gesture of friendship? No friend ever kissed her like that before.

"I'm nearly finished here, Jill. I've told you before, when I leave, you won't see me again."

"Won't see you?" The words refused to make sense.

"Trust me, Jill."

"But ..."

His Adam's apple bobbed as he swallowed hard. "Don't make this harder than it already is. I wish things were different ... but, they aren't. They never will be."

"It's over? Just like that?"

"I'm sorry."

Believing him didn't stop the ache in her heart. Backing away, she turned and hurried to the porch.

As she snatched up her laptop, Tia rushed out to her, squealing. "There you are! Mother, Mrs. Fenton, and I are going into town to finish shopping for the party. Please say you'll come."

Jill shook her head, searching for words that wouldn't betray her confusion.

The girl's brown-eyed gaze flicked behind her, and her face paled. "S-s-snake!"

Jill whipped around as a big, coppery-colored reptile struck Clay from behind. She gasped as he lurched forward and looked behind.

The snake reared and struck his mid-calf again.

Sam raced from the carriage house with a long, forked stick and pinned its head to the ground.

"Hold this, Mr. Merrick." He handed off the stick. "I'll get the gunny sack."

Unable to tear her gaze away yet uncertain how Clay might react should she come to his aid, Jill remained frozen to her spot on the porch. "Tia, go get the first aid kit."

Lenore came out on the porch. "What is all the fuss?" She looked beyond the porch and blanched as Sam hurried back to grasp the snake behind its trapped head.

"Don't worry, Mr. Merrick, it's not poisonous. It's just a harmless pine snake."

Air whooshed from Jill's lungs. Clay would be all right.

He twisted, first trying to see the bite site, then flicking his gaze to the snake. "How do you know?"

Lifting the snake to dangle its five-foot length, Sam checked it. "See? Coloring something like a copperhead, tail like a rattlesnake. No fangs. No poison. You still have some nasty scrapes that will need tending though."

Sam lowered the reptile into the gunny sack, tied it shut, and put the sack on the ground. "You must've disturbed it by pulling that wall apart."

Clay twisted around again. It didn't appear as if he could quite examine his wound.

Tia and Mrs. Fenton arrived with the first-aid kit and stopped short.

Lenore glared at her housekeeper. "Well, what are you waiting for?"

Mrs. Fenton shuddered. "I can't stand snakes."

"You don't expect me—"

Jill thrust the drinking glasses and her laptop at Tia, snatched the first aid kit, and ran to Clay as Sam crouched to examine the wound.

"That snake got you good, Mr. Merrick."

She knelt beside Sam and opened the kit.

"Wash the wound and use that swab to put some antiseptic on it," Sam said. "I'll get a cold pack." He picked up the heavy gunnysack and left for the carriage house.

Jill's hands trembled as she touched Clay's bare leg to clean the wound. Reaching for a swab, she applied the antiseptic as Sam had instructed. After winding sterile gauze around the injured calf several times, she finished securing the bandage with tape just as Sam returned, shaking a cold pack.

He handed it to Clay. "Hold this over the bite area. It'll keep the pain and swelling down. I'll get the Jeep so we can get you to the doctor."

"I don't need a doctor," Clay growled.

Sam stared him down through bushy eyebrows. "You'll see a doctor unless you want infection to set in. Mrs. Bradwell, Mrs. Fenton, Tia. You three better come quick. We can't waste time."

"Please come with us, Jill," a breathless Tia begged.

Neither Clay nor Lenore would appreciate that. Not to mention, the Jeep would have no room for her. "Go along. I'll be fine."

Tia held out Jill's laptop. "Mrs. Fenton took the glasses to the kitchen."

While Tia and the others scurried for the Jeep, Jill retreated to the veranda.

Kicking up yellow dust, the Jeep sped away, and a heaviness pressed on her heart. No room for her was the story of her life, and this time not only in her family but not in Clay's life either.

She opened her laptop and tried to concentrate on her project, but the right words wouldn't come. She put it aside and paced the porch. Button scampered after make-believe prey and tugged at her shoelaces, tumbling around her feet. With a sigh, she gave up and carried the laptop into the house, the kitten following in her wake.

Whatever Clay's reasons, his priorities didn't include her. Yet their attraction was real. That kiss had been real. Oh, what was she doing to herself? Dwelling on this would drive her crazy. She had to think about something else.

Anything, Lord!

She paused before the door to her mother's room. Hmm. Why had it taken her so long to realize this was that perfect opportunity she had been waiting for? Finally alone in the house, she could search her aunt's room for her mother's journals.

Cold beneath her fingers, the knob turned, and she pushed the door open. A huge four-poster bed dominated a room full of dark, bold furnishings nothing like her mother's. Nothing spoke of her mother except the delicate desk on the far wall. She hesitated, not feeling right about stepping across the threshold uninvited.

Button regarded her with quizzical eyes and then shot in.

"No!" Jill scrambled after him.

She stopped in the middle of the room and looked around. She was already in, so what was the harm? She'd take a quick look and get out, no one the wiser. Besides, this might be her one chance, and those journals—if she found them—would tell her all she needed to know.

She carefully examined the writing desk with its graceful legs and multitude of cubby holes. Rats! No hidden drawer, no false compartment.

Her gaze found the fireplace. Did it have a hidden recess? Brick by brick, she inspected it. Nothing here either. Moving methodically around the room, she rapped on the walls. None emitted a slightly different sound. So far, her house history experience proved useless, and she was running out of possibilities.

She pushed a wisp of hair away from her face and gazed around the room.

Floor boards! Quickly moving the small furnishings, she rolled back the large flower-patterned rug. On her hands and knees, she scrutinized each varnished board but, unfortunately, all remained firmly in place.

Sitting back on her heels, she combed her fingers through her hair. It was no use.

"Just what do you think you are doing?"

At Lenore's sharp, throaty voice, Jill stumbled to her feet.

Chapter Twenty-One

From the doorway, the naked hatred in Lenore's eyes chilled Jill. She rose slowly to her feet.

How had her aunt returned so soon? She didn't have to look around to know how disheveled the room appeared. She had expected to put it back in order with no one the wiser, but at the moment, she couldn't even think of a reasonable explanation for her behavior that wouldn't further enrage her aunt.

"Get out!" Lenore's dark eyes bored into hers. She stepped away from the door. "Get out!"

Snatching her laptop from the bed, Jill fled the room. Button shot past her, reaching the third floor before she did. By the time she shut the door, he had crouched beneath the bed, peering at her. Her trembling legs threatened to buckle.

Her simple need to find her mother's missing journals had made matters worse with her aunt. Not that Lenore cared. Her aunt had already given her enough excuses to quit trying to build a relationship with her.

But, Lord, I love you, and as awful as she can be, I want her to love you. Is there any hope?

Covering her face with trembling hands, Jill let the tears leak through her fingers.

As if matters weren't bad enough between Jill and her aunt, Lenore's mouth had twitched Sunday morning when Tia gained her father's permission to accompany Jill to church.

189

Jill mentioned her misgivings as she and Tia approached the church steps. It wasn't too late for the girl to change her mind and join her mother at the family church.

Tia waved her hand. "Don't worry, Jill. Mother will get over it. Besides, it will do her good not to get her way for a change." She smiled winsomely. "Come on. Let's go inside. Can we sit in the front? I don't want to miss a thing."

No doubt, one of the things Tia didn't want to miss was an unobstructed view of a certain red-headed guitar player. Still, it was good to see her young cousin sing hymns and listen in rapt attention to every word of Pastor's McGee's sermon.

A few minutes into the sermon, he raised his hands before the little congregation, a warm intensity in his eyes. "Receive this morning whatever the Lord has to give to you."

Tia bolted upright. Her eyes grew wide with fear as she stumbled into the aisle. With a hoarse cry, she crumpled to the thin red carpet.

The congregation gasped while Leo and Pastor McGee hurried down from the platform to meet Jill on the floor beside her cousin. "She's having a seizure," Jill whispered. "Pastor, I need your suit coat."

He stripped it off and handed it to her. She folded it as she had seen Clay do and placed it beneath Tia's head. "Help me move her onto her side."

Leo gently pulled Tia onto her side, his eyes dark with concern as her body began to jerk.

Jill blocked his attempt to restrain her. "She'll be all right. Just don't let her hurt herself on the edge of those pews."

Leo positioned himself on one side of the aisle. Jill did the same on the other.

Pastor McGee stood up. "Our young sister is having a seizure. Let's ask the Lord to intervene." As he and the congregation prayed, Tia's jerking slowed and an incredible peace came over her face. She lay still. Leo held her limp right hand in his, his gaze focused on her pale face.

Tia opened her eyes and smiled weakly. As she moved to get up, Jill put her arm under the girl's shoulders. "Leo, we have to get her to a quiet place where she can rest."

"No! Just help me back to the pew. I don't want to miss the rest of the service."

"But you need your rest."

"I …" Tia blinked. "I'm all right, Jill. At least, I think I am. Please."

"If you do need to rest, you will let us know, right?" Leo said.

The girl nodded.

While Leo and Jill helped Tia onto the pew, Pastor McGee addressed the congregation. "Are there others who would like prayer?"

Again Tia assured Leo that she was fine, and he returned to the platform to play soft hymns on his guitar while the prayer time continued.

"I can't believe it, Jill. I'm not tired," she whispered, her eyes bright with joy. "Something wonderful has happened!"

All the way home, her cousin bubbled with excitement. At Windtop, she ran up onto the veranda to hug her mother, her father, and her brother.

Uncle Drew looked to Jill and back to his daughter. "What's this all about? It wouldn't be that young man we saw you with at the picnic, would it?"

"Oh, Dad, don't tease. I like Leo, but that isn't it at all." She plopped onto the wicker love seat next to him. "Let me tell you."

Jill slipped into the house. This was a time for family.

She had not gotten to the stairwell before her aunt's sharp voice reached her ears. "Jill Shepherd, you come right back here!"

Not what she wanted, but she did as she was told.

"Now what is this about a seizure?" her aunt demanded of her daughter.

"Don't worry, Mother. You can see I'm fine. I'm not even tired."

As her aunt's gaze darkened, Jill held her breath.

"Isn't it wonderful? Do you think I won't have to take that awful medicine anymore?"

Carver snorted. "Right. You'd be an accident waiting to happen."

Lenore's face flushed a mottled red. "What kind of fanaticism do they preach at that church? You are responsible for putting her life in danger, Jill."

The words stung Jill to silence.

"Oh, Mother," Tia chided, "she never said a word to me. Neither did the pastor. It was my dream last night."

Lenore pursed her lips. "Now dreams?"

"Please listen. Last night, I told the Lord all about my fears and hurts. When I fell asleep, I dreamed that Jesus told me that everything would be all right. He touched my head, and I felt such peace."

Lenore smirked. "And you think that means you are healed?"

Uncle Drew put up his hand. "What if Tia is right, dear? Look at her."

Her aunt jammed her fists on her hips, and Jill cringed. She hadn't come to Windtop to tear the family apart. Yet every move she made only worsened matters.

"Without her medicine, Drew Bradwell, she will die."

"But I'm all right," Tia insisted.

"You will take your medicine until the doctor says otherwise, young lady, and that is that!" Lenore glared at Jill. "And don't you dare encourage her in this insanity."

Jill drew back. "But I—"

"Mother," Tia interrupted, "She didn't have a thing to do with this. She took me to church. That's all."

Uncle Drew stood up and took his daughter's hand. "Look at her, Lenore. She's had a seizure and should barely be aware of the world around her."

Lenore's dark eyes darted from him to Tia. Her red lips twitched. She pressed them together. Turning on her heels, she stormed into the house. Jill jumped out of the way.

Mrs. Fenton came to the door, a perplexed frown on her face. "Dinner is ready."

Prickly silence surrounded them at the dinner table. Jill swallowed a few bites before she excused herself and left the house. Following the brick walk through the gardens, she sought out the vine-covered gazebo. Cool. Inviting. A quiet place to think.

She stepped into its shaded sanctuary, and Clay stood up. Startled, she backed away.

"Don't go, Jill. Please."

She paused inside the entryway. It stung to be near him, to know he didn't want her. She forced her thoughts in another direction. "How is your wound?"

"The doctor gave me a tetanus shot and released me. He said you did a first-rate job." He held her gaze. "But that's not why I asked you to stay. Please. Sit down with me."

She lowered herself to the edge of the bench opposite him, wary of what he might say.

What could he say to help her understand? But even if he failed, he had to try. "I'm sorry about yesterday. I can't ask you to forgive me. I don't deserve—"

"I forgive you."

The soft words startled him. Though he didn't deserve her forgiveness, she offered it anyway.

He nodded, unable to look her in the eye or get past the knot in his throat. He sat for some moments before he could speak again. "I didn't mean to be cruel, Jill. I wish I could explain it to you, but I can't. Not yet. Maybe never."

Her lips trembled. "What are you hiding, Clay? Please, tell me."

"Jill, get out of here as soon as you can. Let me take care of the problem, and when I do, you'll be safe."

Warmth leapt into her eyes, and his gut clenched. He groaned. "Don't look at me like that."

As if struck, she shrank back and stared into her lap where her hands lay limp. "You care, but you don't want me to care for you. Why?"

"Believe me. It's for the best." He released a long breath. "I can't forgive as easily as you do. I don't know how you do it." He shook his head in bewilderment. "I didn't want to, but I hurt you yesterday. Moments later, you helped me without as much as an accusing glance."

"You needed help."

"I know. You help anyone in need," he said. "I also see how the Bradwells treat you in your own house. You could toss them out, but you don't."

"They're family."

"They don't act like it," he growled.

He forced a frustrated breath. "If I were free to love you the way you deserve, Jill, the way I want to ..."

Who was he kidding? He loved her. He desired her. He just couldn't have her. Not without going back on his word. Not without letting Janice's killer go free. Yet, if he was right, the same killer was behind two attempts on Jill's life. He couldn't bring Janice back, but he could keep Jill safe if only she would let him.

He dared to look Jill in the eye. Never had he seen such sad eyes, and it was his fault. "Don't love me, Jill."

A terrible lump rose in his throat. It was too late. She loved a man who had no future to offer her. Not even himself.

"Your grandma told me how Janice died," she whispered. "I'm so sorry. It was awful."

Raw anger flamed his heart at the memory. He bolted to his feet. "Yes," he hissed. "And where was God? Why didn't he stop that piece of trash from running her down and letting her die in the freezing dark?"

She reached out but, thankfully, stopped short of touching him. "I don't know, Clay. I have questions like that about my mother. All I know is that God is good, and we ... I need to trust him to work everything out at the right time and in the right way."

His jaw muscles twitched. *At the right time. In the right way.* He had waited long enough for the law and God to act.

He slammed his fist against the doorframe and stormed out of the gazebo.

The next morning as Jill reached the entrance hall with Button in her arms, Lenore muttered at the foot of the stairs, "Five days before the party and now this." Her aunt called up the stairs, "Hurry, Tia! Who knows how long before the doctor can squeeze you in?"

Jill stopped mid-step. "Is she all right?"

Lenore fixed her with a stony stare. "Of course she's all right, but someone has to straighten out her nonsense." She brushed past Jill. "Tia!"

"And thank you, Jill, for adding to my already overburdened schedule," her aunt said with a stiff back to her.

She regarded Lenore quietly. How awful to be so angry all the time. "Is there something I can help with while you're gone?"

"You have helped quite enough already," her aunt snapped.

Tia skimmed down the stairs.

"It's about time!" Lenore's gaze swept her daughter before she ushered her toward the door, calling over her shoulder to Jill, "See Mrs. Fenton. She has a list of what needs to be done."

The housekeeper sent Jill into the library. Ever curious, Button explored the conservatory plants at the far end of the room while Jill dusted every shelf and knickknack in the library itself, polishing the furniture and shining the glass breakfronts on the bookcases. She came to the oak book stand near the desk and removed the ponderous family Bible in order to polish the stand to a fine sheen.

As she placed the book back on the stand, she paused to open it. Through the years, Bradwell names had been faithfully recorded inside its ornate front cover with the dates of their births, deaths, and marriages. Yet how many of her ancestors actually read this Bible?

Button came to sit at her feet. He fixed her with large golden eyes, tilting his gray head to one side.

As she moved to close the cover, the tiniest corner of a stray paper protruded from its gilded pages. She pulled it out, and her heart stuck in her throat.

Small, well-formed words in her mother's handwriting stared back at her. *My Dearest Jill.*

She wobbled to the chair behind the desk and lowered herself carefully onto its warm leather. Her heart thundered as she realized it had been written on the day of her mother's death.

Her gaze lingered on the opening words. *My Dearest Jill.* Even after she had run away, her mother continued to love her.

Tears blurred the words on the page. Before any could escape and mar them, she snatched a tissue from the box on the desk and wiped them away. Then she read:

You may never see this page, but I feel compelled to write. I have so much to tell you.

First, about your father. When I was young, I ran away to marry him against my parents' wishes, so please don't blame yourself for leaving to find him. In some ways, we are so alike. I understand your need to try though my deepest hope is that you do not succeed.

My dearest daughter, I will always love your father. I wish I could tell you why finding him might harm you. But then, if you already have, you know why, and my heart grieves for you.

As for leaving as you did, I blame my silence about him for driving you away that night. How hard it must have been for you during your last years in school, locked away from everyone and everything because of my fear. Please forgive me.

When the police told me you drowned in the channel during that storm, my heart refused to believe it. As long as there is breath in my body, I will never believe it. I don't think Maggie does either. But my purpose in writing is to tell you something far more important.

Yesterday I went outside. Yes, I did! For the first time in a long time. The sunshine looked so inviting, and I longed to care for the rosebush by the porch steps. Years ago when your father sent it, I planted it at Windtop because here is where we met and fell in love. On that very spot, we shared our first kiss.

Anyway, I was so engrossed in working the soil around it, I never heard the woman come up the drive. Her unexpected appearance frightened me, and I ran into the house. I watched her from the window as she put a paper under my trowel. I waited a long time after she left before I went out to get it. I read it over and over through the night, and …

The letter stopped mid-sentence.

Her mother had wanted to tell her something exciting. Why had she not finished? Who or what interrupted her?

A knowing chill spread through Jill's heart. In her trembling hand, she held the first real evidence that Susannah Bradwell Shepherd had not killed herself.

An anguished cry burrowed up from her heart. Choking it back, she clutched the letter and ran from the house.

Chapter Twenty-Two

*W*ave after wave of wind roared through the treetops from the island's northern heights, gaining volume as it approached and receding as it passed. Jill had beat a coming storm like this on the night she fled the island to find her father. This time, however, she wasn't fleeing the island.

Racing to the carriage house, she snatched the keys from a nail inside the open door, launched herself into Windtop's Jeep, and gunned the engine. As the Jeep jounced west toward the heart of the island, she felt every jarring bump of the sandy road but didn't let up. She had to reach Echo Lake before the storm broke.

Nestled near the center of an island which measured only eight miles by three, most days the placid lake offered peaceful privacy. She badly needed that peace and privacy right now.

There! There it is.

Turning off the road, she parked beneath a giant beech tree and propelled herself on foot the last few yards. Dark clouds roiled above. Lightning streaked the sky. A sparrow cried piteously as it darted into the surrounding forest.

Here she had come many times as a teen when life overwhelmed her. It had comforted her to gaze upon the waters that remained strangely calm no matter how high Lake Superior's storm-driven waves lashed the island cliffs. Those waters had offered her peace in the midst of her storms.

Here she had imagined the father she never knew casting a line, slowly reeling it in while waiting for her. Tall and strong, he seemed the promise of safety that she dearly craved. At the sound of her footsteps, he would turn with a welcoming grin, and she would run to him.

Here she was again, stumbling past the tall wild grasses to reach the lake's shore. This time, she sought her God whom she had come to know in the last few months. He was now the One who soothed her heart. He was also the One who sent her back to this island.

She held her mother's letter up toward the rain-gray sky. "Heavenly Father." She choked out the words rising from her tattered heart. "Please say it isn't true. Tell me Mother wasn't murdered. Tell me ..."

But how could he?

Collapsing on the sandy shore, she sobbed, her head soon tight with pain. Her heart couldn't take it if her family had anything to do with her mother's death.

Deafening thunder cracked as if a giant tree were rent from top to bottom. Chill rain poured from the sky as Jill sprang to her feet and ran for the shelter of the Jeep. Through the windshield, she stared with unseeing eyes into the blinding downpour.

Don't trust anyone!

She pulled her mother's letter from her jeans' pocket where she had thrust it to protect it from the rain. So Maggie Pierce had been right after all.

Leave, if you can.

It was too late. She would never escape the killer who had already tried twice to end her life. She shuddered. Did that killer live in her house?

Jill hugged her waist to stave off the damp chill encasing her.

If only Clay would tell her what he knew instead of insisting she leave. Didn't he understand that if she wanted to live, she had to stay and fight for the right?

The rain slowed, pelting the Jeep with scattered raindrops. From sodden leaves overhead, they dripped in an uneven staccato while sunshine burst through the cloud cover. As quickly as the storm had begun, it vanished.

Jill lowered the Jeep's windows and breathed in the clean, damp air. As she sank back against the seat, she recalled Ruth's words. *You have grave and dark days ahead, but don't let anyone frighten you away. Don't leave until you have completed all the Lord has sent you to do!*

Did that all include finding her mother's killer?

Pressing her lips together, she turned the key in the ignition. The engine roared in response. She backed the Jeep onto the East-West Road.

She had work to do, and God willing, she would finish it.

Jill's damp and gritty clothing chafed as she made her way up Windtop's grand staircase. No doubt, her hair looked as unkempt from her stormy excursion. She had to hurry in order to hide the letter, clean up, and collect her wits before facing the family.

But when sunlight showered down bits of rainbow color from the skylight, the second-floor railing beckoned. She gripped its silken surface and peered below as her imagination played its version of her mother plunging to her death. With a sharp intake of breath, she stepped back.

"Cousin." Carver stood so near she could feel the heat of his breath. "Indulging in your favorite obsession?"

Whirling around, she fought to breathe evenly and clenched her fists to keep from slapping the smug expression off his grinning face. She owed him nothing, and he'd get nothing.

He checked her over from head to toe and chuckled. "Like mother, like daughter."

She gritted her teeth. "What's that supposed to mean?"

The clicking of a woman's high heels on the entrance hall floor below ended as her aunt took to the stairs with quick footsteps. "May I ask, Jill, what you found so important that you left Mrs. Fenton to finish all the work?"

Jill stared at a woman both tall and strong enough to kill her petite sister-in-law.

Lenore's red mouth twitched. "You refuse to answer."

Jill trembled in the dampness of her clothes as her aunt's gaze swept her. "For heaven's sake, where were you? Never mind. Make yourself presentable before dinner. Carver, I hope you have a moment. We need to talk."

Maneuvering around her aunt and her cousin, Jill escaped. A hot bath, freshly washed hair, and dry clothes … she longed for all three, but as for dinner …

She had other plans.

Jill entered the dining room, clutching the shoulder strap of her purse where her mother's unfinished letter lay hidden. Uncle Drew's soft gaze found her, and her imagination flashed to him pushing his sister over the railing.

No way could he do that. To save her sanity, she had to get away this evening.

Her uncle's brow furrowed. "You don't look well, Jill. Are you all right?"

"I'm fine." A bold-faced lie, but she was in no position to share her agony with him. "I just want you all to know I have other plans for tonight." She backed away.

"Don't go yet, Jill. Please," Tia said. "I have wonderful news, and I want you to hear it."

Wonderful news in this house of heartache?

"I'm telling my story at church!" the girl gushed.

Carver howled. "Why, Sis, how quickly you've become a first-class fanatic. Excellent work, Jill."

Uncle Drew leaned in from his place at the head of the table. "What's this all about?"

"Pastor McGee asked me and I said I would." The girl's brown eyes sparkled.

Jill swallowed. That was good news.

Tia rushed on. "Oh, and I'm going to play the organ Jill donated to the church."

Lenore slapped the flat of her hand on the table. "You are not!"

"When does this take place?" Uncle Drew asked.

"Wednesday night and I want you all to come. Please, Mother."

"Absolutely not!"

"Carver?"

"Sorry, Sis. You know church and I don't mix."

Tia's glow faded. Her voice softened with pleading. "Dad?"

Uncle Drew hesitated, and then nodded. "I'll see what I can do."

Tia threw her arms around his neck. "Thank you, thank you, thank you." She looked up. "You'll come, won't you, Jill?"

Despite the pain in her chest, she managed a subdued smile. "You know I will."

"Well, now," Uncle Drew said, "shouldn't we eat?"

As the others sat down to their dinner, Jill slipped away without another word. Amelia would know if her suspicions about her mother's letter were right.

The city's warm evening fog enveloped Amelia's home as Jill approached. Though the front room was brightly lit, she observed no movement beyond the screen door or windows.

She paused at the bottom of the porch steps. Maybe she shouldn't trouble her friend with her suspicions. Yet she had to tell someone she trusted, someone who was blessed with wisdom.

A quavery voice came softly through the screen door. "Lord, I don't know what to do, and I'm so afraid!"

Jill crept onto the stout porch and drew near the window. Was Amelia in trouble?

The dear elderly woman knelt at her living room chair, her eyes closed and her head bent over folded hands propped on the seat cushion. "Is Sonny looking for Janice's killer? I'm so afraid he's planning something awful." She snatched a tissue from a nearby box and blew her nose. "Please, Lord, don't let him …" Her voice choked off.

Jill pulled back from the window. A trembling seized her until her legs threatened to cave beneath her.

Clay was planning something awful? Was this what he had been keeping from her, the thing that would keep them apart?

Dear Lord, if it is, please stop him. Bring him to his senses before it's too late.

What about Amelia? Should she stay and comfort her? But how awful if her friend knew she had been listening to so private a prayer. Better that she should leave quietly and spare her friend who had enough trouble of her own.

She eased away.

"Thank you for hearing my prayer, Lord." Amelia's voice was shaky. "Now please send someone to help me get off my knees."

Jill stopped. Maybe God meant for her to hear Amelia's prayer and be nearby to help.

She knocked on the screen door. "Amelia?"

"Jill, is that you? Please come in."

On her knees by the chair, Amelia looked up with teary eyes and a pink nose. "I've been praying," she confessed. "I must look a mess."

"Would you like me to get you a cold washcloth?"

"No, just help me up, please. I'm afraid these old knees don't work as well as they used to."

Jill helped her friend settle into the chair.

"I'm so glad you came. Did I forget that you were coming?"

Jill shifted uneasily. "No, I just dropped by, but I do have good news. Tia is telling her story and playing the organ at church Wednesday night."

"She is?" Amelia clapped her hands. "Then we *must* celebrate. Are her parents—?" She interrupted herself, suddenly more somber. "How did her parents take the news?"

"Her father may come. Her mother and brother said no."

Amelia sighed. "I see. Well, do you think they would mind if we had a little party afterward? Would Tia like that?"

"I think she would love it, but I'll ask to make sure."

Amelia tipped her gray-haired head, gazing intently. "Jill, you don't seem yourself tonight. What's wrong?"

She blinked to stem her sudden tears. "Remember the story your friend Ruth told us about Mother?"

Amelia nodded.

Drawing a folded paper from her purse, Jill held it out. "I found this at the house today."

Amelia took the paper and picked up her reading glasses from the table next to her chair.

Jill followed every lift of her friend's eyebrows and fleeting change of expression. Finally, Amelia put the letter down on her lap. "Ruth will be thrilled to know your mother read the tract she left."

"I thought the same. But would you tell me ... does my mother sound like a woman about to—" Jill couldn't say the words.

"—commit suicide?"

Jill nodded. The ache in her heart nearly squeezed the breath from her lungs. Suicide had been hard enough to accept, but murder?

Amelia looked at the letter again. "I didn't know your mother, but these are not the words of a woman about to take her life."

"Everyone says Mother felt she had nothing to live for once she believed I had died."

Amelia held the letter up. "But she believed you were alive."

"Exactly!"

"The whole letter is loving and sensible and—"

"—clear-minded?" Jill offered.

Amelia bobbed her head. "And if your mother were going to take her life, I think she would have finished this letter. Don't you?"

Chapter Twenty-Three

Jill closed her laptop and set it on the Jeep's passenger seat. The click of its latch added finality. For two days, she had escaped to Echo Lake to lose herself in the mind-numbing frenzy of writing the house history Nona needed. Now the project was done, and she had no more excuse to hide from the Bradwells.

Or Clay.

Closing her eyes against the lake's sunlit waters and the forest's verdant thickets, she breathed in the air's fresh, woodsy scent and listened to the melodious chirping of songbirds. She'd have to go back to Windtop soon. It was nearly time to get ready for Tia's big night at church. Especially if she intended to e-mail the Rogers' project to Nona and take her mother's portrait and trunk of memorabilia along to ship them to Chicago.

She backed the Jeep onto East-West Road. One thing was sure. The moment she knew the truth about her mother's death, her stay at Windtop would end, and she'd never look back.

But will you forgive?

The sudden voice in her heart startled her. So, God had noticed her spiral into seething anger these past few days.

Forgive her mother's killer? "I can't," she whispered.

Then I cannot forgive you.

The sadness in those soft words did not condemn her. They simply confirmed what she already knew from reading her Bible. If only her heart held such forgiveness, but it was no use pretending.

"It's too much to ask, Lord."

Gripping the steering wheel so hard her fingers hurt, she pressed her foot on the accelerator and roared east along the forest road.

She couldn't outrun God, but right now, she didn't want to listen either.

The moment Jill ran up Windtop's porch steps, Tia jumped up from the wicker loveseat. "Oh, I'm so glad you're here. I can hardly wait for tonight, but I was afraid you wouldn't … but now … well, I'm a little nervous. And excited." Tia paused, the joy draining from her face. "I wish Mother would come."

"She hasn't changed her mind then?" *Silly question.* Her cousin's downcast face said it all. "And your dad?"

"Mom said not to count on him, and she's right. He usually gets sidetracked at the mill."

"Maybe this time she'll be wrong."

Tia shook her head somberly. "Even if he comes, you and he may be the only ones. I'm praying, but every time I ask Carver, he only laughs. I'm really worried about him, Jill. Would you pray with me?"

Right now Jill didn't feel like praying. Would God even hear her when her heart was in such shabby condition? Yet, how could she disappoint her young cousin?

When they finished, Jill hugged the girl. "I'm going to town early. Would you like to come along?"

Tia's brown eyes lit up. "Yes! I'd have time to talk to Dad."

Jill turned away. Her coming to Windtop had brought Tia God's unspeakable joy, but she had lost that blessing.

Would she ever find her way back?

A first lonely star winked from above as Jill helped Amelia cross the street for church early that evening.

"Anything new about your mother?" her friend asked.

Jill shook her head. "Unless I find some way to get into the house while the security system is on, I have no proof her death could be anything but suicide."

Amelia lifted her walker up the curb and stepped up behind it. "You know, I remember old stories about the time when Windtop was built. There were a lot of forest fires around here back then. Is it possible your house has some built-in escape route?"

Why hadn't she thought of that? She completed enough house histories to know what to look for, and the blueprints in gatehouse cottage might be a great place to start. "It's worth checking out, Amelia. Thank you."

Sadness invaded her friend's faded eyes. "If only the answer to Sonny's problem were as easy." She allowed Jill to help her up the church steps. "I still say you and Sonny would be good for each other."

Jill stifled a sigh. As much as she wished their circumstances were different, in a few days, their lives would separate. He had already made his choice, and it didn't include her or God.

She settled beside Amelia in the front pew while Tia quietly played the organ and Leo accompanied on his guitar. Uncle Drew slipped into the pew beside her.

Her flesh crawled. Had he taken part in her mother's death? Barely able to muster a welcoming smile, she quickly directed her attention away.

The soft light of the mid-summer evening shone like pale gold through the long windows behind the sanctuary. The sweet fragrance of the fresh floral arrangement on the communion table below the pulpit drew her gaze. An open Bible perched on a tabletop stand. So much like Windtop's family Bible where she had found her mother's letter.

Her heart stilled for a moment and Uncle Drew patted her hand.

She glanced at him. Only kindness shone in his brown eyes. How could those be the eyes of a killer or a killer's accomplice?

People continued to file into pews, smiling and greeting one another. Some shook hands. Others hugged. Uncle Drew appeared to soak in each detail.

When Pastor McGee approached the pulpit, Tia slipped away from the organ to sit beside her father. A quiet expectancy hushed the congregation.

"Welcome in the name of Jesus. Do you remember the day you first asked him to be your Savior and Lord?"

A warm murmur spread through the sanctuary, many heads nodding. Jill looked around and caught Carver standing at the back of the church.

"Tia." She tipped her head in Carver's direction.

Tia grinned as if her heart would burst.

About to look away, Jill caught her breath.

"Amelia," she whispered. "Clay just came in."

Tears flooded her dear friend's eyes, and Jill took her hand. *Lord, please touch hearts in this service.*

Leo softly strummed "Amazing Grace" on his guitar while Pastor McGee told the story of the favorite hymn's author, a man so wretched before he gave his life to Christ that people avoided him. "But Jesus Christ changed his life completely. Tonight, we will hear a young girl share her story of forgiveness. We all need forgiveness, don't we?"

Many in the congregation nodded.

"Only a week ago, Tia Bradwell sought God's forgiveness and gave her life to Jesus."

"Glory to God!" one man said.

"Tia, would you join me at the pulpit?"

Jill's young cousin hurried to the pastor's side.

He smiled into her upturned face. "Will you please tell us what Jesus means to you?"

Lord, Jill prayed, *please give Tia words that will change hearts—especially Clay's and mine.*

Tia took the cordless microphone Pastor McGee held out to her. "Jesus means everything to me." She went on to tell how the onset of her epilepsy and later, her failing to feel her mother's love had scarred her life. "Until I let Jesus become part of my life last week, I had no idea how wonderful his love could be." She looked at her father. "I didn't deserve it, but he forgave my sins and healed my heart. I'm not bitter anymore. God is showing me how to face my problems his way. He's given me a whole new life."

The congregation applauded as Tia returned the microphone to Pastor McGee.

"Now let's pray for our new sister in Christ to grow strong in the Lord," Pastor said.

Joining in, Jill felt the unmistakable presence of God. "I know, Father," she whispered. "I know. I don't want to forgive, but for your sake, I will."

Letting her mother's killer stand between her and the Lord was too great a price to pay. She needed God and his forgiveness every day, so she'd let him deal with whoever killed her mother. Maybe one day, she would feel that forgiveness she had extended. Right now, it was a mere act of her will she wished she could feel but just didn't.

Uncle Drew beamed at Tia with watery eyes, took a handkerchief from his suit coat, and blew his nose. As he tucked it back into his pocket, Jill caught his eye and her heart warmed. She smiled.

God had touched her heart and her uncle's, but what about Carver. How was he taking all this?

She glanced back. Her cousin had vanished, but Clay stood in the shadows near the door, staring at the floor. He opened the door and left.

Sagging against the pew, Jill ached in the depths of her soul.

While Jill poured a cup of punch and gave it to her uncle, she stole a glance at Clay standing near the fireplace in his grandmother's home. At that moment, Pastor and Mrs. McGee arrived with Tia and Leo.

Her cousin rushed up to her and hugged her impulsively. "Jill, Pastor just made me the new church organist. Isn't that wonderful? None of this would've happened if you hadn't come."

Jill offered a wan smile. *Well, God, thank you for this one good reason for sending me back.* If only it were enough, but the puzzle of her mother's death lay on her heart like one of those boulders Clay wrestled from the stone wall at Windtop.

Tia threw her arms around her father's neck.

"Thank you for coming tonight, Dad." Her voice choked up, and Uncle Drew held his daughter in his arms.

Turning quickly away, Jill fought the powerful longing to know her own father's love. Yes, she was happy for this father and daughter, glad Tia was no longer the frightened, angry girl she had been. Yet none of that removed Jill's own longing.

She poured punch into the cup she held, and Clay's strong hand covered hers with a gentleness that made her heart flutter. He leaned in, his warm breath on her neck as he whispered, "Meet me on the porch later."

When he stepped back, he wasn't smiling, and her joy shriveled. She nodded and hurried into the kitchen to begin arranging Amelia's supper on the table. As she settled a large platter of sandwiches among the other offerings on the dining room table, she glanced at her cousin.

Tia kissed Amelia's cheek. "Mrs. Tanner, everything looks wonderful. Please let me return the favor. Come to my party this Saturday."

Amelia's eyes widened. "It's nice of you to ask, but—"

"I would like to invite all my new friends," Tia rushed on. "That's all right, isn't it, Dad?"

Uncle Drew favored his daughter with an indulgent smile. Amusement settled into his eyes. "Well, I—"

"Say no more," Amelia said. "I appreciate your invitation, Tia, but perhaps another time."

Pastor McGee shook his head. "Thank you, but my wife and I already have plans."

"But Leo can come, can't he? You will, won't you? One extra guest will be all right, won't it Dad?"

Uncle Drew nodded, his gaze resting like a blessing on his daughter.

The matter decided, everyone crowded around Amelia's table and filled their plates while Jill refreshed their punch cups. When they had settled down to eat, she noticed Clay across the room, his gaze never leaving her.

Heat crept up her neck. A silly reaction unless he had changed his mind.

She placed a narrow slice of chocolate cheesecake on a plate and joined the others in the living room area. With the prospect of meeting Clay later, she hardly tasted her favorite dessert.

Not long after, Pastor McGee checked his watch and stood up. "What do you think, Helen? Is it time we head for home?"

"Can Tia and I walk for a while?" Leo asked.

"If her father gives his permission," his uncle said.

Uncle Drew nodded. "All right by me. I'll help Mrs. Tanner put everything back in order here. I think Jill has done enough for one evening. Maybe she would like some fresh air too."

Jill studied her uncle's round face. Had he overheard Clay earlier?

Clay found Jill on the porch swing. When she looked up and moved over, he took it as an invitation. The swing jounced as he sat beside her. Not knowing quite how to open the subject that she had fought him on so vehemently before, he set the swing into a gentle motion, stirring a pleasant breeze in the warm night air as he collected his thoughts. Not an easy thing to do with her so near and the waning moon shining down on the fragrant flowers hugging the porch.

"What was your father like?" she asked, her gaze in her lap.

He flinched. What was this sudden invasion into his past? "Why do you ask?"

"I never knew mine. I just wonder what it's like, having a father." Her voice came so soft and wistful that it hurt his heart.

"I … uh … well, he was an ordinary man." He hadn't talked about his father in a long time. It was too painful.

"Did he love you?"

She gazed into his eyes with such hunger to know, he swallowed and went on. "Sure. I loved him too."

"Did you do things together?"

"He was a big baseball fan, so we played ball and went to games. He coached my Little League team." Here's where it got hard, but there was no way to avoid it. "Until he died."

Jill stopped the swing and stared at him. "How old were you?"

"Twelve." He'd rather not think about this.

"I'm so sorry, Clay."

He grasped the swing's chain with his right hand. "It was a long time ago. Let's change the subject, okay?"

She nodded, her gaze still soft with sympathy.

He should get to the point of their meeting here. "I wasn't angry with you the night Grandma tried to set us up. I was angry with myself."

Curiosity lit her eyes. "Why?"

"Let's just say you're a very distracting woman at a time when I need to stay focused." He pressed his lips to stem the pain. Strange that it no longer bit as deep.

He leaned forward, resting his elbows on his knees so that he wouldn't have to look into her eyes. Clasping his hands together, he rubbed his chin with his knuckles. "You're a lot like Janice. She lived in a way that made me question my not-so-close relationship with God. You do the same."

"I never meant—"

He sat up and put a finger gently to her lips. "She didn't either."

Leaning back, he reached his arm around her shoulders. She snuggled in and his gut clenched. *This was how it should be. How it would be, if only . . .*

He kissed the top of her head, her silky hair fragrant beneath his lips. His heart ached. "Please, Jill. Give up your search, and go back to Chicago."

"I can't."

The anguish in her voice made his heart sick. He eased away and groped for a way to make her understand. "You're in real danger."

"I know." Her agony cut him deeply.

"Then why not listen to me?"

"Why do you want me to leave?" she shot back. "Amelia thinks you've followed Janice's killer here. Is she right?"

"What?"

"You heard me," she said, her voice hardly above a whisper. "She's scared to death that you plan to . . . to do something rash."

"Did she tell you?" Had Jill broken her promise? Had she talked with his grandma about this?

"She doesn't know that I overheard her praying when I came to visit. She wasn't expecting me."

His breathing slowed to normal. Jill had kept her promise then.

"Why are you here, Clay? Do you know who killed Janice?"

He clamped his mouth shut. She was only guessing.

"If you know, why not let the police handle it?" Her gaze pleaded with him as much as her words.

He turned away. She didn't know how useless that could be. The law was trapped by rules that let criminals go free. It wasn't right. Not in his father's case, or his little sister's, and for all he knew, in Janice's.

Jill caressed his forearm, sending pleasant shivers through him. "Please, Clay, don't break your grandma's heart . . . and mine. Don't ruin your life."

Did she think he wanted to do those things? What he really wanted was a life with her. "You don't understand."

"Help me understand."

He ground his teeth. Did he have to rip open the pain of his past to convince her? So be it. "What did Grandma tell you about Dad?"

She wagged her head slowly, her eyes somber. "Nothing."

"When I was twelve, he stopped at a gas station convenience store to pick up milk. He walked in on a holdup, and some young punk gunned him down. The police never found the killer."

Jill paled. "Oh, Clay."

"Seven years later, my little sister died in a drive-by shooting. She was hardly more than a baby. The killer got off turning state's evidence for another crime." He gritted his teeth. "Real life crime-solving isn't like the movies, Jill. Victims don't always get justice. I won't let that happen to Janice."

"So, you do know who her killer is," she whispered.

He looked at his feet. "I'm not positive. But I will be."

"When you find that piece of evidence you've mentioned before, don't do anything rash, Clay. Not if it means you'll—"

"I'm trying to stop a cold-blooded killer, Jill. One who will kill again. And until I do, I don't want you around. That's why you must leave before it's too late!"

She reached up, her fingers soft against his face. She traced the contours of his jaw, sending shivers down his body and intensifying his longing for her.

"Clay, I'm frightened. Who wouldn't be? But I can't run. I'm here to accomplish something important. I have to stay and finish whatever it is."

"You don't even know what it is, and yet you're willing to risk your life?" *Incredible!*

"Nothing will happen to me unless God allows it."

"Janice talked like that. Look where it got her." He ground out the words. "I don't want that happening to you."

"Trusting God didn't get her killed, Clay. That was someone else's doing. We can't always protect the ones we love. We can't always protect ourselves. But we can do our best to trust God to make it come out all right in the end."

He looked away and ground his teeth. What nonsense!

"Besides, it's too late. The danger at Windtop would simply follow me to Chicago. I'd be looking over my shoulder all the time, wondering when it would strike. I'm better off staying here and facing it now."

Good grief! She really believed that? "You don't know what you're doing."

"But you know who the killer is, don't you, Clay?" Her gaze pierced him as she gripped his arm. "Who, Clay? Who is it?"

He clenched his teeth. If he told her, she'd get in the way and get hurt. Why was she so stubborn? Why couldn't she just trust him?

He eased her fingers from his arm and stalked into the night shadows. She was making his job much harder. What if he couldn't stop the killer? It could cost her life.

Time was running out. He could feel it in his gut.

Chapter Twenty-Four

Keeping to the inside of the forest edge, Jill angled toward the gatehouse. Since Clay refused to help her, she would find the answers to her mother's death on her own. The minute he left for Hanley Field to bring Lenore's long-time friend to Windtop, she knew she'd found her best chance to study Windtop's blueprints. She had slipped out of the house while everyone else was busy with last minute preparations for Katherine Wentworth's arrival.

She paused in the shadows of the tree-sheltered drive and peered both ways. All clear. Hurrying across the drive, she let herself into the gatehouse and went straight to Clay's drawing table. Bound at the top, Windtop's great sheaf of blueprints lay where she had last seen them.

Her heart thrummed as she turned over the pages of exterior elevations to get to the floor plans. If Windtop had a hidden escape route as Amelia suggested, she should find clues to its whereabouts among all the lines and symbols that identified the construction details.

Over and over she scrutinized each page, but nothing caught her eye. Icy disappointment seeped through her veins. She arranged the pages as she had found them. If Windtop had an escape route, Clay made sure no one would discover the information so easily.

She fisted her hands. The blueprints had failed her, but she had another trick that might reveal a hidden passageway. The method would take longer, and she would be in constant danger of discovery, but all she needed was a steel measuring tape.

Jill knelt on the floor of the carriage house. Just as she remembered, Windtop's old toolbox held two such tapes. She tucked one in the pocket of her loose-fitting shorts, carefully closed the box, and made sure it didn't look disturbed before she headed for the house.

She hurried through Windtop's front door, hoping no one would notice her. No such luck!

A harried flush on her cheeks, Lenore appraised her from head to foot. "You look decent enough. Keep watch, and let me know the minute Mrs. Wentworth arrives. Tia is getting ready and I must do the same."

Without another word, her aunt rushed up the stairs.

Jill blinked. In a backhanded sort of way, Lenore had both complimented and included her, even depending on her as if she belonged. For a moment, Jill dared to hope that her fears about her mother's death would prove untrue, but at the moment, she didn't have much time to think about it.

The door to the master bedroom closed as a car crunched gravel outside and pulled to a stop before the front door.

Elma darted from the library, carrying fresh towels and scurrying toward the stairs. The poor thing never appeared at ease.

Jill stopped her. "Tell Mrs. Bradwell her friend has arrived."

Elma nodded and scrambled up the stairs. Moments later, she called down over the railing. "Mrs. Bradwell says to entertain Mrs. Wentworth until she is ready."

In that case, she had better go out and greet the woman.

Tall and in her forties, Katherine Wentworth emerged from the car and glided up the porch steps. Exquisitely dressed in a summer-weight suit that flattered her slightly plump figure, she smiled graciously and extended her hand. "You must be Tia."

Taking the woman's soft hand, Jill returned her smile. "I'm Lenore's niece, Jill Shepherd, Mrs. Wentworth."

"Kitty," she invited.

"Welcome to Windtop, Kitty." Jill opened the screen door for Lenore's guest to enter. "My aunt has been looking forward to your visit."

"So have I."

"Please come into the parlor." She led Kitty through the entrance hall. "Lenore will be down in a few minutes."

Kitty surveyed the room before seating herself on the gold brocade sofa. "So this is Windtop. Lenore must be thrilled to finally be the mistress of this grand old house."

A small gasp drew their attention. Tia stood at the parlor entrance. "Oh, but Jill—"

"Kitty, I would like you to meet Tia."

Kitty extended her hand. "You are just as lovely as your cousin."

Tia blushed and came forward. "Thank you." As Mrs. Wentworth reseated herself, the girl tilted her head toward Jill, confusion in her eyes.

Thankfully, Mrs. Wentworth didn't notice. She continued to reminisce. "When your mother and I were college roommates, she said one day she would live here. Of course, your father was so shy, I didn't think it would ever happen."

"Kitty!" With a rustle of long skirts, Lenore rushed in to hug her friend. Kitty rose to meet her. "Please forgive me," her aunt went on, "for keeping you waiting."

"I didn't mind at all," Kitty said. "It gave me a chance to meet your lovely niece and charming daughter."

"Really?" Lenore slipped her arm through Kitty's, turning her toward the entrance hall.

"What an exquisite place to host your party," Kitty remarked as the two women prepared to leave the parlor. "You must be so proud of your home."

Lenore flicked a nervous glance at Jill. "Yes, well, we must get you settled after your long journey. I see the girls failed to offer you refreshments. Please accept my apologies."

She paused to look back at Jill and Tia. "Tell Mrs. Fenton to serve tea in the library in about fifteen minutes. After that, I assume you girls have plenty to keep yourselves busy."

As Lenore retreated with her friend, Jill gaped after her. Had she heard Kitty right? Did she imply that Lenore knew about Windtop before she met Uncle Drew? That would put a whole new spin on Lenore's obsession with Windtop.

The possibility continued to nag her that afternoon, even while lost in helping the other women with an avalanche of party details. Fortunately, with Kitty's experience, everything quickly fell into place. Jill didn't have a moment alone to make use of the steel measuring tape. Instead, she fell into an exhausted sleep that night, praying for a better opportunity tomorrow.

Early the next day, two rectangular pink-and-white striped party tents arrived by rumbling truck. From the talk during breakfast, Jill gathered that one tent would shelter a varnished dance floor, and the other a banquet hall, each complete with crystal chandeliers. Lenore had spared no expense, and understandably, she and Kitty intended to supervise the set-up beyond the gardens and gazebo.

Jill removed the linen napkin from her lap and pushed back from the dining table. She had a hard time keeping herself from grinning. This was just the opportunity she had hoped for. With those two busy, she was free to search Windtop for that hidden escape route for a while. She itched to begin.

But she didn't get far.

"Jill." Her aunt's voice held an edge that pushed Jill's buttons. "Bring two lawn chairs, and tell Tia to join us."

Jill inhaled a calming breath. A slight delay, that's all. She could handle it.

On the lawn near the tent sites, she arrived to set up the chairs.

"How unfortunate you couldn't use your lovely house for this occasion," Kitty lamented against the clatter of boards and the workmen's noise as they prepared to lay the flooring.

Lenore sighed. "My first choice, of course, but you know how guest lists grow. This was the best answer."

Jill unfolded one chair, much relieved that Lenore, Kitty, and even Tia would be busy outside, leaving the house free of intrusion. *Thank you, Lord.*

Kitty shaded her eyes against the morning sun. "And your idea of transporting guests from William's Landing in vintage cars is inspired."

Unfolding the second chair, Jill glanced up in time to catch Lenore's proud smile. "That was Carver's idea. Since we collect them, he believed they might add a unique touch."

"Well, I can tell you, my Ben and his friends are looking forward to the fun of driving them, even as temporary chauffeurs."

"May I get you ladies anything else?" Jill asked.

"No, thank you." Kitty smiled graciously.

Lenore waved Jill off, appearing unaware that she was more than happy to leave. As she moved away, the women's conversation faded, and she noted Mrs. Fenton and Elma gathering fresh vegetables from the garden.

Clay and Sam were lining the graveled walkway to the tents with alternating pots of pink geraniums and white. With a quick smile, Tia hurried past her to join her mother.

Perfect!

Within minutes, Jill snagged the steel measuring tape from her room, along with a notepad and pen. She could almost taste victory. If that hidden route existed, she was sure to find it.

Jill wiped her moist brow with the back of her hand and checked her watch. She had forgotten how tedious the work of measuring every interior wall could be. Worse, the first floor had netted her exactly nothing. She wasn't doing any better with the second floor.

She mumbled under her breath, "Lord, I know it's here somewhere. Why can't I find it?"

The others had gathered on the veranda for lunch. If she had any sense, she would join them. She could use a break, a cold drink, and something to stop her stomach from growling. On the other hand, how much time did she have left before the house teemed with people again?

Groaning, she moved on with measuring the second floor, but the extra half hour did her no good. She blew a stray lock of hair away from her face and went down to join the others.

Lenore dabbed her lips with a damask napkin and set it beside her plate. "You've been such a help, Kitty. How can I ever thank you?"

"It's been my pleasure, and I'm sure my son and his friends are enjoying your lovely home in Munising since their arrival this morning."

Jill poured herself a tall glass of peach iced tea, relishing the cold glass against the palms of her hands.

Lenore sighed. "I wish you all could stay at Windtop."

"We'll be fine in town," Kitty assured her.

Lenore raised her brows. "We?"

Kitty took Lenore's hand. "I hope you don't mind. I plan to stay at your home in Munising tonight."

"But—"

"Don't worry, Lenore. Someone has to look after those young men, and we will arrive in plenty of time for the party tomorrow. In the meantime, you will be so busy that you'll be glad we aren't underfoot. And before I leave here today, I will have done all I can to help you."

Kitty noticed Jill and smiled. "We missed your delightful company at lunch."

Lenore stood. "Uh … yes. Unfortunately, we now have work to do. Please excuse us."

Kitty smiled apologetically and joined Lenore. They left the porch, walking toward the party tents where workers were unloading tables and chairs.

Tia tilted her head to one side. "I don't know what it is, but something's not quite right about all this," she whispered. "I feel it in here." She touched her breastbone.

Jill frowned. She felt it too.

"Tia," her mother called sharply. "Are you coming?"

The girl moaned. "See you later."

Jill grabbed the last croissant stuffed with chicken salad and munched on it as she headed back into the house. She didn't have a moment to waste. But would she find what she was looking for? Or simply rule it out?

The afternoon waned with no sign of space discrepancy on the third floor. Returning to the second floor, she rechecked some areas, then blew a weary breath. If not for her mother's letter, she could believe that Windtop never had an escape route. But most likely, she wasn't quite skilled enough to detect it.

In need of a short rest with fresh air, she sought the secluded balcony at the end of the second-floor hall. Sitting on its wooden bench, she leaned against the wall behind her, welcoming a soft breeze wafting off the bay.

Stumped! That's what she was. She didn't have a clue what to try next.

As the rumble of car motors grew, she raised her gaze to catch sight of a fleet of classic cars arriving. Six shiny black, red, green, and buff cars, each unique, approached the carriage house. Carver had the lead in the red car. He parked it on the lawn across from the carriage house and leapt from it to direct the remaining drivers. One by one, the young men parked side-by-side and bounded out noisily, each covering his vehicle with a beige car cover. With the protective car sheaths in place, they followed her cousin as he headed toward the party tents.

Those young men with Carver must be Kitty's son and his college friends. They were so carefree, full of fun, and completely oblivious to the pain permeating Windtop.

Jill shook herself. She would not allow herself to sink into grief. Somewhere in this house, she would find the answer to her mother's death, no matter what it took.

She stood to re-enter the house and caught a movement in the shadows within the open carriage house door. She peered at the figure of the man standing there.

What was Clay up to?

Stepping through the open doorway, Clay looked around. Not a soul in sight. Good. He'd never get a better chance than now.

He let his gaze sweep the covered cars and moved closer. If the one he sought was among them, he'd see tell-tale signs of damage. By now that damage would not be easily visible, but if the car used to kill Janice was among them, he would find it.

He stole from one to another, peeling back the edge of the covers over the passenger's side fenders and staying alert for anyone who might return. This sleek, red Porsche might be it. He crouched and ran his hand over every inch of the painted metal. It was as smooth as a candy apple, and just as he expected, not a detectable sign of repair—at least from the outside.

He doubted that Janice's killer had purchased a whole new fender. The transaction would have alerted the law. If this was the car, the fender had been expertly repaired.

He glanced around once more, sweat beading on his brow. Then, easing himself down onto the grass, he reached up along the underside of the fender.

From the shadows of the balcony, Jill observed Clay. What was he doing and why so secretive? With a sick, sinking feeling, she realized it had to have something to do with Janice's death. *Lord, please. Whatever he finds or thinks he finds, help him change his mind and do what is right.*

As Clay moved out from beneath the car, she quickly stepped back. She couldn't let him catch her gawking.

Slipping back into the house, she wanted to cry. Clay was obviously moving forward with his plan with no one to stop him. She gripped the second-floor railing and looked below. Well, she and Clay had one thing in common. They were both stubborn. In his case, it could spell disaster. In her case, she had no choice. In her deepest heart, she couldn't accept her mother's suicide. It just didn't make sense. All she needed was some way to flush out the killer.

She smiled slowly as an idea formed. Bringing her fists down on the railing, she whispered. "That's it!"

"What's that, cousin?"

Jill jerked around. How had Carver managed to sneak up on her like that?

"You look pale, Jill." He moved closer as if genuinely concerned. "Are you feeling ill?"

Pale? Ill? She glared at him and turned away. When he touched her shoulder, every nerve in her body tightened. She shrugged him away.

"We're all worried about you, you know." He played it so well she could almost believe his feigned concern.

She pressed her lips together. Of course they were worried, and whoever was responsible for her mother's death had better worry.

"Have you considered seeing a psychiatrist?" he said. "Not pleasant to contemplate, but wouldn't you want to know if you inherited your mother's unfortunate mental weakness."

Jill whipped around. "What a wicked thing to say!"

He shrugged. "Suicide runs in families, Jill, and with the strain you've been under lately, well, who knows where it might lead if you don't get help?"

Chapter Twenty-Five

Jill had itched to slap Carver's face. His words still stung as she finished fastening the dress she would wear to Tia's party.

Mental weakness, my foot! What he really meant was mental illness. Her mother had been fragile, yes, and delicate, certainly. She had even been frightened at times but never mentally ill.

Jill brushed her hair with quick, strong strokes.

So the family believed Susannah Bradwell Shepherd had ended her life because she was mentally ill. Well, tonight Jill would prove them wrong.

Sweeping her hair up, she secured the mass of curls cascading to her bare shoulders. Just like her mother's. She released spiraling wisps to frame her face and tipped her head from side to side. Did it duplicate the arrangement in the portrait now at her place in Chicago? Was it close enough to startle the killer?

In a soft rustle of floor-length skirts, she turned slowly before Maggie's mirror to examine the lovely white gown she had taken from her mother's trunk before sending the rest on to Chicago. "What do you think, Button?"

The kitten eyed her from his perch on the bed. He jumped to the floor, and with his tail held high, he left the room.

"Not exactly my type of occasion either," Jill muttered as she adjusted the dress's off-the-shoulder neckline and added her mother's string of pearls.

Standing back from the mirror, she made a last check, her heart racing a few beats. If she didn't know better, she would believe that her mother looked back at her.

Just the effect she hoped to work at the party. Not that she wanted to take the focus off Tia. She only wanted to unnerve a killer. She lifted her chin. So what if the game was dangerous? She intended to win.

Moving through the quiet of the house, she started down the stairs. No need to hurry. Dressed in Victorian finery, the Bradwells had left for the party tents well in advance.

In the shadows of the second-floor hall, she paused at an unexpected sound. A faint but frantic scratching noise, like ... *oh, no!*

She dashed forward. "Button, stop!"

Pawing at the base of the paneled wall outside the master bedroom, the kitten ignored her. She snatched him away, but with single-minded determination, he wriggled free and sprang back to resume his pawing. She moved him gently aside and found a bit of white cloth embedded at the base of the wall.

Her heart leapt in her throat, and she found she couldn't move. Button had found the elusive passageway.

Off-center to the massive fireplace on the opposite side of the wall, the escape passage was likely encased in its brickwork. But where was its entrance release?

She stepped back to study the wall's intricately carved surface. Decorative wood medallions were placed at the corners of both the upper and lower panels, the motif repeated throughout the hall. She pushed those on the panel above the bit of cloth. Nothing. She attempted to turn them. They refused to move.

Maybe a sequence would work.

After trying different combinations with no success, she pushed two at her shoulder height, and a four-foot width of wall slid open without a sound. Blood pounded in her ears.

As she grew up, she had lived in this house every summer for as long as she could remember. How had she not stumbled across its secret?

A chill snaked through her. The bit of cloth was ample evidence that someone else knew.

She crouched to retrieve it. An inch of delicate handmade lace surrounded a square of white lawn. Her stomach knotted. Lenore presented that very handkerchief to Tia this morning. "Every Victorian woman must carry one," her aunt insisted.

Oh, please, Lord. Not Tia.

Jill forced herself to breathe slowly. Why grab the first obvious answer? A handkerchief was flimsy evidence. Her aunt probably had more like it and a better reason for wanting her mother out of the way.

Sudden tears overtook her. No! She must not cry. She couldn't arrive at the party red-nosed and teary eyed. Above all, she had to keep a clear mind and calm demeanor.

She peered into the dim passage with its brick walls. A metal stairway wound into the darkness below. That didn't mean much. She had seen similar devices while conducting research on at least one other house for which she had prepared a genealogy. Those had concealed a passage but only to other parts of the house. This one might be no different.

She shivered as it begged her to explore, but she didn't have time now.

Windtop's front door opened below, and footsteps, decidedly feminine, clicked across the entrance hall. "Jill?"

Throwing the handkerchief inside the passage, she touched the two medallions. Button shot through the opening just before the panel slid back into place. He would have to wait a few minutes. She hurried to the second-floor rail.

Tia looked up at her. "Mother sent me to find you. Are you ready? Our guests will arrive soon." The girl radiated a joyous poise in her lovely Victorian ball gown, her hair like a shimmering waterfall behind her shoulders.

Glancing at the paneled wall behind, Jill sighed. Both the kitten and the passageway would have to wait. "Coming."

Tia squealed as Jill descended the stairs. "Oh, great choice. You look every bit as pretty as your mother in that dress."

Jill assessed her cousin's clear-eyed gaze. *Thank you, Lord!* Tia was not the one she sought.

One down and three to go.

Twilight settled softly over the freshly cut lawns as Jill accompanied Tia. The great pink-and-white-striped tents glowed from the light of chandeliers within, and the soft music of a stringed quartet floated on the night air. If not for unanswered questions about her mother's death and the dark passageway begging her to explore its secret, she could have enjoyed this lovely occasion.

They reached the wide entrance of the entertainment tent, and Tia slipped into her place in the reception line between her father and her mother.

Lenore's cold gaze raked Jill. "I hoped you would choose something more suitable than that tasteless old thing."

Uncle Drew stopped tugging at the high, stiff collar of his Victorian evening wear. He half-smiled and sighed. "You look ... so much like your mother, Jill." His eyes misted, but the first guests approached, pulling his attention away.

Jill moved aside, continuing to observe her aunt and uncle who were now fully engaged in receiving guests. Neither of their reactions was decisive. Lenore was her usual critical self. Uncle Drew simply appeared to miss his sister. If one or both were concealing a crime, she had no proof. How awful to be suspecting her family like this. But she had to stay open to any possibility.

The ache in Jill's heart accelerated as she moved into the cavernous reception tent. Round, linen-covered tables rimmed the perimeter of a polished dance floor. Each table was accented by a tall, fluted vase of fresh flowers and trailing ivy at its center and surrounded by eight polished wood chairs. Its beauty belied the ugliness slithering beneath the lavish occasion.

She chose the nearest table, looking down at her mother's lovely dress before seating herself. So far, her attempt to unnerve a killer had failed. One Bradwell remained.

Near the far wall of the tent, Carver played the charming younger host to Ben and his friends. She could be wrong about him too. She could be wrong about this whole murder idea. All she had to go on were Maggie's suspicions and her mother's unfinished letter. She would have to slip away and explore that passageway.

A shadow fell across the table, and she looked up. Clay, in black tie and tails, stood a few feet away. Her foolish heart leapt until she caught the anger as his gaze swept her attire.

"What do you think you're doing?" he hissed.

Looking him straight in the eye, she kept her voice low as she ground out her words. "Trying to flush out a killer."

"Trying to get yourself killed." He pulled out a chair and gestured for her to sit down.

She lifted her chin. "I don't think so. Not as long as the Lord has anything to say about it."

At the deepening concern in Clay's gaze, she set her chin and walked away. He would not stop her from finding the truth about her mother's death.

A feminine hand arrested her flight. She looked down to find Kitty seated at the next table. "Are you all right?" the woman asked.

Jill forced a smile. "A little difference of opinion. That's all."

"Well, settle it soon, dear. He obviously cares a great deal for you."

Jill tilted her head. "Not enough, I'm afraid."

"That's too bad." Kitty nodded toward the reception line. "Just look at Lenore."

Following the woman's joyful gaze, Jill observed her aunt, head held high, a gracious smile on her face, and one hand occasionally fluttering to the antique brooch at her throat. Lenore surely gloried in her role for the evening.

"She's the picture of her great-grandmother," Kitty mused.

Jill blinked. "I … don't know what you mean."

Kitty appeared mildly puzzled. "Madeleine Beaupre, first mistress of Windtop. You know, the woman in Lenore's family photo album."

Lenore? A Beaupre? Jill sank into one of the chairs at Kitty's table. "Are you sure?"

"You didn't know?"

Jill shook her head, unable to choke out a response. That explained a certain orphan's obsession with Windtop.

Kitty shrugged. "I shouldn't be surprised. Lenore never breathed a word of it to me either. Not until after that weekend she went home with me for our first college break. She wandered through our old home, utterly entranced. When we returned to the dorm, she pulled out her family album and the pictures of Windtop. 'One day I'll live there,' she said. The next semester, she met your uncle, they fell in love, and here she is. It's interesting how some things are meant to be."

A chill pressed on Jill's heart. *Yes, interesting.* Her aunt must have tracked Uncle Drew down and maneuvered him into marrying her.

"How are you ladies getting along?" Her uncle smiled broadly as he pulled out a chair.

Kitty finished sipping iced tea from her glass. "Jill and I were reminiscing about Lenore and Windtop. But, of course, you know all about her great-grandfather."

Uncle Drew scrunched his brow.

"The Frenchman who built this house," Kitty prompted.

Jill caught him paling slightly before he sat down as if his legs might not hold him. "No."

Kitty wagged her finger at him playfully. "Like most busy men, you simply have no memory for unimportant details."

The slightly gray tinge gathering along her uncle's jawline and his almost inaudible voice said otherwise. "She was an orphan."

"After her grandmother died. A very sad event for a ten-year-old. It's a good thing she had the comfort of remembering her grandmother's wonderful stories of Windtop. Lenore is quite proud of her heritage." Kitty's brow crinkled. "Are you sure she never told you?"

Uncle Drew shifted uncomfortably. "Some of it."

Kitty raised her brows slightly. "Oh."

"Is there more?" Jill asked.

"Maybe I've said too much already," she said. "Are you sure you want to hear it?"

"If there's more to the story," Uncle Drew said, "I'd like to hear it."

"Well ..." Kitty appeared uncertain.

"Please. For Lenore's sake," he said.

"All right, but I don't know much more." She paused a moment longer. Jill leaned slightly forward to catch each word.

"Lenore took her grandmother's death very hard. She arrived at the orphanage with two possessions, the brooch she is wearing tonight and her grandmother's scrapbook."

Jill leaned on the table, crossing her arms and gripping her elbows. So that's how Lenore knew so much about the Beaupres.

"When she was thirteen years old, she happened to read a magazine article about your family, Drew, and was immediately drawn to you. She kept up on any news about your family. When she heard about the college you would attend, she made up her mind to do the same. Isn't that romantic?"

"But private college is expensive," Jill said.

Kitty grinned. "You know Lenore. When she wants something, she makes a way."

Uncle Drew nodded solemnly. "You're talking about her winning a scholarship to the college of her choice."

"Exactly!" Kitty's eyes sparkled. "It was meant to be. You two fell in love, and Lenore regained her ancestral home."

Jill struggled to catch her next breath. The years of strife made an ugly sense now.

Kitty studied her, then Uncle Drew. "You two really didn't know, did you? How strange."

Jill's chest tightened. *Strange nothing!* Kitty just confirmed what she had known since she was a child. Her aunt preyed on others for her own gain.

"If only I had known," Uncle Drew mumbled.

Jill gazed at her uncle. Would he have done differently?

"Mrs. Wentworth." Carver's cheer broke through the fog of Kitty's revelations. "Mother wants to see you right away."

He nodded to his father and paused to acknowledge Jill. "How lovely you look tonight, dear cousin, and may I say, dressed most appropriately."

He held an arm out to Kitty. "Are you ready?"

The moment they left, Uncle Drew slumped in his chair. "Why didn't I guess?"

"So you didn't know any of this when you agreed with Grandma and Grandpa that Mother and I should inherit Windtop."

Her uncle's ashen face began to regain its color. "I had no idea."

"But you must have known Lenore would object." How could he not?

He groaned his eyes dark pools of agony. "I did it for her own good. Her obsession with Windtop seemed unhealthy. It never occurred to me that she would make you and Susannah miserable all those years. I tried to stop her more times than I can count and was never successful. Finally, I just gave up."

Jill remembered all too well. "Then why did you beg me to return, Uncle Drew? With Mom and me out of the way, Lenore would have gotten Windtop and been happy." *And I wouldn't be agonizing over whether or not my mother was murdered.*

"You have no idea how happy I was when I discovered you were alive, Jill. Every time I look at you, I see Susannah and know a part of her lives." He tried to still his trembling hands. "But, forgive me, I urged you to claim Windtop, not just because it was your inheritance, but to save my wife."

"From what?" Jill crinkled her brow. Her uncle looked so weary.

"About a year ago, Lenore took to wearing those old-fashioned dresses. Her doctor warned me she was in danger of an emotional breakdown. Her years of obsession over Windtop had weakened her health and the strain was taking its toll. I hoped that keeping this place from her would also keep her safe."

"And I ruined everything by inviting you all to live here. You couldn't refuse. Oh, Uncle Drew, I'm so sorry." Jill laid her hand on her uncle's sleeve.

"You believed you were doing the right thing," he said. "You meant well."

Sure. She also meant well when she left the island to find her father. Why hadn't she seen the pattern before? Her impulsive solutions often ended more in hurt than help.

"Hey, you two." Tia rushed up and bent to kiss her father's cheek. "This is no time for all this serious talk. Dad, will you come with me? I have something to show you."

"Give me a minute, Tia. I'll be right back." Uncle Drew left the table.

Tia plopped down in a chair, her joy like the fragrance of the table flowers. "Why did I ever fight Mother about this party? I am having the best time. Especially with Leo." She sighed and gazed across the floor.

He smiled and waved in acknowledgment.

"But he's right. It's time I gave Dad some attention."

Uncle Drew returned and Tia led him away.

Jill scanned the guests and her breath caught in her throat. They were ambling toward the dining tent. The moment she had been waiting for had arrived. Her best chance to escape to the house and explore the passageway undisturbed was right now.

A familiar, outstretched hand arrested her attention. She looked up to find Clay gazing at her. Her pulse quickened.

"I'm leaving," he said. "Could we talk?"

She placed her hand in his and let him lead her into the night.

Outside of the gazebo, stars shimmered overhead. Subdued strains of chamber music reached them while Jill's hand lay so warm and yielding in his. This could become a memorable night if he found that elusive way to break through her stubborn resolve.

"You're leaving tonight?" Her soft words came to him as if she were pleading with him not to go.

Clay claimed both her hands and ran his thumbs gently over her fingers. "It's time I moved on."

"But I thought … have you changed your mind about catching Janice's killer?" Her gaze simmered with a desperate hope.

"For now."

She nodded, the sadness in her eyes telling him she hadn't missed the nuance. His hunt wasn't over, merely postponed.

"And your next project?"

"Hopefully restoring a historic hotel in Haiti. The client wants to discuss the details early tomorrow morning. She's considering other firms."

"I wish you well," Jill whispered. Wistful words, as if she would miss him even after all the stupid things he'd said and done.

He gently guided her chin up to look deep into her eyes. "Do you?"

"Yes." Her soft lips, so ripe for the kissing, trembled.

He gazed at her for a long, painful moment. Did she care enough? Could he convince her? "Then come with me, Jill. Let's both just walk away."

"What about catching a killer?"

"You're more important." He would take care of that killer once he had Jill safely out of harm's way.

She said nothing as if wrestling with her decision. Then her chin quivered, and she stepped away. "I want to, Clay, but I can't. Not yet."

Her iron resolve had slipped back into place. Nothing he said would make a difference. He didn't want to leave her, but neither could he force her to go.

He kissed the palm of her hand, not trusting himself to seek her lips. She had his heart as surely as it once belonged to Janice. To keep Jill from harm, he'd have to play it the hard way.

"Good-bye, Jill."

Jill stood mutely as Clay walked away. She strained to stop herself from running after him. His suggestion tugged at her, but she knew she could not leave Windtop with so many questions about her mother's death unresolved. The answers were so close. If Maggie and Clay were right, she had all the more reason to see this sorry mess to the end. She couldn't live the rest of her life not knowing when a killer might strike.

The party's bright lights and distant laughter held no charm for her. With Clay gone, along with her heart and her hopes for their future, all she had left was the task that lay ahead of her.

Lenore's guests were gathering around tables in the dining tent, anticipating the late evening supper about to begin. Her aunt, Uncle Drew, Carver, and Tia seated themselves at the head table. As far as Jill could tell, everyone was accounted for.

Her heart lodged in her throat. Now was the perfect opportunity to check the passageway. She skimmed through the shadows on her way to the house.

How was it possible to seek the truth with such determination, yet fear it so deeply? At least Clay had walked away. Whatever she discovered, he would never know. He would be safe from whatever followed. Maybe, sometime in the future, he would share his suspicions with the police. Maybe, after tonight, she could do the same.

The house loomed in the night sky, its hidden passageway calling her. She hurried toward Windtop's back entrance.

Lord, please help me find the truth and accept whatever it might be.

Chapter Twenty-Six

$\mathcal{L}$ilting strains of stringed instruments and a faint din of conversation drifted on the damp night air as Jill slipped into the kitchen and set the security system. Alert for the slightest sound of another person in the house, she moved through the dining room, the library, and entrance hall and stole up the stairs.

Evening shadows dimmed the second-floor hall.

Her heart thudded. Did she dare turn on a light? Better to use the antique oil lamp Lenore kept on the hall table. It should provide enough light to accomplish her task.

She opened the small table's narrow drawer and searched for the box of matches. Moments later, the lamp's wick flamed to life, casting a faint pool of light. After replacing its glass chimney, she left to check the rooms on the third floor.

All clear. She needed one more thing.

Entering her room, she groped in her purse until her fingers curled around a small, bright-beamed flashlight she kept for emergencies. That should illuminate the dark passageway.

Returning to the second floor, she paused at the railing, again listening for any telltale sound below. All remained quiet.

She swallowed the lump in her throat. Now to activate the medallions on the paneled wall and face what lay beyond.

Her shadow loomed large in the passageway's cavity. She stepped inside and turned on the flashlight, praying for enough time to see where it led and get back to the party before anyone missed her.

Grasping her long skirts, she plunged down the iron staircase, following its spiral descent into the darkness below. Surrounded by stone walls, she reached the level where a cool dampness enveloped her.

A light shone below.

With a soft gasp, she turned off her light to listen. No footsteps or detectable breathing accompanied the dim, steady light.

She crept down the last few steps and peered into the lighted area. A wide, damp tunnel carved through rock stretched before her. Overhead, at far intervals, hung a string of dim electric lights. Who left them on? Did she dare go farther?

Venturing forward a few steps, she stopped and listened again. Nothing more than a faint dripping reached her ears. It was probably moisture from the stone walls.

A different light loomed ahead. She moved toward it. The overhead lights ended where another passage opened to her right. Her heart thudding in her chest, she turned to face the opening. A slight incline of the stone floor lost itself in darkness with no light switches visible at its mouth. With that incline, the second tunnel would eventually open in the forest.

Shuddering, she backed away from the shadowy tunnel and turned to stumble the last few yards to stand where the main passage ended at a large opening above Trout Bay. A crooked tree growing in the cliff's face hung over the opening and pale moonlight filtered through its leaves.

Numbness swept over her as she gazed into the bay's dark, lapping waters. She could no longer hope against hope. The passageway gave unprotected access to Windtop and to her mother.

Throwing a sports bag packed with his clothing into the back of Windtop's Jeep, Clay slammed the hatch. He'd made all the necessary arrangements. Later, when the Bradwells' guests were delivered to their boats, Carver would ride along and retrieve Bradwell's boat from its berth at the marina. He would then pick up the Jeep near Williams Landing and return it to the carriage house.

Clay was free to leave. At the marina, he'd transfer everything from the boat to his truck and drive through the night. He should arrive just in time to meet with his new client tomorrow.

Yet if everything appeared so right, why did he have this uncomfortable sense that something was badly amiss? Whatever it was, he had no time to figure it out. If he didn't leave now, he'd lose out on a chance at his biggest contract so far. The one that would not only keep him in business but get him out of the country the minute he settled his score with Janice's killer.

He climbed into the Jeep and took off. He'd return early the day after tomorrow and take care of his unfinished business, and no one would know, least of all Jill.

The headlight beams pierced the forest shadows along the island's sandy road as he kept a sharp eye for deer or bear. Yet he couldn't dislodge his longing for Jill. The same sort of longing he had seen in her eyes. He slammed the steering wheel with the heel of his hand. He shouldn't leave her like this. She was sure to do something foolish while he was gone. *God, please keep her from harm.* Did God even hear him?

Movement in his peripheral vision gave him a split second before a large buck stepped onto the road directly in front of him. Adrenaline shot through his veins. He veered sharply to the left, barely missing the huge animal.

Momentary triumph froze as his front tire struck something solid in the dark. Tossed a foot in the air, the Jeep slammed back to earth while he jammed on the brake to miss a tree and wrestle the vehicle to a stop.

Arms aching and heart pumping, he inhaled deeply to steady himself. As far as he could tell, he had missed both buck and tree by a fraction and hadn't suffered more than a bruise or two. He grabbed a flashlight from the glove compartment and went to check for any damage.

Resting at an awkward angle, the Jeep seemed to be all right until he came to the front, passenger-side tire. He trained the pool of light on it.

Flat!

The tree stump behind the Jeep, sporting fresh scrapes on its bark, was the culprit. He yanked open the back hatch to pull out the spare. It was soft. When he couldn't find the air pump, he knew he wasn't going anywhere.

Someone didn't want him to leave. "All right, what's going on?"

His heart began to thud in his chest. A strong sense of Jill in danger overwhelmed him. She needed him. *Now!* Fear boiled up in his chest as he turned back to Windtop at a dead run.

Was God letting it happen again? "She trusts you just as Janice did," he muttered.

Will you trust me?

Clay blinked and stumbled. He'd never before heard the voice of God in his heart. Janice had and so did Jill, but not him.

Now God chose to talk to him?

A flicker of hope flamed to life as he churned down the road toward Windtop. *God, help me get to Jill in time, and I'll never doubt you again.*

Jill shivered in the dampness of the stone tunnel Lenore, no doubt, knew from all the stories her grandmother had told her. This was also the explanation for Windtop's missing antiques.

And her mother's death.

Her body trembled so violently she wasn't sure she could continue to stand. Her hopes that Maggie was wrong vanished. Once made known, this discovery could destroy the entire family. But then, what would her aunt care as long as she gained Windtop?

Lenore! It always came down to Lenore.

Jill's breathing came in spasms. "Lord, please don't let her get away with this!"

Forgive, child.

Weeping, she shook her head. "I can't. I can't!"

She crumbled within. The very words Clay had spoken about Janice's killer. She understood them now. Some wrongs were too awful to forgive.

It was one thing to forgive her uncle for failing to protect them when her mother was alive, but this? How could God ask that of her?

"I don't want to forgive!"

If you do not forgive, I cannot forgive you.

She had known all along it could come to this. Hoped it never would.

She buried her face in her hands. "Lord, please help me. For your sake, please make me willing. Help me to forgive again because right now, I don't want to."

Her whispers echoed in the stone tunnel, and she froze before glancing around the passageway. She saw no one, but a niggling that she was no longer safe overwhelmed her. An intense urge to run gripped her at the same time a violent trembling seized her knees. She turned to retrace her steps, her heart pumping faster than her feet. Skidding on tiny pebbles, she stumbled toward the unexplored passage.

What was that?

She paused to listen. Only a steady dripping came to her as she peered into the darkness. This was probably the quickest way back to the party but also the only way a threat might reach her.

The whisper of a sound moved closer, and a prickling raced along her skin. Smothering a cry, she grasped her long skirts, lifted them out of the way, and ran for the stairs.

Her footsteps rang out as she dashed up the metal steps. Another heavier set sounded discordantly behind her, gaining on her. Gasping for air, she pushed harder. A faint light shone above as she neared Windtop's second floor. She strained toward it in reckless abandon.

The exit! She leapt into the cavity, slapped the two buttons on the back of the panel, and flung herself into the hall. The panel swung silently into place.

And slid open again.

Chapter Twenty-Seven

Clay raced along Windtop's gravel drive. *Help me reach Jill in time, God. Forgive me. Jill was right. You were never to blame for Janice's death. You never wanted her to die like that, and you don't want Jill to die at that madman's hands either.* Why else would the Jeep lie disabled with him racing back to Jill?

The house appeared dark except for a faint glow on the second floor. He tried the door. Locked. He hurried through the gazebo garden.

"Merrick."

He turned toward the sound of Bradwell's voice.

"You're still here?"

Clay glanced behind Bradwell. "Have you seen Jill?"

The man shook his head. "But I'll help you find her."

"I'll find her myself." The man would only slow him down. He didn't have a moment to lose.

He quickly canvassed the party, his gut tightening. No one had seen her for some time. She had to be in the house. If she was, he had only one way to get to her. He strained every muscle to reach the hidden entranceway in the forest.

There!

He opened the hatch, and Button shot out. His heart leapt into his throat. Jill had found the passageway.

★★★

Jill backed away. Carver stepped out, grinning. His chest heaved nearly as hard as hers. "So, dear cousin, you discovered Windtop's secret."

239

Every nerve in her body worked against her. This explained why, when as children they played hide and seek, he always found her but she never found him until, like magic, he appeared. He knew all along about this passageway.

"You're frightened. Your mother was too. Often. Those last few summers proved especially amusing. But then ..." He shrugged. "She caught me with a few trinkets."

"You were stealing."

He ground his teeth. "Not stealing, cousin. Taking what was rightfully mine. I am, after all, Windtop's rightful heir through both my father's and my mother's sides of the family."

Jill edged away. "The law wouldn't see it that way."

"The law doesn't matter. Where are you going?"

His mocking concern sent prickles dancing over her skin.

The muscles along his jaw twitched. "I haven't finished yet."

She glanced through the railing to the front door below. She'd have to disarm the security system. Could she do it before he caught her?

"You may as well not look for help," he said. "No one knows we're here."

Jill snapped her attention back to Carver and his crooked smile as he inched toward her.

"I kept an eye on you all evening," he said. "When you left the party, I knew you had found the handkerchief. Clever of me to leave that clue, wasn't it?" His cold gaze sickened her, turning her muscles to jelly. She stared, afraid to blink.

"I had to do something, cousin. You're quite clever. In time, you would have figured it out. I couldn't allow that. You see, I don't belong behind bars, so I had no choice. Just as I had no choice when your mother discovered my clever enterprise."

His admission hit her like a club to her stomach.

She forced herself to breathe. "You—!"

Carver put up the palms of his hands. "Now, now. Don't beg me to reconsider. Your mother tried that, muttering some nonsense about my eternal soul."

Jill sucked rapid breaths. Her mother had tried to talk to him about Jesus?

He yawned. "It did no good, of course. Her demise took mere moments."

Carver narrowed his eyes to cold slits. "And, now, dear cousin …" He lunged to grab her.

She dodged, his hand grazing her arm.

He moved slowly forward. "You're quick, but why make this difficult? Merrick can't rescue you this time."

Clay? She tensed. "What have you done to him?"

"Nothing. He left on his own."

Carver lunged and trapped her upper arms, his fingers digging in painfully. She jerked again and again to free herself, but he held tight. "Stop!" he roared.

Stop? Was he crazy? She kicked and jerked until, finally, he shook her so hard that her hair fell loose around her shoulders and her neck throbbed.

He pressed his face so close she could smell alcohol fumes on his breath. "Accept it, Jill. Like mother, like daughter." He dragged her toward the railing. "Just another suicide."

She continued to fight him. "No one will believe that!"

"Oh, yes, they will. Your near-attempt in Chicago. Your odd behavior lately." He grinned. "And your suicide note."

Jill glared at him. "I wrote no such thing!"

"Oh, but you did." He trapped both her hands in the iron grip of his left and pulled a paper from the pocket of his dinner jacket.

She stared at the letter she had written the night Tia begged her to stay. "I found this treasure in your wastebasket."

Jill slumped. Her words could be taken as a suicide note. Drew and Lenore would believe him, and the police would believe them.

Carver tucked the letter away and grabbed her chin, forcing her head up. "Look at it this way, cousin. I'm doing you a favor. You are about to reap your eternal reward."

Laughing at his little joke, he relaxed his grip.

Jill wrenched herself free. "Only God has the right to take a life."

"Well, then …" He pulled her back, pushing his face close to hers. "Call me God!"

Digging his fingers into her flesh, he dragged her closer to the railing.

"No!" She wriggled and writhed, kicking at his legs. She tried to bite him.

He slapped her face with a stinging blow. "Enough!"

She drew back and clenched her teeth. Now only holding her with one hand, he grasped at her with the other. As she jerked away, his fingers tangled in her necklace, and the strand broke, scattering pearls at their feet.

Carver's feet slipped out from beneath him. Surprise flashed across his face. His hands flew up in the air as he fell backward. Striking his head on the corner of the hall table, he slid to the floor as the oil lamp rocked and toppled. Plunging through the uprights of the railing, its oil chamber shattered on the entrance hall's parquet floor. With a whoosh of flame, the fire spread.

Jill's breath caught. The old house would go up in no time! She raced for the passageway. Carver groaned, and she stopped to look back. Even he didn't deserve to die like this. Crackling fire and smoke began to rise from the entrance hall, making its way through the wide stairwell to the third floor.

"Carver, get up!"

When he didn't move, she ran back and tugged at him. "We've got to get out of here."

He sat up, rubbed his head, and shook it. His eyes rolled and then focused. As he stumbled to his feet, she dashed for the metal stairs and heard him right behind her.

He grabbed her arm and swung her around. "No one runs from me," he growled. "Not you and not Merrick's little witch."

Jill stared unblinkingly. "You killed Janice."

He sneered. "No one refuses me either. She got what she deserved."

"You're ... crazy!" she whispered.

His upper lip curled as his pupils turned to dark pinholes. The tiny muscles in his jaw jumped. "You'll never say that again!"

He still meant to kill her? *No way!* Screaming, she slammed her heel down on the top of his shoe. She would not be his next victim.

Howling, he cursed and released his grip.

A fist shot past her head, and the door to the passageway closed.

Clay pounced on Carver before they hit the floor. He caught the scum in a choke hold and tightened it. What a pleasure to see the beast's face turned red, then purple.

"Stop, Clay! You're killing him." Jill pulled at his shirt.

Clay held on but turned to face Jill. "This piece of filth killed—"

"I know. Let the law punish him." The words quivered on her lips. She released him and stepped back.

He yanked on Carver's throat. "He tried to kill you!"

"Clay, if his life ends, so does yours … ours. Please. Don't."

His gaze locked with hers. Was this really what he wanted?

You have a choice, child. Jill or …

He released his hold, and Carver fell back on his elbows, coughing as flames engulfed the wide stairwell.

Clay grabbed Jill and thrust her in front of him. "Let's get out of here."

Jill had taken only a few steps when Clay grunted and plowed into her. Propelled forward, she fought to keep her balance and whirled around to see Clay punch Carver. Her cousin backed up. Before Carver could ready himself for another charge, Clay lowered his shoulder and rammed. Carver staggered backward into the railing. With a loud crack, the old wood gave way.

Teetering, Carver flung his arms overhead. His eyes widened as Clay sprang forward. For a split second, Carver hung in the thick, rising smoke above the flames. Then, screaming, he plunged into the crackling inferno.

Chapter Twenty-Eight

Jill froze. The roar of flames licked up the walls while clacking debris fell to the entrance hall. Clay turned to her, his right fist clenched, his skin pale, and his eyes vacant. She laid her hand on his chest.

Shivers wracked his body as much as hers. Was he in shock? Did he feel as sickened as she did?

Fire engulfing the stairwell had almost reached the second floor. The acrid smoke rising through the wide stairwell must have filled the third floor, for it now snaked along the ceiling high above them. Coughing, she rubbed her nose. Her eyes stung. The heat was becoming unbearable. She turned and opened the passageway just as a chunk of flaming debris crashed on the floor behind Clay.

With a hacking cough, he leapt clear and caught her by her waist, propelling her before him into the passageway. "Go!" He coughed again. "I'm right behind you."

He must have activated the passageway door, which slid into place, cutting off the smoke before much could enter.

Racing down the metal steps, Jill heard Clay follow and pushed to increase her speed. The image of Carver plunging to his death played through her mind in a repetitive loop. Her cousin crashing through the railing, suspended in midair. Clay lunging. Carver's scream as he fell.

With a smoke-scratchy ache in her throat, she raced downward. Could they make it out in time? Or would the dry building above them come crashing down, taking them with it?

Her heart thrummed in her rib cage. Clay had risked his life to come back for her, but Carver had died. They reached the bottom of the steps, and her stomach spasmed. She bent over and retched.

The crackle of fire and shattering glass reached them through the damp night air as Clay grasped Jill's hand and helped her from the passageway into the forest. An eerie play of flame and shadow danced beyond the treetops with enough light to glimpse her stricken face.

She launched herself at him, clinging. He closed his arms around her, holding her close. If only he could tell her everything would be all right, but very soon, they would have questions to answer. Those questions would bring the whole ugly story to light. As for him, he would accept whatever the law decided.

He slipped his right hand into his jeans pocket for a moment and pushed the button from Carver's shirt deeper. She didn't seem to notice. He stroked her silken hair, its faint odor of smoke reminding him of how close she had come to death.

Thank God, she was safe now, and Carver would never kill again.

Jill clutched his sleeve, her trusting eyes seeking his. "How do I tell my uncle that his son is dead, that he murdered his sister and tried to kill me? I can't do that to him."

Clay cradled her head between his hands and wiped away her tears with the pads of his thumbs, leaving streaks of soot. If only he could find a way to spare her what waited for them when they joined the others. No family, no community, wanted to know they had harbored a killer in their midst. Or that the outsider they had learned to trust had really come among them to take vengeance.

"We have to tell the truth, Jill. It's the only way."

Tell the truth and trust God. Both Janice and his grandmother would recommend that.

"I can't bear what it will do to Uncle Drew. To Tia. Even Lenore. I wish I had never come back." She began to cry again.

A hot iron lodged in his chest.

"Don't ever say that, Jill." If she hadn't come, he would never have known her. He would never have regained his relationship with God. "But you're right. Bradwell is a decent man. He doesn't deserve what his son's choices brought on him and his family."

She clutched his shirt. "Will anyone believe us?"

God, that's up to you. And they would need the best help heaven could offer.

He wrapped her softness in his arms. "We'll do what we can to make them believe. Your family. The sheriff. Everyone."

How hard he had tried to save her from this moment. Now, all he could do was take what was coming to him and shield her the best he could within the bounds of truth.

"Are you ready?" he asked.

She nodded and directed her gaze toward the fire. He took her hand and led her toward Windtop's open lawns.

Please, God, not for my sake. But for hers.

Lenore's guests stood a distance from the roaring inferno, gripped in a shocked hush. Flames had breached the roof and poured into the night through the third-floor windows. A piercing wail rose into the starlit night.

Lenore.

Jill cringed. Chilled slivers broke out on her back. Clay's strong hand held hers as she surged ahead, making her way to the front of the crowd where her family huddled.

Her aunt clutched Tia's arm and shrieked in a keening wail. The girl tried to comfort her mother while the family doctor prepared a syringe. Leo stayed at Tia's side.

As Jill reached them, Uncle Drew pulled Sam aside. "What did you say to my wife?"

"Well, sir." Sam furrowed his brow. "I saw a dead man in the entrance hall."

"You're sure?"

"Yes, sir. The railing above broke and he fell. I couldn't get in, but even if I had, it wouldn't have done any good. The fire was already bad." Sam lowered his head. "Mr. Bradwell, I think that man was your son."

Her uncle stared as if trying to understand, and then bent his head.

Jill plucked at his sleeve. "Uncle Drew. I'm so sorry."

His brow crinkled as he looked from her to Clay. When Clay nodded, her uncle's face turned pale, then greenish. His gaze settled on her.

"Jill, your arms. Your neck. They're bruised. Who did that?"

How could she tell him? The ache in her heart robbed her of adequate words.

Uncle Drew's shoulders slumped. "It was Carver, wasn't it? What happened?"

"We fought, sir," Clay volunteered.

"About what?" He looked from Clay to her.

Jill stepped closer to her uncle. "I discovered that he'd been stealing from Windtop, and he didn't want anyone else to know."

A gasping sob choked her uncle, drawing Lenore's attention. The woman's frenzied gaze swept Jill from head to foot.

With a horrible screech, her aunt tore away from the doctor and swooped down on her. She gripped the skirt of Jill's soot-sullied gown. "You set our house on fire. You left our son to die!"

An unearthly wail from deep within her aunt sailed into the night air and careened into a livid rage.

Jill backed away, but Lenore held tight. Clay stepped between them and gripped her aunt's wrist, prying the woman's fingers from the ruined dress.

Lenore's gaze raked his disheveled shirt and soot-smeared face. "You killed him. You both killed him."

With Uncle Drew's help, the doctor took her aunt's arm and injected the sedative. As it took effect, her voice turned to a moan. "Murderers! Murderers! You'll pay."

Uncle Drew eased his wife away. She slumped against him. "They killed him, Drew," she whimpered. "I saw them. I saw them do it."

"No, dear. You didn't see anything. You were with me."

A classic town car screeched to a gravelly halt, and Kitty's son bounded out from the driver's seat to open the back door.

"But they did it, Drew. They killed our son. They set our beautiful house on fire." Lenore's voice died. Uncle Drew helped her into the car's back seat where she lay down with her head on his lap. The doctor leaped into the front passenger seat.

As the car drove away, Tia sidled up. "Jill, you didn't—" she asked, barely above a whisper. "Did you?"

Jill put an arm around her cousin. "No, but we were in the house with Carver."

Her cousin's brown eyes searched hers. "What really happened?"

"I think …" *O Lord, please help me tell the truth without causing her unnecessary pain.* "Your brother followed me into Windtop. We argued, and he accidentally upset the oil lamp and set the house on fire. I tried to escape, but he came after me and Clay stopped him."

Tia turned to Clay. "I thought you left for Chicago."

Clay released a heavy breath and lifted his head to meet the girl's gaze. "I almost did, but I came back to make sure Jill was all right."

"How did you know she needed you?" Tia appeared to wrestle with the idea.

"Yes, how did you know?" Jill asked.

"I guess you'd have to say it was a God thing. I knew you needed me."

"But how did you find her?' Tia scrunched her brow. "I mean, the security system was on."

"Your brother wasn't the only one who knew about the forest entrance to the passageway. I reached the second floor just in time. We fought, and when he fell against the railing, it broke away. By that time, Jill and I had only moments to escape the fire."

Tia's chin trembled. "Did my brother tell you he killed Aunt Susannah?"

Jill sucked the night air. "You knew?"

"If my brother knew a way past the security system, it only makes sense." Silent tears leaked from Tia's brown eyes.

Leo put an arm around her cousin's shoulders as the rising roar of tumbling lumber and brick pulled their attention to the house. The glowing framework of the upper floors caved in. Sparks and flame shot into the night and acrid smoke permeated the air.

The horrific spectacle continued, and Jill held her cousin's hand until the din of Windtop's demise quieted. Jill had told Tia all she thought the girl could bear. Soon enough, the rest of the details would come to light, and none of their lives would ever be the same.

Over the next week, the sheriff, the coroner, and the fire chief sorted out the details surrounding Carver's death. They took pictures of the bruises on Jill's neck and arms, questioned those at the scene, and searched Windtop's ruins to confirm both the cause of the fire and the cause of death. In the end, they decided that no charges would be made. Once the necessary papers were signed, they released Carver's remains for burial.

In the meantime, with Lenore in the hospital under sedation, Jill stayed with Uncle Drew at his home in Munising where she could comfort Tia. When her aunt remained too ill to attend Carver's funeral, Jill helped Uncle Drew and Tia with the arrangements.

Now, standing beside her uncle and her cousin in the island cemetery, she shed no tears. Much as she wished none of this heartache had happened, it was over. There was no going back.

A few family friends and business acquaintances gathered around them while the priest offered prayers at Carver's grave site. They looked on with sadness as the remains of her mother's killer were lowered into the earth only a few feet from her mother's resting place.

First her uncle, then Tia, and then she added one shovel full of dirt to the hole. Others did the same.

Jill gazed at the dirt splattered casket. It was done now. She stepped away.

Amelia whispered, "How are you doing?"

"I'm all right." Actually, she was relieved now that her mother's murderer was no longer at large, and her family had no more need for secrets.

Standing stiffly at the open grave, Jill clung to her one consolation. As difficult as it was, she had told her uncle and cousin and those in authority the whole story. Clay had done the same. Now, all she could do was keep loving and praying for them and herself. She could also finish grieving the loss of her mother with no more need for self-incrimination.

Mourners began leaving, trickling away in groups of three or four. While Uncle Drew and Tia bid them good-bye, Jill carried a single red rose to her mother's grave. Pressing a kiss to its soft petals, she placed it on the marker.

Amelia touched her shoulder. "One day, you will see her again in heaven."

Jill nodded. All was now at rest between her mother and herself. Though these past weeks were anything but easy, Nona was right to insist she return.

"Are you ready to go, Jill?" her uncle asked.

She and Amelia followed him to the family car. They rode in silence except for Jill's little gasp as the car turned, not toward Williams Landing, but toward Windtop.

"A little unfinished business," her uncle said.

Charred ruins lay in stark contrast to the forest's lush green. Gazing into the gaping, black hole that had once been Windtop, Jill recalled her laughter as a child in this house, her mother's soft smile, and the twinkle in Maggie's eyes as their beloved housekeeper shook a finger at her for some harmless mischief.

She also recalled her aunt's vicious wrangling, spawned by this inheritance, and her mother's eventual withdrawal from Uncle Drew and his family. How sad. Then her own flight from the house and her mother's tragic death in her absence brought more loss. Even her mother's beautiful rose bush had perished in the blaze, never again to offer its rich, fragrant blossoms. And somewhere in those black ashes, Button had perished.

Too numb to shed another tear, Jill crossed her arms and rubbed her shoulders. Windtop's destruction had also removed any chance she might discover who her father was. Perhaps that was the way the Lord wanted it.

A shadow fell on the ground at her feet. Clay stood near, gazing at her with tender reserve and holding a scarred container in his hands.

She offered him a sad smile and turned back to the charred ruins. "All your beautiful work destroyed."

He held out the container to her.

She took the box from his hands and brushed a finger over the initials on its lid. Her mother's journal box. "Where did you find it?"

"The firemen found it lodged in the main chimney. It's fireproof, so any papers in it most likely survived." He shuffled his feet but made no effort to touch her.

"Thank you." She gazed into his sad eyes, her voice thick with emotion. *Oh, Lord, where is he with you?* No matter how long it took, she would never stop praying for him.

Clutching the box, she turned blindly toward the gazebo, its boards still white beneath the summer sun. Inside, she sat on one of the built-in benches, staring at the box.

Amelia was already seated in its cooling shade. "Are you going to open it?"

Jill shook her head. "I don't have the key. It was lost in the fire."

"Well, maybe a locksmith can help you."

Footsteps scuffed and clicked on the brick walkway. Tia stood at the gazebo's entrance. "Can Dad and I join you?"

Jill set the box aside while her cousin and uncle entered.

Uncle Drew cleared his throat. "Jill, I want to thank you."

She blinked. "Thank me?"

"Tia and I both want to thank you. Carver is gone, and my wife is in the hospital, but during these past weeks, you brought change into our lives. Change for the good."

Tia looped her arm with her father's. "My life is so much better."

"This past week," Uncle Drew continued, "while I prayed so desperately for my wife—for all of us—I asked the Lord into my life too. I hope that maybe someday, Lenore will do the same. In the meantime and no matter what lies ahead, I believe our lives will get better. We know enough now to turn to God for the help we need."

Jill could only stare in wonder.

"I wasted so many opportunities," he continued, "preoccupied with that mill while my children grew up. If I had taken a stronger hand with Carver ..." His shoulders jerked as he fought to compose himself. "I ... can't change any of that now, but with God's help, I intend to be a better father to my daughter."

Tia's mouth curved in a wobbly smile. "Oh, Dad!"

Uncle Drew reached into his suit jacket. "Speaking of fathers ..." He removed an envelope and held it out to Jill. "This came in the mail today."

Jill took the heavy vellum envelope and read her name penned in long, bold strokes at the center. In the upper left-hand corner, the return address included a name. *"John Ashley Taylor."*

"Your father," Uncle Drew said. "He legally changed your last name and your mother's at her request."

With trembling fingers, she touched her name. Her father had written it. "You knew him?"

Uncle Drew shook his head. "I knew of him, but for Susannah's sake and yours, our parents swore me to secrecy. They and Susannah were certain no good would come of any contact with him."

"But why?"

"Circumstances were complicated then, but I've spoken with your father and believe they may no longer matter. Now it's up to you, Jill. You might at least want to read what he wrote."

Jill broke the seal and withdrew the elegant sympathy card. She read the message twice.

"He wants to see me, Uncle Drew. He included his cell phone number."

Tia jumped up and hugged her. "This is what you've wanted, Jill. What I prayed for you."

"He also sends his sympathy regarding our loss," Jill continued.

"I take comfort," Uncle Drew said, "in that, if my son's tragedy had to be, it brought us new beginnings, Jill. Including that fine young man who obviously loves you so much."

Amelia smiled. "I believe he's referring to my Sonny," she said. "It's no secret to the rest of us how you feel about each other. So, will we hear any good news in the near future?"

Jill lowered her eyes. "I ... I don't think so."

Uncle Drew slapped his knees and stood up. "Well, that's between you two. You'll work it out. I'm just glad Carver's death proved accidental though I had no doubt it would."

Jill searched his round face. "You didn't?"

"Sam witnessed enough to make that clear. Carver crashing through the railing and Clay grabbing at his shirt to keep him from falling."

"He did?"

"He still had the shirt button when you two joined the rest of us that night."

Jill tried to wrap her mind around what her heart had been telling her all along. Clay was innocent of any wrongdoing. "Would you three excuse me?"

She had to find Clay and ... didn't have far to go. He stood at the end of the brick walkway.

Her joy suddenly deflated. She hesitated. She hadn't wanted to, but she had doubted him. He deserved someone who believed in him no matter what.

Now only a whisper away, she looked up into his love-filled gaze. "Clay, I wasn't absolutely sure …" The words died in her throat. She couldn't speak such despicable things. "Please forgive me."

He put a forefinger gently to her lips. "If not for you, I would have done exactly what I came here to do. Yes, Carver's death was an accident—but only by a split second."

"You didn't kill him. That's all that matters."

He grasped her hand. "You're wrong, Jill. That's not all that matters."

"It is."

"Listen to me." He stopped to clear his throat. "That night when God sent me back to you, he asked me to trust him. This past week, he and I have been doing a lot of communicating."

They had? A happy tear slid down her cheek.

"You were right, Jill. No matter what happens or how bad things might look, we can trust God to make it come out all right. At the right time and in the right way."

Lord, Clay came back to you! The wonder of it sent shivers of joy through her entire being. Her heart throbbed for both God and him. "I only know that I love you, Clay."

He opened his arms, and she snuggled into his embrace. While she listened to the strong, steady beat of his heart, he sighed and buried his face in her hair.

Suddenly he shifted, arching awkwardly to look over his shoulder. She looked up.

"I hope you don't mind a foursome," he said.

"Foursome?"

"God, you, me, and …" He nodded toward their feet. "… our little buddy here."

"Me-ew."

Jill peered down. "Button!" She bent to scoop him up, laughing as he purred with his deep rumble.

"I spotted him a few days ago," Clay said. "The little rascal allowed me to feed him but wouldn't let me near him until last night. We're finally best buds." He scratched Button behind the ears.

The kitten arched his neck and closed his eyes, his whiskers spreading out like a fireworks display.

Jill laughed. "I fully agree, Button." She gazed up at the man who, God willing, she would love for the rest of her life.

As he lowered his head, she raised her lips to meet his promise of a lifetime of love.

THE END